THE SWEDE by Andre

Chapter one

The heat got to Anders where he lay on the dry grass, staring at the short straw between his fingers, convinced that the bastards had set him up. He sat forward covered in sweat, glanced side to side very slowly, then picked up his shirt and left through the park gates. Coming onto the street, he kept his head down for a moment while he fumbled in his pockets for his spectacles. Then putting them on, he saw both John and Andrew on the road ahead of him, crossing through threads of traffic. It had begun, he thought, and he sat down edge of the kerb thinking about John's plan, and his role in it. He wished there was another way, wished that the farmer he had picked for in Gatton had paid his wages. Being broke was no fun, he thought, especially when far from home.

Staying on the roadside with cars passing in front of him and the sun's glare over his face, he squinted at John and Andrew, cursing himself for leaving Gatton with them. He thought then about his circumstances, how things had gone badly since he met them on Lindsay's farm, how John had persuaded him to join them at the meat factory. His old job of picking cabbages was tough, but at least it never questioned his morals. Now he was stuck in Rockhampton, waiting to

1

work the dreaded kill room, where he, a vegetarian, would help slaughter over twelve-hundred cows a day.

The irony caused Anders to smirk for a moment. He could appreciate the irony. But what he couldn't appreciate was John's sneakiness, the way he left out bits of information, the way he never mentioned the kill room or the compulsory vaccination shots, which they needed to work there, which they still hadn't received. Anders wasn't smirking now. The thought of being John's puppet had annoyed him.

It also annoyed him that they were doing this in the midday heat. There was no shade where he sat and the sun kept burning his shoulders. He put on his shirt now trying to refocus his mind on John's plan, reminding himself that it was necessary. They hadn't eaten since leaving Gatton and were, as John kept dramatically telling him, on the brink of starvation. He checked their progress and licked his lips. His mouth felt dry. He spat what spit he had left, spitting between his knees and with the tip of his shoe, smudging it into the dry, grey dirt. Then he stood facing the shop entrance. It was happening. Soon it would be his turn.

They had entered but still he waited, sticking to John's orders and counting to sixty. Then he moved his feet making his way through traffic with engine smoke all around him. His knees were going, and reaching the other side he leaned on them feeling dizzy. He tried to spit again but his mouth was too dry. Then looking up, he noticed a small dog tied to a lamppost by its lead, bouncing on its back legs and barking at him, and a bearded tramp staring from between two yellow bins, watching him with drunken yellowy eyes, slumped on a makeshift bed of cardboard. Anders paused, picturing himself in an Australian courtroom - the dog and the tramp in a witness box describing him, a pale-faced Swedish man looking shifty as hell outside a shop doorway. The heat and his imagination, he knew, were getting to him. To clear his mind he took a breath. Then he came up, peered over each shoulder and entered the shop.

That was days ago now, but John hadn't let the incident drop since.

He rose looking angry. He came down his bunk ladders, yawning, dropping to the floor, scratching his behind with both hands. He was a big man, a stout man, with shortly cropped hair like a crew cut, chubby red cheeks and small piggy eyes. From a doorway he watched Anders on the balcony decking, slumped over a table drinking coffee. He knew John was watching but paid little attention. His fringe was wet across his forehead. His shirt was open, its cloth damp with sweat. He continued to ignore John, staring only into a willow tree that leaned drunkenly over their balcony, where a possum nested and visited him each night. Now it was dark he waited, hoping it would come again.

'Where's Andy?' John asked staying in the doorway, scratching his groin through a rip in his underpants.

'Out.'

'I've figured that,' he said. 'Where and why?'

Anders drank coffee. It was strong and black and his face twisted painfully as he swallowed. He only drank it to ease the hunger pains. It was all they had. 'He left earlier, something about a message from Dickie.'

'What does Dickie want?' Anders didn't answer. 'I asked a question.'

Anders stood up and staggered round the table, holding it as though standing there was a great effort.

'What does he want?' John asked again.

'I don't know what he wants, just a message to give.'

'About the bar tab?'

'I really don't know.'

'It better not be the bar tab,' John came onto the decking flexing his neck and shoulders. 'If Andy's been using that bar tab I'll kill him,' he said standing still for a moment, looking down at red insect bites on his arms. 'I'm just asking what it's about,' he said. Then slapping his own cheek, he jogged slowly back into their room.

'What's wrong,' Anders said.

'Something buzzed in my ear,' he said. 'They're in, they're in already.'

Barefooted he staggered over clothes and suitcases, working his way through the narrow room, looking sandwiched between kitchen top on one side and bunk beds on the other. Then stopping and reaching forward, he pulled a readymade rolled up newspaper from underneath his pillow. Watching him, Anders yawned and then smiled shaking his head. He was used to this nightly ritual, John in T-shirt and underpants, waving his newspaper like a baton.

'I got it,' he said chasing something into a corner, slapping his newspaper on the wall. 'It's a mosquito.'

He paused listening to its buzz, stepping towards it and squinting his eyes, then closely studying a crusty slice of wallpaper. Never had Anders met anyone so obsessed with insects. They annoyed everyone, he knew that, but John simply detested them, he detested them all, especially the sand flies which came from the nearby river and the mosquitoes that according to John, only attacked and drank his blood.

He moved to the kitchen top and lit two candles. 'Something landed on my face then,' he said swinging again. 'Something touched me.' He turned suddenly, swung at an innocent moth circling the light bulb above him. He kept swinging and missing it, hitting the bulb, almost taking it from its wire. 'They're all out tonight,' he yelled facing Anders, splashing insect repellent over his face. Then he was off again, following the same mosquito. 'They're all out.' He opened a kitchen cupboard. Two cockroaches scuttled round a ketchup bottle. He flicked one with his fingertip watching it struggle. 'They're everywhere.' He flicked it again. He swore at it. Then he turned and messed with his bedding, there was more swearing as he began lifting his mattress and ranting about bedbugs. He pulled up his T-shirt, pointing and swearing at red blotches on his belly.

'Take a seat and relax,' Anders said.

'That's easier said than done,' John said. 'How can you be a vegetarian with all this going on?'

He threw down his newspaper, took both candles to the table and joined him. They sat in silence for a while, John staring at the swinging bulb and the moth enjoying its freedom. 'I'm hungry,' he then said. 'Have you called Lindsay yet?' He picked up Anders's phone, was now scrolling through messages.

'I do every night. It's always the same outcome.'

'Well we need that money,' John said, and there was silence again while he watched Anders open a small tin with Swedish writing on the outside, counting what looked like mini teabags. Anders called them snus, and the snus contained tobacco. He took one pressing it underneath his top lip, holding it there against his gum.

'It's my money,' he said sounding different with snus in his mouth, 'remember that.'

John stroked his face sullenly. 'That's neither here nor there,' he said. 'Keep trying him, we need that money, especially after you messed up my plan.'

'Please, John, not tonight.'

'Yes tonight, tonight and every night.' John snatched the snus tin. 'I think I'll have one. In fact I'm having two.' He stuck his fingers inside, grabbing.

'John, please, it'll be weeks before my mother sends another batch.'

'Okay you selfish shit.' He threw the tin on the table. 'Okay,' he said. 'I'll have a coffee. Make me a coffee.'

Anders didn't say anything, he didn't rise or move, he just sat there using his shirtsleeve to dry sweat from his forehead.

'I don't know why you have them anyway,' John said. 'They make your lip all puffy. I've noticed that. Sometimes you look like a cat. Are you listening to me, cat-face?'

Again, Anders said nothing. He just got up and walked into their room more steadily now, dropping his shirt into an open suitcase. He stood bare-chested, his body tanned and hairless, his arms thin and slender. A cloth hung from his pocket. He took it and wet it under the water tap, laying it out over his face. John watched him for a moment then followed him inside.

'Go away, John,' Anders said, speaking through the cloth.

But John stayed close to him. He took something from the kitchen cupboard, facing it and turning it over in his hands, twisting his brow as though staring at some ugly looking idol or relic.

'Ready to explain yourself?'

'I'm tired, John,' Anders said, 'I just told you to go away.'

'Christ almighty lad, tell me what happened.'

Anders lifted a flap of cloth then let go. 'Put it back,' he said, seeing the can in John's hand.

'Why bring it back? Why take it in the first place?' John was looking at the can. 'We're on the brink of starvation and you take this.' He bashed the kitchen top with the can as though trying to get Anders's attention, but Anders stayed still, head back, breathing through the cloth. 'You'll tell me what happened right now.'

'I didn't mean to take it.'

'Yeah. I bet you didn't, lad.'

'Leave it, John, we're both tired.'

'I'm not leaving anything, lad. You've still not explained yourself. Why this can? Tell me.' John left the can on the kitchen top. He returned to his chair, turning it so he could face Anders from the balcony. 'We had a good plan going for us,' he said. 'It was my plan and it was a good one.'

'But I never wanted to. I've never stolen in my life. It wasn't fair, forcing me that way wasn't fair.'

'Yes but we pulled straws,' John said. 'We all had our roles to play and the plan was simple. We go into town. We find the nearest shop. We create two diversions. Mine, to hang out near the counter top pestering the till worker about tobaccos and whiskeys, and Andy, to fake vomit with his head inside that deep-freezer. It was perfect. Okay, neither the shopkeepers nor the customers paid us much attention. But we still played our roles. And you, all you had to do was take us some grub, you had it easy.' John sucked his lips looking redder than usual.

'How did it go so wrong?' he said, 'Why so much crashing about for creamed corn?'

'I panicked.'

'Yes but creamed corn wasn't part of my plan,' John said. 'I was expecting rashers and chops, sausages, ham, beef.'

'The boy was on me,' Anders said, and removing the cloth and wetting it again, he saw John wasn't paying him any attention. He was well into his rant now, same as he was each night since the incident.

'A chicken wing would've been nice. We're starving. Why not grab a luncheon meat, some kind of meat stick?'

'I'm a vegetarian.'

'Okay, okay, what about cheese?' John said. 'There was cheese wasn't there? You vegetarians eat cheese for a living, cheese and fish. That's why your farts smell so badly.' He spoke fast. 'What about fish, a tin of fish, a block of cheese?'

'I took what I could.'

'You took a can of shit because you're a spineless bastard and because you want my farts to smell like your farts.'

Anders moved the cloth to his neck, wearing it like a mini cape. He then sighed as he remembered John's plan for a moment. How they had pulled straws. How the role of shoplifter had fallen to him. How the tramp laughed as he entered the shop, those yellow eyes following him. Then he remembered walking round and touching things, his face pale and twisted with panic as he picked things up and put them down again. His mind was a fog that day, and he struggled to think clearly through panic and hunger.

'I thought the plan was a good one,' John went on. 'I remember being glad to see you when we caught up.' He put his hands over his stomach, slouching in his chair. 'My mouth was actually watering.'

'Yes, I noticed that.'

'And we stood there in the park. Remember?' John kept going, 'Remember that bit?'

'I try to forget.'

'I remember it. I remember your daft face and the can.' John stood up. 'I might've bashed your head with it.' He hit one hand against the other whilst eyeing up the can. 'Put it away,' he said. 'I'm sick of seeing it. Throw it out.'

Anders walked to the balcony, hanging his arms over the edge, facing the concrete car park below. 'Just eat it and shut up.'

'I don't want to,' John said. 'I like ham on white. I like roasted beef sandwiches with English mustard. What I don't like is creamed fucking corn.'

'Okay then, have that egg in the fridge.'

'I don't want that egg in the fridge. I put it in water. It began to float.'

Anders was laughing. He kept his face turned away from John and looked into the tree. The Possum will come soon, he thought, but there was no sign yet, just leaves, branches and darkness, and he squinted while staring up at them. John was still going, standing now, coming close and speaking into Anders's ear. 'I want beef soup, warm bread, cold butter,' he spoke excitedly, he spoke as though ordering dishes at a restaurant. 'I want hamburgers, fried onions, brown sauce. I want brown sauce, Daddies brown sauce. I want cornflakes, icy cold milk, lots of sugar. I want tasty things, yummy things. I don't want creamed corn,' he shot out his last sentence then repeated it loudly causing Anders to jump. 'I don't want creamed corn, do you understand that?'

'And do you understand I don't want to be here with you, living above this filthy pub?' Anders faced John, raising the volume of his voice to match John's rant. 'Do you understand I don't want to steal my food, or work a kill room, or wait to be vaccinated for God knows what.'

'Don't raise your voice to me,' John said, 'I'm the one to be angry here, lad. You messed up my plan.'

Anders had more to say but decided not to bother. He turned again to the car park, trying to ignore him.

'I want yummy things,' John spoke with his head down. 'Not egg. Not creamed corn. I'm a northerner and we northern lads like our brown sauce, not to mention our gravy.' He licked his lips and kept speaking. 'We love gravy, us northern lads.'

Then he paused suddenly. He backed into a corner and stayed there with the Possum facing him. 'Your rat friend is here,' he said.

'That's no way to talk about Andrew.'

'No, that big rat you're obsessed with. It's here.'

Anders glanced over his shoulder. 'Come here, little one.' But it stayed edge of the balcony, curling its tail around itself and tilting its head, then lifting its pink nose and sniffing the night air.

'Don't be nice to it,' John said folding his arms. 'They're scavengers. Ignore it so it goes away. Are you listening to me? I don't want it here. How can you be a vegetarian, look,' he pointed, 'it stinks.'

'I love it,' Anders said offering his hand, 'I look forward to it each night. It's the only good part of my day.' He bent forward speaking to it the way one speaks to a playful puppy dog. 'Hello, little one, hello, hello. I like your whiskers, they're very nice.'

'Jesus,' John said, and keeping his arms folded and eyes on the Possum, he walked slowly back inside their room, took a kettle from the kitchen top and filled it with water. 'You're one sad bastard,' he added over the sound of the tap.

Anders ignored him, speaking as though no one else was there, as though floating in his own happy bubble, just him and the Possum. 'Does little one like that idea, a bit of papaya, a bit of mango for little one?' He danced his feet and moved his fingers in front of the Possum's face, as though sprinkling imaginary fruit onto the decking. 'Some fruit for little one.'

'It's not little, it's pretty big for a rat,' John yelled with steaming kettle in hand. 'Don't encourage it. It stinks.'

'It's beautiful,' Anders whispered, watching it return under the willow tree.

'It stinks,' John said. 'Did you hear me?'

Anders was barely listening. He looked at the Possum for a very long time and saw much of himself in it. *We're misunderstood creatures you and me,* he thought, *only watching the world go by you and me, and nothing more. Two of the same we are.* He sat with both hands crossed in his lap, nodding. To him the Possum provided therapy, and sitting there and smiling he imagined it as his protector, laughing at such a thought.

'It's not funny,' John said. 'We're starving. I was expecting yummy things.'

Chapter two

Andrew had returned not sober. He was a skinny boy with long legs, a boyish freckled face, and a mop of ginger hair that hung scruffily over his eyes like a donkey's fringe. His skin was pale. His clothes were worn and baggy and splashed with lots of beer stains. He pulled up his jeans but they kept slipping down again, sagging on his hips. He looked at Anders and John with a grin. Anders found him vulgar, loud, cocky and annoying, sometimes pleasant and sometimes likeable, and much like he did with John, he put up with him.

'I bring news,' he said. 'I bring good news.'

'You're pissed,' John said, grimacing from the balcony. 'You've been on the tab.'

'It's true... I had a Tooheys or two.'

'You're drunk and you've had more than two,' John said. 'You've been on the tab. I know it.' He puffed his cheeks, struck a match on the table and watched it burn slowly. Beyond him and along the road were lines of tall trees with campfire smoke above them, drifting up, disappearing into a purple, cloudless sky. The road and the trees were silent. Country music played from the bar area below.

'Calm down I can't hear Kenny Rogers,' Andrew said pulling up his jeans. 'I've not touched that tab.'

'You take the piss,' John said, 'You do, lad.' He stood up sipping his thick black coffee, moving the mug as he spoke. 'You sneaked two bags of goon the other night, one red, one white.'

'What's goon?' Anders asked from underneath his blanket, sitting up with book in hand.

'Cheap wine,' John said, 'very cheap and nasty stuff, apparently there's egg in it.'

'Sounds like a lovely drop.'

'It's what Abos drink when they ain't sniffing paint,' John added.

'Aborigines, you mean, how about some respect.' Anders leaned over his knees to face him.

'Hard to respect them when they sit outside train stations giving me shit,' John said. 'Drinking goon and sniffing paint.'

'John,' Anders said coming down his bunk ladder, 'not so long ago those people had their land taken away. They suddenly had to adapt to western life.'

'Yeah,' John said, 'a better life.'

'That's so ignorant,' Anders spoke while Andrew faced one way then another, wearing the expression of a confused child caught centre of a grown up conversation, simply grinning. 'That's not for you to say,' Anders went on. 'How would you cope if someone bulldozed your home, your city, demolished your computers, your transport, your machines. How would you cope? How would your piles cope in the wilderness?'

'He'd rub 'em with a dot leaf I suppose,' Andrew said with both Anders and John ignoring him.

'Where's this going?' John asked walking on the balcony. 'I'm not sure where this is going, lad.'

'The Aborigine lived in the wilderness for many years,' Anders said, 'adapted to its harsh lands, survived in it, thrived in it, and some still do. They like it there. It's their home, their way of life. These so-called civilisations we westerners bring them, the so-called better life as you put it, is, you'll often find if you read your history books, not wanted and for some never will be. For some it brings nothing but fear and depression, the end of a life they once cherished, and as the generations move on, they lose their survival skills, lose their independence, and after a time they become just like the fucking rest of us, dependant on governments, nothing but vegetables sat in front of TV screens eating sodium covered snacks. Jesus Christ,' he said, 'the thought makes me want to reach for the cheap and nasty wine too, with or without the egg.'

'I think you better calm down,' John said picking up his coffee, staring into it. 'And while you're at it, scribble the word sodium across your arse-cheeks and pencil dive over the balcony.'

Anders said nothing. He returned up his ladder, lying on his crumpled blanket and bed sheets, moving the heel of his hand over his forehead, pressing it there as though suffering a migraine.

'You will leave that tab alone.' John had turned his attention back to Andrew now. 'Are you listening to me?' He drank some coffee. 'I know you had Guinness the other night, a big box of Guinness.'

'Have you heard him?' Andrew looked up at Anders. 'Have you heard that puffer fish? That constipated gerbil, standing there clamping his cheeks and holding one in. You wanna get some fibre in your diet. You wanna eat the skin on your potatoes more often.' He staggered to the balcony doors. 'Back me up here, lad.' He turned to Anders but he was still and said nothing. 'John's holding one in, isn't he?'

Anders kept silent, fed up with them arguing. If they weren't getting at him, they were getting at each other. It was, he thought, as though they had a contest going on, as though they were trying to score points from one another, seeing who could ruffle who. And it seemed to Anders, that whenever John was getting at Andrew, which was often, Andrew would begin with childish comments, or throw things, or make up songs, usually about John's piles and his creams. One song in particular, Anders remembered, went as follows.

John has gone for miles, yet still he keeps those piles, those grapes of wrath, those stinging beads, Anusol is what he needs, give it him hard, give it him quick, through the cream tube, out the stick, sooth his rosebud, sooth his flower, touch and go, for an hour...

Their arguments often ended that way, and Andrew, the more immature, the more competitive of the two, wouldn't stop until he felt a win, a hint of victory, and this was every day now, and Anders found himself either involved in or stuck in an argument. The sooner they had money, he thought, the sooner they were out of this stifling room and working with food in their bellies, everything would be better, and thinking that way along with his nightly visits from the Possum, kept him going.

'Just listen to what I'm saying, lad,' John said with his feet on the table, trying, Anders thought, to look cool and relaxed. 'Just stop running up that tab,' he said. 'Being broke is one thing. Being in debt is another. Especially to our landlord, so take it easy.'

'I am,' Andrew said. 'Dickie told everyone at The Old Crow not to serve me.'

'Did he? So why you pissed then?'

'Because Henry got me a few,' Andrew laughed before continuing. 'You should've seen Dickie. He was in a right state. He came out raging at the barman, grabbing his shirt and everything. "Why he got a schooner," he yelled, "tell me, tell me," he kept yelling. "I'd like to know why, cunt-face, tell me why. Why he holding a schooner in my bar?" he kept on that way. He got up in this guy's face and got a sweat on. Then he came for me, calling me a cheeky pommy cunt. I tried not to laugh but it was hard, he was sweating so much.'

'Annoying him isn't clever,' Anders said, bunk wood creaking as he sat up. 'We're still broke, remember that.'

'That,' Andrew said, 'is about to change.'

'Why?' John asked widening his expression, looking interested suddenly.

'Because we got our vaccination shots.' Andrew was grinning again. He went to the kitchen top, facing Anders. 'That's why Dickie wanted me. He took the message.'

'Good,' John said, 'Where and what time?'

'Town centre in the afternoon.' Andrew paused. He turned leaning over the sink, burping and spitting between words. 'I'll check again later,' he said holding his stomach. 'That bastard served me a dodgy one.' Then laughing he looked up towards Anders. 'You okay up there, lad?'

'I'm fine,' Anders said. 'I just don't like needles.'

'That's unfortunate,' Andrew said.

'Well what can I do?' Anders turned sullenly onto his side and through a gap in the bunk-wood, watched John come into the room. He took shaving foam. He lathered his cheeks, neck and chin. Then he bent over the sink with his dirty razor, shaving over used coffee mugs.

'Who's Henry?' he asked, holding his razor to a trickle of tap water.

'He got me a few,' Andrew said, and like Anders, he watched John shave.

'We've established that,' John said. 'But who is he?'

'Well I don't know his life story.'

'But you've been drinking with him all afternoon, just answer my questions.'

'He's a nice guy, will that do?' Andrew grinned. 'Now stop getting agitated or you'll pop a pile.'

'A nice guy, eh,' John said.

'That's what I just said. But his roommate though, Steve, he's a bit odd.'

'Odd?'

22

'Yeah. He stares a lot, you know. He's one of those people you can't figure out, gets you thinking, you know, and you suspect things. He's odd. I don't know how else to put it.'

'I've never seen this Henry and Steve,' Anders said speaking between the planks.

'Well you wouldn't,' Andrew said. 'They only arrived today. They're staying next door in that six bunker with the Chinese kid, the one we saw taking an up close photograph of someone's shoes.'

'I don't remember that,' Anders said.

'Me neither,' John said, razor blade tug-tugging on his skin. 'Are they working?'

'Both are working, will that do now?' Andrew tilted his chin to peer at Anders. 'You're paler than me up there. What's got you so badly, the needle?'

'I'm a bit tired,' Anders said quietly, 'that's all.'

'Tired? From what? From being in this room all day? From listening to John fart?'

'I guess so.'

'What's gone on in here?' Andrew said. 'Why's he paler than an albino snowman?' He put an arm on John's shoulder but John returned to the balcony, where he stood dabbing his cheeks with a tea towel.

'We're turning in soon,' he said. 'Why don't you go now,' he said, 'go back downstairs with the other drunks?'

'But why's he being a queer fish?'

'Go back to the bar,' Anders said.

'Has John been farting too much?' Andrew looked at Anders and smiled. 'Has he been hitting eight-point-nine on the sphincter scale?'

Both ignored him.

'It's a simple question,' he said, 'please answer.'

Anders reached for his book, found a page and pretended to read.

'Do you have a problem with John's farts?' Andrew continued. 'Is it John's fault,' he said. 'Are his farts not funny enough for you? Is John losing his touch or his parp so to speak, could that be it? I remember him back in Thailand, at Chiang Mai hostel he was famous. They appreciated a good farter there. The famous tooter they called him, and the drunken cockney used to say jokingly from his bunk, "you were only supposed to blow the bloody doors off," and the other travellers would always sing to him as he entered the room, asking the famous tooter to play them something, and he did, he always did. Except for one time when he was over tired and a little grumpy, and when no tune came, the other travellers ran off, leaving me to wonder where they had gone to and why. But later that night I saw them. They had returned with bowls of sticky rice. All lining up orderly by the tooters bed, and one by one he ate their rice, he ate it with his fingers, and then like some kind of galactic explosion, like an awakening of a geyser...'

'That's enough,' John shouted from the balcony doors. 'That's more than enough. Go back downstairs now.'

'But I'm not done here.'

'Tell him to pack it in, John.'

'Pack it in,' John said coming into the room. 'Go back downstairs.'

A grin appeared on Andrew's face. 'Maybe I should go,' he said. 'Another drink with Henry would be nice.' But before leaving he turned to Anders making a circle with his thumb and forefinger. 'Your arse,' he said to confirm, 'tomorrow, that's where the needle is going tomorrow, pop, pop, pop.'

Chapter three

An hour had passed. John finished another coffee, flipped the light switch and closed the balcony doors. It was dark now, but slits of light still sneaked in from the corridor outside, and some of moonlight from underneath the balcony doorway. Now up on his elbows, Anders saw in those slits of light, John dropping his underpants and climbing the bunk ladder to his left, bare bottom showing. 'Oh, I almost forgot,' he said jumping off the ladders. 'I can't sleep without the old Chopper Harris on full whack.' Anders knew what was coming. He tensed up now and listened to John's feet going across the floor, and to his hands fumbling in the darkness for the switch.

'Please not tonight, John,' Anders said.

'Yes tonight, and every night while it's this hot.' John stepped back, nodding. He watched the ceiling fan for a moment, its large propellers turning just above Anders's face. Anders stayed tense, clenching his shoulders as though trying to fit into a small space, hanging onto his mattress with both hands, fearing decapitation. He sighed. One or two seconds passed. He sighed again, louder, longer.

'What is it?' John said. 'Speak up man. I can't handle you making those noises. Lying there like a wet lump of turd, making those noises.'

'But it's the fan, it's so bloody close.'

26

'And it's so bloody hot,' John said pushing his blanket away.

'Let's open the balcony doors then, get a nice breeze coming in.'

'No. Shut up now.'

'Please, it scares me.'

'I'm not opening those doors. I'm not giving those sand flies a chance to run amok on me.'

'You're being unreasonable.'

'No I'm not. You are.' John pulled away more bedding. From his hips down, he was completely naked. 'You are,' he said, 'with your irrational fear of being decapitated. No, no, no,' he said, 'the fan stays on and that's final.'

'But it's right above my face.'

'Don't speak so soft, lad.'

'I can feel it tip of my nose.'

'You're supposed to feel it, lad. It's a fan and it's staying on by the way. And you can take that as I say it, because what I'm saying is bang on, lad.'

'The breeze, you're supposed to feel the breeze. Not its propellers.' Anders got out of bed. He was stumbling near the kitchen and feeling for the switch, and then flipping it, he hung round the foot of his bunk ladder, waiting for the propellers to slow again. 'There, I feel better already,' he said climbing back into bed.

'So that's it,' John said. 'I'm to boil in my own filth.'

'Listen to me. I don't want to be killed,' Anders yelled pulling his blanket over his waste. 'What if I sit up suddenly and it slices my head?'

'But it's okay for me to boil in my filth, is that what you're saying to me?'

'If you're so hot take off that T-shirt. Everything else seems to come off. I've noticed that, everything, including those soiled underpants you left down there on the floor, so why keep that T-shirt on? Why if you're so bloody hot are you wearing a T-shirt?'

'The T-shirt protects me from the sand flies.'

'You and those sand flies,' Anders said. 'That fan will kill me and you're bothered about insect bites.'

John was silent after that and for a while, Anders became distracted. He listened to drunks in the corridor. They kept knocking on doors and asking people for things, beers and cigarettes. Hope they don't knock here, he thought, not unless they want an egg. Then he heard the scuttle of John's feet again, and soon, felt that irritable fan swishing over his nose. He sighed. He turned watching John climb back up his bunk

28

ladders. Then he swore very loudly in Swedish, pushed his bedding away, moved carefully under the fan's propellers, and climbed down to the spare bunk below.

Chapter four

The corridor was dark and that's where he lay, on his back staring at her, feeling his pockets with his fingers. She stood over him clutching her shoes and her handbag in the same hand, holding them on her hip. 'Come on, Andy, find the bloody thing.' She kicked him and he laughed. 'Found it or not?' Again, he laughed. 'You're bloody useless,' she said trying the door handle.

   Nothing gave, but then she looked down seeing him with the key, laughing with it, jabbing it into her thick ankles. 'Ouch! Quit doing that.' She bent down to rub them. Then it was silent. He got up and began leaning on her, and then staggering drunkenly towards the door, trying the lock. 'You're not much good with those hands, Andy,' she said elbowing his ribs. 'This may be a disappointment.' She then swore and looked at her feet.

   'I dropped it,' he said, patting the carpet where she stood.

   'My goodness you're one dozy sod. My two year old has better navigation skills than you.'

   'I thought I had it though. I thought it was in.'

   'Story of my life,' she laughed, she cackled. 'Is my beer down there?'

   'No,' he said. 'You threw it. Now shift your foot, the key is under your foot.' He pinched her ankles.

'I told you to quit that stuff, I wasn't joking.'

'I got it,' he said. 'Move you're big arse.'

He twisted the key in the lock. The door opened and she rushed in covering her wide nostrils with her handbag. 'Christ on a bike,' she said. 'You boys bloody stink.' She tripped on a suitcase as Andrew followed behind her, falling over. 'Bloody hell!' She rolled on top of him, her dark frizzy hair dangling in his eyes, her yellow teeth showing through it as she laughed, witch like, cackle like, a laugh that could wake the dead never mind the living.

'Jesus girl, get off me.' Andrew spat clumps of greasy hair. 'Roll over,' he said prodding her belly, losing his fingers in her rolls of fat. 'Roll, I said roll.' She rolled and crawled through a pile of dirty clothes towards the spare bunk, touching Anders's face in the darkness. He sprung up from under his covers, turning, confused, fearing a stranger had broken in.

'Someone is here, John.' He said reaching for his spectacles, but then remembering he had switched beds.

The two lovers stumbled up laughing, and without a hint of grace the big girl wrapped her arms around Andrew and began kissing him aggressively, pushing her weight on to him, dominating him, manoeuvring him towards the bunk. 'Right then,' she said throwing

31

herself backwards, and, pulling Andrew with her, they kissed on top of Anders while he gagged on his pillow. The pillow was in his mouth now and he made funny noises, sexual almost. 'I won't have this,' she said moving him with her backside, thrusting it at him, knocking him to the floor. Suddenly he could breathe again.

'Someone is in our room, John. Do something.'

John leaned over his bunk looking downwards, squinting and fingering sleep from one eye. He stared at Andrew and the big woman. There they where, tangled in Anders's bedding, with Anders on the floor on his back, resembling a woodlouse that had been flipped over. When he managed to turn, Andrew rugby tackled him and the woman followed laughing her witch like cackle. She felt Anders's face for the second time. 'I don't agree with this,' she said reaching for him. 'He's getting away now.'

'He bloody well isn't,' Andrew said, quickly grabbing his underpants.

'Let me go,' Anders said.

'What do you think, Marian? Shall I let him go?'

'I think you ought to bring him to me,' she said. 'I want to slap his arse,' she laughed, she sat up. 'He felt me up in that bed. I won't have it. I'm not that sort.'

'I'd say an apology was in order then.' Andrew tugged the waistline of the underpants like a leash, ripping the fabric.

'Yes, yes, for sure. Bring him over.' She reached into the darkness, touching bunk-wood and bedding. 'Where is the skinny runt?' She threw the blanket aside and pushed off the floor. 'Is this him?' Her hands were on his face again. He yelled into them. 'He needs to calm down.'

'We got a lively one, Marian?' Andrew gave the underpants another tug. 'Come back here and apologise to our Marian, she's our guest.'

'He still not apologised then?'

'I'm working on it.'

'I want a proper apology.'

'I said I'm working on it.' Andrew lost grip, then turning he faced her. They were beginning to argue when Anders ran passed, pouncing onto the bunk ladder like a gecko.

'No, no, you don't escape that easy.' Working as a team, they stood and each got a leg, pulling him from the ladder. Andrew fell with him, grabbing his hair and his face and then wrestling him with Marian looking over them, trying to move away.

'What the hell,' Andrew yelled suddenly. 'You trod on my ankle.'

33

'Who cares,' she said watching Anders recover and pounce for the ladder. 'The skinny runt is escaping again. I've had no apology whatsoever.' She followed him as he climbed, underpants sagging. She went for him but missed clapping her hands together. He kept going. Then wearing a victorious grin, he reached the top and sprung forward leading with his forehead.

There was no time to register the stupidity of this badly thought out escape plan; the pain was blunt, sharp and instant. No longer grinning, he turned with his heels rocking on the ladder's step, his eyes opening and closing, as was his mouth. A feeling of fogginess ran over him. He reached out not knowing which way was up or down, left or right. The room seemed to spin as fast as the propeller that had struck him, and at that moment he dropped landing in Marian's arms.

'You again,' she said lifting him like a baby, bending down to show Andrew.

'That's the one,' Andrew said rubbing his ankle. 'Got an apology yet?'

'Not yet, and I can't see me getting one at this rate either, look at him, look at the state of him.' She lay him on the floor, leaned over him, pulled Andrew towards her and stuck her wet, studded tongue inside his mouth. Their bodies arched over him as they kissed. He crawled away with his bed-sheet and got up swaying, hands reaching out for something to hold onto. His saggy underpants dropped. He stood there in front of Marian, stooping to pick them up again, staggering, holding them to his hip. Unsteadily he climbed his ladder, pausing now and then to feel his forehead, leaning one-way then the other. He reached the top. He kept low under the fan and moved snakelike, belly to the mattress.

'I saw him then.' Marian pushed Andrew away. 'I saw what he did.'

'What,' Andrew asked drying his lips on his vest. 'What did you see?' He smiled waiting for her to answer.

'Him,' she said, 'it's the ignorant one that's too almighty to apologise. He dropped his pants in front of me. I caught him doing it.'

Anders listened, a lump had sprouted on his forehead and he moved his fingers over it in circles, moved them very slowly.

'I'm sure it was nothing,' Andrew said standing up, hands in both pockets, walking backwards.

'You must've seen it,' she said and her eyes followed him. 'I'm not that kind of girl. He obviously wasn't listening when I said that, or chose not to, probably chose not to.'

'I don't think he'd flash you though.'

'You think I'd make it up?'

John cut in asking for quiet.

'Was that him?' Marian asked from the floor, looking round in the darkness. 'Was that him?' Andrew didn't answer her, he just ran the water tap and drank from it.

'Enough down there,' John added. 'Take it outside now.'

Marian stood up. 'He has front doesn't he? Dropping his pants while I kiss another man, then asking me to leave. He certainly has front.'

'Show her the door,' John said. 'Roll her out if you have to.'

'There he goes again, he's exceptional,' she spoke behind Andrew. He had the fridge door open and light glowed over his feet. 'What you holding?' she said.

'Something,' he laughed, 'I got something,' and arm over head he threw it across the room, watching John turn under his covers.

'What was that?' John said. 'I'm all sticky.' No one answered him. He felt his forehead. He asked again. 'This is getting out of hand,' he then said, 'I won't have this.'

'And I won't either.' Marian was marching towards Anders's ladders, spitting on her palms, rubbing them together like a shot-putter gearing up for the big throw. 'I won't.' She gripped the ladder. Her arm flab wobbled like jelly as she climbed, breathing heavily, wheezing almost. The bunk rocked. Anders had tensed up and looked now side to side fearing this crazy woman. She was nearing him. He felt her shadow.

36

'Right then,' he heard her say, and her hand was under his covers between his thighs. He felt it moving upwards, warm and sweaty, then on to his testicles, squeezing them like a rubber stress ball.

Horrific sounds filled the room. Like a fish out of water he thrashed his body, screaming and swearing in Swedish. Andrew laughed. John sat up dabbing his forehead with his covers. Marian smiled, tightening her grip around Anders's scrotum, tugging now. He felt sick. He felt cold sweat over his chest. 'Knulla!' he cried in his home tongue. 'Knulla! Knulla! Knulla!'

His head went side to side. His feet kicked out. His heels dug into his mattress. Marian gave him the works. 'Yelp!' he cried. 'Let a go go. Let a go go.' He spoke nonsense words, something between English, Swedish, and good old gibberish. 'Yelpy-yelp-yelp! Let a go go, let a go go of me balaks! Me Balaks, aj, aj, aj. Noodles! Fucking noodles! Spanish omelettes wearing wigs. Several sausages in the sea.'

She let go but her smile, he noticed, looked very sinister. He turned to protect himself. He brought his knees up high, curling like a cooked prawn. She trod more steps and brought her fist high in the air, asking if he had ordered a knuckle sandwich. 'Well have you?' she said leaning in. He wanted to say something. He pointed to the fan. But it was too late. Blood splashed his bedding. She was falling now, falling backwards.

Cutlery rattled inside drawers. Mugs fell into the sink. A second or two passed. Then she sprung forward on the floor, her fingers touching her cut cheek. In the darkness, she began to cry and grab items. She brought John's underpants from the floor and rubbed her face with them, blotting blood and tears. The room was silent but for her crying and the hum of the fan. Then she got up and patted the walls for the light switch. On it went. Blinding light got to them and they all squinted their eyes.

'Who's he?' Marian said looking at John, her voice stuttering and weak. 'How many of you are there? What's on his face?'

'I threw an egg,' Andrew said proudly.

'Well throw one at him too,' Marian screamed in Andrew's face. 'He hit me. The one up there hit me, look.' Tears ran into her cut. 'Go punch him up for me,' she said, her voice growing weaker as though the blow of the propeller had knocked all the brazenness out of her. 'Go get him,' she was trying to yell but her words came out all squeaky. Andrew backed up, he had distanced himself now and sat in the corner, red eyed, looking tired and sober in the lighted room.

'That it then you coward,' she said following, breathing her garlic and beer breath over him.

'He never hit you,' Andrew said. 'I think it was the fan. I think you should go now.'

'But he did. He hit me.' She tried showing him the blood on her hand but he didn't look up.

'It was the fan,' Andrew said speaking with his forehead on his knees. 'I think you better go.'

'It was the fan,' Anders agreed, still curled on his mattress, hoping she would accept this and leave quietly.

But she frowned and with her finger, she prodded Andrew's shoulder. 'You're going up there right now. You're going to punch him for me, yes?' She prodded him twice more. He didn't move or speak. 'Punch him in the face, yes?'

He kept his head down staying silent. Then he looked up. The bunk was creaking and rocking above him, with John crouching half-naked on his mattress, swaying. 'I'll be doing the punching,' he said, 'don't worry about that.' He dropped to his backside and, missing out the ladder, flung himself off the bunk's edge. Anders, Andrew and Marian watched as he landed, penis showing, looking small and bent, nesting in a sponge of orange pubic hair.

'What the hell is this,' Marian yelled. Then turning and looking round the room, she took her stuff and wobbled towards the door. 'I didn't sign up to this.' She held the door handle. She looked back over her shoulder. John was staring at her, breathing heavy. 'I'm out of here,' she said. 'I'm going to fetch my brothers,' she said. 'I'm getting my apology one way or another and my brothers will beat the ignorant one for this.' She pointed to her cheek. 'He thinks he can hit me does he? He thinks he can feel me up and drop his pants while I kiss a man?' She was leaving now and the door closed behind her, but her voice went on ranting down the corridor and down the stairs, ranting about her brothers.

'Get up!' John said. 'Your girlfriend has gone.'

Andrew stayed on the floor laughing.

'Don't you dare laugh at me,' he said, lifting Andrew by his hair. 'Get up.' He punched him. 'Stand up.' He kept punching him, backing him up towards the balcony doors. 'Stop,' Anders said coming down his ladders. 'That's enough.' He tried coming between them, ducking away from John's punches. 'Enough John you're killing him.'

'Good,' John said, 'bastard put egg on me.' Another punch sent Andrew through the balcony doors. His body hit the decking. 'Teach him to put egg on me.' John was over him. He kept his fists clenched looking dangerous, as though ready for more. 'Get him cleaned up,' he said to Anders, 'and change your underpants for God sake, they're pointless.' Anders kneeled beside Andrew. 'Clean him up,' John said. 'Put him to bed.' Now he took a towel. 'I'm going for a shower. I want him cleaned up when I get back.'

After John had left, Anders turned Andrew over. There was blood on his lips and nostrils. 'Are you okay,' he said, but Andrew just grunted, coughed, and spat blood. Anders then tried lifting him by his arms, staggering with him, falling sluggishly forward. Both were on the floor now, almost face to face. 'Come on, work with me.' This time Anders put his arms around Andrew's chest, lifting him onto a chair, leaving him slumped there, feet apart, chest moving up and down like a boxer between rounds. 'Stay there,' Anders said, 'Your nose is bleeding.' He went inside for a moment, the tap was going and he quickly returned with a wet cloth, dabbing it over Andrew's face.

'I'm okay,' Andrew said, 'Get that off me.' He got up holding the chair for a while, spitting more blood. 'Where is he?' he said going into the room. 'Where is he?' he paused in the doorway, feeling his nose with his fingers. 'Where did he go?'

'Come inside, I'll make you a nice hot drink.'

'I don't want a nice hot drink.' Andrew was in the corridor now. 'I want a fight. I'm going after him.'

Anders stood centre of the room, holding his underpants up with one hand. He wanted to say more, but knew reasoning with him was pointless. John and Andrew could be as stubborn as each other, *let them fight*, he thought, *why should I bother*. He thought about packing his bags and leaving himself, but his head was hurting too much, so he switched off the fan and filled the kettle with water.

'I don't want coffee,' John said entering the room with the towel on his waist. 'Why is the fan off? Why is he not in bed?' He took off the towel. He used it to cover his eggy pillow. 'Where's Andy?' He was on his ladder now. 'I told you I don't want coffee.'

'He went after you,' Anders said, spooning granules into his mug. 'And the coffee is for me.'

'Well he doesn't have to go far. If he wants another fight I'm here.'

Anders switched off the light. The balcony doors were still open and moonlight glowed over the kitchen top. In that light, he separated his bedding and hung a blanket around his shoulders and chest, giving him the look of a spiritual person. Then he looked down the corridor. Five minutes had passed now and he expected Andrew to have returned. Then there was shouting on the road. 'Does he want some,' John said.

'Wake me if he wants some.' Anders said nothing. He went to the balcony. He leaned on the wooden edge, which creaked and wobbled, as it was old and almost broken, like most things in their room. He stepped back watching Andrew disappear into the tall trees, still shouting John's name as he headed down towards the river.

Shortly afterwards two men got out of a taxi. They spoke by the roadside and one lit a cigarette, pointing it towards their room above The Old Crow. Anders watched with a churning in his stomach. The kettle clicked. He turned sharply as though someone was behind him. Suddenly he felt very hot. He dropped his blanket and stepped backwards over it, returning to the room. He then closed the door searching for extra locks. There was only one. He checked it twice, then made a coffee and returned to the balcony. Now he saw they were crossing the road. They're coming for me, he thought, Marian wants her apology.

Chapter five

Bang! Bang! Bang! The door kept going and the two men shouted behind it. 'Let us in.' Bang! Bang! 'Open up.'

Anders quickly finished dressing himself. Now in small shorts and a tight vest, he leaned on John's bunk speaking into his ear. 'Wake,' he whispered. But John turned over facing the wall, groaning in a sleepy kind of way. 'The two brothers are here,' Anders said. 'They're going to beat me, wake up.' John kept sleeping. 'You're a bastard.'

Anders stepped away from the bunk, went to his suitcase, picked up his shoes, then stood there and looked outside. He considered climbing into the willow tree, hiding there with his friend, the Possum. Bang! Bang! Bang! 'Let us in.'

He ignored them while doing up his laces, then going outside, and looking silly in shorts and shoes, he reached over the balcony's edge for a drainpipe. The slack wood swayed as he leaned on it, cracking, struggling under his weight. He stepped back fearing it would break. 'Let us in right now.' Then he grabbed a tree branch, but his arms were too weak and briefly he just hung there, arms trembling. 'We know you're in there.'

Bang! Bang! Bang! 'Let us in!' Only one of them spoke now, and he sounded Australian.

Anders went back inside, he put on his spectacles and stood near the door.

'Go away,' he said, struggling on each syllable. 'It's late. I'll call for someone.'

'Call for someone then,' the Australian said. 'Let us in, we're with Andy.'

'But he's not here,' Anders said.

'Well let us in anyway.'

'I'd rather not.'

'I'm not asking you, I'm telling you.' Bang! Bang! Bang!

'Okay, okay, I apologise.'

'Let us in!'

'She's got her apology, now go away.'

'I'll be up that drainpipe in a minute.'

Anders turned. He tugged John's covers, patted his shoulders. 'Wake up, John. I think we're in trouble.' John grunted again and with one arm, he reached for his blanket and pulled it over himself, snoring.

Bang! Bang! Bang! 'Let us in,' the Australian yelled.

Anders put both hands on the door handle. It rattled in his grip.

'That's it,' the Australian said. 'Now open up.'

He opened the door and staggered backwards as the Australian charged in, grinning, then nodding, then grinning and nodding. 'We're in,' he said. 'Now hold this.' He passed Anders a full box of beer cans, laughing, watching him struggle, staggering backwards some more. 'Where's Andy?' he asked. But Anders couldn't speak. As though his tongue had doubled in size, his words were now blocked. He faced the Australian, a big man with a shaven head, a black goatee beard and dark patches under each eye, as though he slept badly. His clothes were dark too, and front of his T-shirt was a print of the bearded Australian outlaw, Ned Kelly.

Another man entered. The second brother, Anders thought, watching him wander past carrying a stench of cannabis. The second brother looked nothing like the first, Anders thought, he had face piercings and long yellow hair, which he'd parted down the middle. His clothes were colourful, baggy and hippy-like, and his eyes Anders noticed, unlike his brothers, had no darkness in them and shone a wonderful blue colour. He was more relaxed too, and calmly headed for the balcony where he sat taking Rizlas and cigarettes and a small block of weed from his pocket, laying his drug paraphernalia on the table.

'I didn't do anything,' Anders said as though on the verge of tears. 'It was the fan.' The Australian stayed in front of him, staring, scratching his goatee beard with his overgrown, dirty fingernails.

'It was the fan,' Anders said again, this time he pointed to it.

'Sure,' the second brother said, 'burning weed over candle flame, rubbing charred bits into an open Rizla with his thumb. 'Where's Andy?'

'I don't know,' Anders said now ashamed of his own words, of how weak, of how stuttered they came out. 'Maybe you have the wrong room.'

'Nah, we don't,' the Australian said with clenched teeth, as though biting on something. 'This room has a terrace.' His breathing became heavy through his nostrils. 'We heard all about the terrace. I love a terrace.' He looked at Anders holding the box, punched through the cardboard packaging with his fist, took a can and opened it in Anders's face. Froth sprayed his eyes. He stood there blinking.

'That box heavy?' The Australian then asked.

Anders looked down. He said nothing.

John was now awake peering over his blanketed shoulder, and taking one glance at the big, bald, beer drinking Australian, lowered himself under his covers again, keeping still.

'Is it heavy?' the Australian repeated. This time Anders nodded, feeling a cold sweat on his spine that caused him to shiver. He wondered why they hadn't beaten him yet, and why the second brother had an English accent. Also, he thought, they look nothing like Marian, maybe they have different fathers or mothers, or maybe they're just friends and she refers to them as brothers in an affectionate way, and as for the beating, maybe they like to get in the mood first, maybe they like a little drink and a little smoke first, maybe they're psychopaths, maybe they like to take their time.

The second brother had his spliff going on the candle flame now, drawing on it slowly, admiring it between his fingers in the moonlight, blowing smoke upwards, as though it was an offering to the gods. The Australian, still sipping his beer, then joined him at the table where he sat waiting his turn.

'What happened to your head?' the second brother asked.

'It was the fan,' Anders said, pleased the subject had come up. 'This is what I'm trying to say.'

'I see.' He drew on the spliff again before passing it to the Australian, who took it and smoked it without taking his eyes off Anders. 'You can leave that box with me if you like, come join us.'

Anders brought the box to the table and sat with them. He thanked the second brother but then felt silly for acting so obediently in his own room. The second brother smiled, opened two beers and passed one to Anders. Again, Anders thanked him. Meanwhile the Australian had turned his chair, looking at John's underpants in the doorway. He asked Anders if they belonged to him, then asked why, whilst jabbing his finger towards them, they were covered with blood and shit. Staring downwards, taking beer as quickly as possible to aid his nerves, Anders ignored both questions while the second brother burned more weed, laughing as he noticed the Australian still looking at the soiled underpants.

'Someone ought to pick 'em up,' the Australian said. 'They're the worst kept undies I ever seen.'

'Would you prefer I close the doors to stop them bothering you?' Anders asked.

'Do what you want,' the Australian said, 'all I'm saying, and I think I'm right when I say this, is they look shitty.'

The second brother laughed again and turning weed over flame he said, 'Andy said you're Anders, is that right?' *The little shit,* Anders thought, *he's told these psychopaths my name.*

49

'Why?' Anders said, hiding his shaky hands under the table. 'What's going on?'

'Nothing,' he said, 'you can relax. We drank beers with Andy earlier, he invited us up for some more, but me and Steve,' he paused, he took his spliff back from Steve and finished it, 'we got held up for ages trying to score weed, then ages again trying to find a bottle shop. Sorry, my name is Henry.' He reached over the table. Anders shook hands with him while Steve tossed an empty over his shoulder, burped extravagantly, and cracked open another.

'Andy also told us you'd be well up for this, that right?' Steve said tasting his beer. 'You're certainly enjoying that one, aren't you?'

'It's nice,' Anders said. 'It's refreshing.'

'I didn't ask if it was nice or refreshing,' Steve said. 'What I'm saying is you're enjoying it, aren't you?' Anders didn't say anything, he just stared between his feet on the floor. 'What I'm saying is this,' Steve went on, 'you kept us waiting. I wasn't happy about that.'

'I wasn't sure who it was,' Anders said. 'It's the middle of the night. I wasn't sure.'

'Well,' Steve said waving his can, 'I wasn't happy.'

Henry leaned over the candle. He lit another spliff, smoking it while asking questions about Andrew. Anders explained about the egg and the fight, and how Andrew had gone looking for John not long before they arrived. Steve seemed very interested. He began grinning suddenly, and his right hand, Anders noticed, seemed to clench and squeeze and crush around his beer can, especially when there was any mention of blood. He took short drags on the spliff now and blew smoke directly into Anders's face, he grinned at that too, staring and grinning as he watched Anders waft the smoke away, then he'd blow more, and stare at his own clenched fist through the smoke, as though admiring it. 'He would've got worse from me,' he said still admiring his fist. 'I'd have let some serious bombs go, if he cracked an egg on me, serious bombs.'

He kissed his fist. Henry saw this and burst out laughing.

'I'm serious,' Steve said, staring vacantly at the both of them.

Anders finished his beer. Henry opened another and passed it to him. Steve reached into the box, took one for himself and produced a small pocketknife. Anders shot Henry a glance from across the table, but Henry waved a hand signalling that everything was okay, that trepidation was not necessary. Anders settled again and like Henry, he watched Steve, now stabbing his beer can with his knife, downing it in one. This was a process he repeated three more times, and each time he told them, whilst beer fizzed onto the decking, that this was how he did it, Aussie style. Then he'd stare at Anders for a while as though waiting for a reaction. When nothing came, he'd show them another can, keeping eyes on Anders as he stabbed it up. 'Us Aussies can drink, you both know that, right?'

Henry laughed.

Tissst! The knife kept going, he moved onto beer number seven, more fizz, more spillage. 'Yeah, that's right,' he said thrusting back in his seat, sucking the can, beer escaping him, wetting his T-shirt. 'Another one down.' He burped. He crushed the can and tossed it over his shoulder. Then he'd do it all again, each time reminding them what number can he was on. 'If there's one thing you ought to know about us Aussies,' he said, 'it's that we can drink.' But he began to slow and by number ten, he was pausing and burping for long periods. He took a short break while he finished Henry's spliff. Then he reached for another. Half way through number eleven his head dropped, his mouth opened, and shortly afterwards snoring began.

Anders sighed and smiled at Henry from across the table. That was enough. There was no reason to discuss anything further. Their smiles said it all. Henry opened another Rizla and burned weed over the candle. Anders watched him the way one might watch an artist creating a masterpiece, and with weed pinched between thumb and finger Henry looked up, and noticing he'd been caught, Anders pretended to look somewhere else, as though embarrassed, as though he'd intruded on a ritual, a ritual of burning weed and tearing up cigarettes. 'You can try this one if you like,' Henry said.

'Would be my first,' Anders said.

'Well,' Henry said holding another spliff to the moonlight, 'you're in for a treat,' he said. 'I make a good one.'

Steve made a noise and they looked at him in his chair, chin on chest, arms limp either side of him, and sand flies swarming around his baldhead. Henry laughed with the candle in his hand, holding it to the spliff, which he drew on for a moment before leaning over the table with it in his fingers. 'Here,' he said to Anders, 'give it a try.' Anders took it and asked what to do. Henry told him it was just like smoking a cigarette, he was to simply drag and inhale.

'Here goes then,' Anders smelt it, put it between his lips.

'Yep,' Henry said, 'that's how you do it.'

He held the weed within his lungs, stared at Henry for more instruction.

'You can breathe now,' Henry laughed. 'Go on, that's fine.'

Smoke drifted across the table. Anders gasped for breath, thumped his chest with his fist, coughed savagely, turned a little pale, and then watery eyed he began to blink. Henry was smiling, and, Anders noticed, was looking at him in a protective way, in an older brother kind of way, and being an only child, Anders took comfort in his presence.

'You'll get there,' Henry said taking the spliff back, drawing on it and blowing smoke upwards in a relaxed manner. Then he kicked Steve's leg, holding the spliff out for him. Steve mumbled, reached both arms forward like a zombie, took it, drew on it for no longer than half a second and dropped his arms again, with the spliff burning between his fingers.

'That's a bit nasty, isn't it?' Henry said.

'He's a nasty bloke,' Anders laughed feeling the effects of the weed.

'Not him,' Henry said, 'the smell, what is it?'

'Oh yeah, think I'm with you now. What is it?'

'I don't know. It's like burning hair, that horrible smell you get at the hairdressers.'

'Yeah, when old women sit having their hair coloured purple,' Anders said. 'It's like that.'

Steve was suddenly lifting a foot, jerking a shoulder and rocking the table with his knees. Beer cans fell. He opened his eyes and threw the spliff into the willow tree. Red ash glowed on the leaves, turning slowly grey. He got up, rubbed his burnt fingers over his jeans while pacing up and down, glaring at Anders as though it was his fault. Then he went back to his chair, got another can and opened it. He slumped down again, leaving the can untouched, staring now and then between his fingers. His mouth opened and closed as though he was going to say something, and then he closed his eyes. They gave him a moment before Henry began prodding him with his finger. 'Is he asleep?' Anders asked.

'Think so,' Henry said, 'think he's going again.' Prod, prod. 'Yeah, he's out.'

'He's erratic, isn't he?'

'He is, and I have to bunk with him.'

'And there's me thinking I have it bad with John and Andrew.'

'They annoy you?'

'Constantly,' Anders said.

Henry passed the spliff to him. He took it, dragged on it, coughed, handed it back.

'What do you think?' Henry asked.

'I think he's a strange individual.'

'I was asking about the weed.'

'Oh,' Anders laughed, 'it's okay, but rather hard to appreciate with him being so jumpy. He keeps staring at me.'

Both looked at Steve, head down, shoulders hung, sand flies all over him. Sudden fits of laughter overwhelmed them. Tears streaked their faces. Henry dropped his arms on the table, spilling beer, knocking cans. Anders reached out catching the candle. He held an arm across his chest, coughing and laughing.

'He does,' Henry said still laughing, 'he stares a lot.'

'Glad you've noticed. It's freaking me out.'

'Yeah but I bunk with the fucker.'

'I feel for you.'

'Really,' Henry laughed, 'how much? You gonna come running to my rescue when the cunt attacks me with a sledgehammer during the night?'

'I'll listen out for that.'

'Thanks, and I'll be sleeping with one eye open.'

Anders lifted his vest drying his cheeks with it, both arms going now and then as the giggles kept coming. 'I recommend you do that,' he said. 'I think that's an idea.'

Henry made another spliff and lit it. They smoked weed and drank their beers together in silence, giggling now and then, but mostly they were silent and there was no awkwardness in this, which Anders thought to be strange. It was as though they'd known each other for

56

years and small talk was not necessary, as though they were happy just to sit and appreciate their own thoughts, and appreciate each other's company in silence, and in this peaceful moment - Anders closed his eyes and slept.

Chapter six

For how long he slept, he was unsure. But on waking again he felt cold, unpleasant, and loneliness came over him. He heard cupboard doors opening and closing. The chairs where Henry and Steve had sat were now empty, and there was a spliff burning out on the table. 'Is that you?' he asked. 'Andrew, are you back?'

'It's me,' Steve said appearing between the balcony doors, holding the can of creamed corn. 'I'm hungry,' he said. 'Tell me what this is.'

'Where's Henry,' Anders said, outstretching his arms, looking into the room.

'He went to bed. It's just me and you now,' Steve said. 'Tell me what this is.' He stared at the can then waved it in Anders's face. 'What is it?'

'Pureed corn, John has it for supper with toast.'

'Good stuff, where's the bread?'

'We don't have any.'

'Why mention toast then?'

'Just saying, that's what he has it with.' Anders yawned and looked round wishing that Henry was still with him.

'Sick bastards,' Steve said putting the can on the kitchen top. 'No wonder you shit blood eating this stuff.' He looked at the underpants again and kicked them. Then he patted his belly, walked up and down the room eyeing up the can. 'I am hungry though,' he said, 'is this really all you have?' Anders nodded and then watched Steve reaching into his back pocket for his pocketknife. By the kitchen top, he began jabbing it into the can. 'I'll eat it,' he said. 'I don't care, I don't care, I'll eat it.' His knife bounced everywhere as he jabbed it, catching him back of the hand, back of the wrist, slashing his knuckles, but still he kept going as though he felt no pain. Anders picked up the spliff and smoked some, keeping his eyes on Steve, jabbing and swearing, thrusting his knife down, twisting it, turning it in and out like a fisherman prying open a stubborn oyster. Sweat appeared across his eyebrows. It ran into his eyes. He squinted. He reached for a tea towel, brought it to his face and rubbed it all over his baldhead. Then he was attacking the can again, jab-jabbing, twisting the knife. 'I'm getting there,' he said. 'This is progress.' But he breathed heavily, sweated badly, and bled all over the kitchen top. The progress was poor. He'd made one or two holes, but the rest of the can was just dinted. He missed again slicing a finger. This time he reacted, jumping in the air shouting, 'Coolangatta! Coolangatta!'

He threw the creamed corn into the sink, ran his tongue up and down his knife and returned to his chair with the tea towel draped over his head. 'I'm not even bothered,' he said sitting down, looking sullen, staring at his bleeding knuckles. 'It stunk. I was almost there but it stunk too much.'

'We have a tin opener,' Anders said, but Steve ignored him and looked away, sucking his knuckles, tasting blood. 'We also have a first aid box.' There was no answer. Steve dropped his shoulders. He looked off over the balcony, vacantly, into the distance somewhere. 'Well,' Anders said, 'I think that's a night. I hear my bed calling me.' He giggled. 'I should imagine you'll need your sleep too. I guess you have work tomorrow.'

'I don't care about work,' Steve said, and he reached out to somewhere within his jeans and placed several tabs of acid on the table. 'And this party ain't over,' he said, 'not yet.'

In his innocence Anders had no idea what they were, and when he saw the print of Jimmy Hendrix's face on each one, he assumed they might be rare postage stamps, collectables maybe. But the thought of that seemed odd. He couldn't picture Steve as a stamp collector, a head stamper, possibly, but no stamp collector. Steve then explained how he got them, how a crazy American had handed them to him at Bryon Bay bus station, and how the American kept calling him the egg man.

Although, Steve told with a frown, he wasn't sure what the egg man bit meant.

'Maybe,' Anders said sitting up straight. 'Maybe because you're bald, you know, your baldhead, egg like, hence the egg man.'

Steve felt underneath the tea towel with his fingers. 'I'm not bald,' he said. 'I shave it. I got loads of hair if I want it. But I shave it. I'm not bald and I shave it.'

'Of course,' Anders said trying not to laugh, still feeling the effects of weed.

'Anyway, forget that,' Steve said poking a tab of acid with his finger, putting it on his tongue. 'We're going on a trip.' He took some beer, washed down the tab and burped.

'But what are they?' Anders asked.

'Acid,' Steve said, 'LSD, trips.' He put another tab on his tongue and again, washed it down with beer. 'Easy see, just like taking bread at church. Now you go.'

'I don't want any, thank you.' Anders said. 'I want my bed.'

'But you must pass the acid test.' Steve laughed, though there was no joy in his laugher, it was a wicked laugh, a cruel laugh, and his eyes played no part in it. He moved the tabs closer to Anders, tapped a beer can with his fingernail.

'I really don't want to, Steve.' Anders pushed the tabs away.

Steve pulled the tea towel from his head. He rubbed his neck with it, dabbed it over his knuckles. 'Look,' he said putting it back where it was, wearing it like an Arab. 'You're not sitting there watching me trip. If you're going to host a party, you join in. Now take a tab, take a tab and take a beer with it.'

'But...'

'Don't argue with me. Just do as you're told.'

'But I'm really tired. I thought you were too. You could barely keep your head up before.'

Steve laughed and leaned over the candle flame, eyes glaring in its light. He signalled Anders closer with his finger. 'I was awake,' he whispered. 'I was awake the whole time. I can be rather patient with things like that. I can wait a long time. I wanted Henry to go. I wanted more acid for me and you, greedy huh?' He rocked in his chair, laughing. The tea towel fell and he caught it.

'But I don't want them.'

'Andy said you'd be well up for this.'

'He probably meant a beer or two, a few beers on the balcony.'

'You and Henry had a good giggle, didn't you?' Steve kept rocking in his chair, rocking then putting his arms on the table, messing with the beer cans.

'It was the weed. It made me act silly.'

'Just take the acid, there's a good boy.' Steve ripped a tab and held it to Anders's face. Anders looked over Steve's fingertip and saw it there. 'Just do half,' Steve said, almost touching Anders's lips.

'Tomorrow,' Anders said trying to buy more time, 'when I'm not so tired, yes?'

Steve picked up a can with his other hand. 'Do it, do it now.'

'Please, Steve, please, it's so fucking late.'

'You're arguing again. Now take your medicine and behave.'

'I'm so tired.'

'Don't argue with me.'

'Tomorrow, please, tomorrow.'

'Thing is, I'm not going anywhere.'

'Was you really not asleep?'

Steve didn't answer. He just rattled the can. Beer swished inside.

'We were only joking.'

'I understand. I have a sense of humour.'

Then Anders got up and when he spoke, he packed his words with as much authority as he could muster. 'Please, I don't like this. Please, I want my bed. Please, this is my room and I will not be dictated to.'

Steve laughed again. He put down the can and rubbed his finger edge of the table to get rid of the tab. Then he sat back waving his arms in defeat. 'I was only joking,' he said. 'I won't force you into anything.' He laughed again and took a fresh can from the box. 'Look,' he said with his fingers on the ring-pull, just finish a beer with me, yes, and then I'll leave.'

Anders still wanted his bed but conceded that a beer with Steve was progress compared to staying up for the rest of the night doing hard drugs. 'Okay,' he said, 'one more beer.' Steve passed Anders a can from the table. It was almost empty and warm and he wasn't sure whose it was, but he didn't care, he wanted rid of Steve, and so he took it, drinking the warm, flat, disgustingly horrid beer as quickly as possible. Steve drank too. Then he was laughing again, nodding and rocking again. 'Was that druggy,' he asked.

'Sorry?' Anders smiled looking up from his can.

'I said was that druggy, I mean yummy?'

'I guess so,' Anders said putting down the can, rubbing both hands over his mouth. 'Is it bedtime now?'

'Nope.'

'What do you mean?'

'You said tomorrow.' Steve was grinning.

'That's right.'

'Well by my clock it's past midnight.' He tapped his watch-face.

Now Anders sighed. He stood again and lifted his arms high in the air. 'You stop this now, Steve,' he shouted. 'Stop this fucking about. It's been past midnight for fucking ages and you're fucking me about, and I'm tired, and I'm so fucking tired.' Anders paused suddenly, eyes studying the table, then studying Steve's hands, left hand, right hand, left and right, eyes flickering between both. 'Where are the tabs?' he said. 'Get up, get up now and help me find them.' But Steve just laughed, rocking back and forth like one of those creepy. mechanical clowns in its box at the fairground, the ones that don't stop laughing. Anders was on his hands and knees now, crawling between table legs and chairs. 'Help me find them!'

'Good drink was it,' Steve said.

'Where are they?'

'Two each will be plenty, would you agree?'

Anders fell onto his back, kicking his feet in the air. 'You bastard,' he said, 'you dirty, rotten bastard.' He got up, tipping out beer cans, moving his fingers in their frothy puddles. 'You didn't. Tell me you didn't. You swine. You scoundrel. You rotten bastard.'

'The pink elephants are coming,' Steve said. 'The acid test has begun.'

Chapter seven

The sky was cloudless and tinged with red. Then suddenly the sun appeared over brown hills in the distance. And though the day was early, it was already a hot one. For an hour Anders had fretted over his next move. He faced the road now thinking about his situation. Then images of Steve came into his mind, just Steve wearing that tea towel and laughing that laugh, and after that Anders wasn't sure, he wasn't sure about any of it, for reality and trip had now merged into one foggy nightmare.

Feeling trapped he moved slightly. The thorns of the bush hurt him and he blinked, wincing in pain. Then he looked down, then up again. There were two pubs across the road and he surveyed them. Eyeing their wooden balconies, they reminded him of The Old Crow and that's where he wished he were right now, sat at the table with the Possum, with memory intact. Then switching his attention to the left, he saw a bistro style cafe, a bus stop, a barbershop, and a ponytailed man walking back and forth over his own footsteps, pinching a cigarette between his fingers. He drew on it and stopped suddenly staring at his shoes. Then he watched himself for a moment. He watched himself smoke in the shop windows. Anders watched him while he watched himself. Anders watched from a funny position, from the bush he was half in, half out, arms bleeding, neck scratched. Again, he thought about his situation.

He puffed his cheeks and looked each way, left, right. There was nothing but dirt path and acacia trees and bush, a long curvy line of bush, which was parallel with the path and the road. He touched the sides of his mouth with his tongue, tasting weed. He sucked his teeth. He dug his elbows into the sandy dirt and dragged his front and then his legs through the bush. He lay in the dirt a while, arms and legs trembling, looking so scratched it was as though he'd been raked. His feet bled. Thorns lay hidden under the skin of his toes and fingertips.

After a short rest, he climbed up a dip towards an acacia tree. This was nearer to the road now and the car smoke got to him. He kept low and coughed a little. Then he crawled towards and over some tree roots, resting his face on a piece of cool bark. Then gently he stroked one side of his ribs, feeling rough scratches with his fingers, and then moved them over his hair, which was thick with dirt and twigs. He puffed his cheeks again and looked at the bush.

The sun rose taking his shade. Then a glow appeared over his body. It's time to move again, he thought, and he set off towards the next tree, a larger one with more foliage. There he kept low with his belly on the dirt, studying the area, figuring a way home. He wished he had woken earlier, or woken on the other side of the bush. Then he wondered how he came to be there at all, stuck, face down in the dirt like that. He stared for a second at his bleeding arms; going back through the bush was not an option, he knew that much, it was painful enough the first time. He touched his legs. He looked at his arms again - the damn thing had shredded him good.

Now on his feet, he began stumbling towards another tree, then another, appearing between each one, walking as though stepping on hot coals, skipping and a hopping, making an O shape with his lips then quickly blowing through them, blowing sharply as though putting out a candle. He fell. He slumped over more roots and lay there sweating. Muddy beads of perspiration dripped into his eyes and he rubbed them with his palms. Then he came onto his elbows and noticed something glistening beside a pile of red rocks. He blinked feeling his eyes again. 'Maybe,' he whispered, and if his spectacles were there, what else?

From behind the tree, he studied the bus stop. There was a bunch of school kids knocking about a football and playing a game of keepy-upy. He watched for a while tallying their progress. He saw a woman there too, sat staring forward, ignoring the gambolling group around her. She looked pleasant in her turtleneck sweater, he thought, pleasant but fed up, and she kept having to slap the ball away from her face or roll it back to them, while the boisterous scoundrels cheered sarcastically.

Seeing them as his biggest threat, he kept watching the road and the bus stop area. He arched forward and sat up. He did this with one foot in his lap and began pinching his toes with thumb and forefinger, squeezing thorns from them. Some bled. Some spat yellow puss. His eyes watered. He turned in the direction of the red rocks again. They seem close, he kept thinking as he pinched more skin, and maybe there's more stuff that way. Moreover, he noted, was a gate further on, which led to a farm or some property that would lead to the other side of the bush. He let go of his foot now and thought about it, thought about being on the other side, wading through high grass with nobody else around him. It seemed a good idea, was nice to have a plan, was nice to know he'd be going home soon.

The idea brought a smile to his face. He set off crawling, twitching his body now and then as salty compounds from the dirt got into his cuts. He kept low, stayed beside the traffic, moving in its shadows. A cattle wagon slowed nearby pushing onto the kerb. At the back of the wagon were cows, pushing their heads between wooden planks, staring over him with their big white eyes. Birds flapped above in the trees, some chased each other branch-to-branch, knocking dusty leaves. Now and then he would pause. He would look around and listen to engines ticking, horns beeping, kids laughing and football bouncing. The traffic was stop-start, slow but steady, and he moved in a similar rhythm, chest and belly on the dirt, heart thudding like crazy.

At the rocks, he found his spectacles and put them on. They hung wonky to the left, and when he touched the right lens, his finger felt a tiny crack. He didn't mind much though. He was happy to find something. He kept them on and peered over the rocks hoping to find more stuff, shorts, maybe a vest. But there was nothing, just bush on one side and road on the other. He looked between them. Again nothing, just dirt, acacia trees and the odd pile of rocks. Maybe they're on the other side of the bush, he thought. Then he looked at the gate and smiled, picturing himself on the other side, running through golden barley in slow motion, as though he was in a pop music video. He began to laugh, he felt good, good apart from the cuts and the headache and the memory loss.

On he crawled with blood, sweat and dirt drying across his back in different shades of red, grey and brown, but his belly was damp, and the dirt below it formed into mud. 'I'm a commando,' he said digging in with his elbows, shuffling on, 'I'm a commando, and I'm dressed commando.' He laughed again. 'Come now, Anders,' he said. 'Behave

71

yourself.' He kept moving. He was close now and not too far from the last tree, where he planned another short rest before making a run for the gate. He settled his breath. He closed his eyes and laughed again at his commando joke.

'What's that?' a kid yelled suddenly from the bus stop. 'That's a sasquatch,' answered his friend. 'It's a big foot,' said another. 'A big foot is a sasquatch you dope,' the first kid said while shaking his head. Then they all laughed, all except for the woman in the turtleneck sweater, she was cupping her mouth with both hands.

Anders froze mid crawl resembling a lizard stopped in its tracks, as though face-to-face with a King cobra. His eyes widened giving him the expression of an alerted owl, a muddy faced owl. He felt a fluttering in his stomach, felt his scalp prickle and his forehead burn. He'd gone all feeble, all doughy, and in that moment, he couldn't pick himself up from the floor.

'That sure is a sasquatch,' a scrawny old man said appearing suddenly, staggering along one of the pub balconies and zipping up his worn green pants. 'I'm into this,' he added. 'Have I missed much?' Then his attention turned elsewhere, to his left, to the cafe, where a blonde woman screamed from the passenger side of her boyfriends red sports car. The roof was down and she stood holding her hands top of

72

her head, bouncing her heels on the expensive looking leather seats. 'Someone shut that bitch up!' he yelled showing a brown tooth. 'I'm getting into this, shut her up!'

But she screamed again, and the old man's crinkled up and sun-scorched forehead began to twitch. 'Sammy,' she screamed. 'Sammy get out here now.'

Sammy, who she now turned to with a scolding look of frustration, watching him eat greedily behind the cafe window, got up fast and came to the doorway. He was a beefy man with arms like weapons of mass destruction and an exaggerated chin like some comic book superhero. He looked slightly lost as he ran a napkin over his face and nodded while she thrust her arm out, pointing at Anders. Again he nodded, he pulled a string of meat from his teeth and stared at her. Then he peered through the cafe window at his breakfast box, at his meaty burrito and selection of sides, at his pulped avocados, diced onions, mustard sauce and daddy sized dose of scrambled eggs. 'My breakie,' he whispered, slowly, gloomily.

'Forget that, Sammy,' she said, 'You got a job to do.'

'But I need my protein, baby. Come on, I need my protein.' He passed the napkin nervously between both hands, glanced over his shoulder at his breakfast box. He stood looking fresh from a morning gym session, his red T-shirt covered in damp sweat patches. 'He'll move on soon, baby, come on now.'

'I don't care, Sammy,' she said. 'You go after him,' she said.

'But, babe...' Sammy squeezed his napkin. Again, he looked through the cafe window. He felt his cube shaped head. He flattened his spiky hair with his fingers. She beeped the car horn, threw her hands in the air and glared at him. He dropped the napkin now and began moving sullenly from the doorway, and taking one final glance through the cafe window, he set off.

The school kids cheered for Sammy as he crossed the road, big shoulders moving, muscular thighs showing from his short-shorts as he weaved through the traffic with a grin. The ponytailed man lit another cigarette, shifting his eyes between Anders and Sammy. Passengers hung from car windows laughing and yelling. Horns beeped. Engines revved. Some folks, one or two in cowboy hats, stepped from pub doorways with their eyes on the dirt path, glass of morning beer in hand, and on the dirt path was a man being dragged along by his German Shepherd. The dog paused dipping its nose to Anders's backside. It sniffed while he blinked. He only blinked. The rest of him stayed stiff.

Sammy kept making progress. His grin broke into a smile and he began to slow jog and raise his arms to the bus stop crowd and the cheers. Anders watched him, now pleased that the dog owner had moved on, struggling, staggering and yanking the German Shepherd away by its lead. Anders got ready, moving his toes, his feet, his legs. The race would soon be on. Anders knew he had to be first, he just needed to get to that gate. Sammy kept coming, kept lapping up the cheers like an athlete entering a grand stadium on cup final day. He was smiling a lot. His face looked awkward now, as though sore from too much smiling.

Anders stood up with his penis showing. There was more laughter, more cheers. The old man with the brown tooth jumped up and down, was eating mashed beans from a mess tin, shovelling them into his mouth with a long wooden spoon. He poured a drop of bourbon over the beans, titled the tin and sipped from one corner. 'What am I missing?' He ran from one end of the balcony to the other. 'Where's he gone?'

Sammy strode onto the dirt path. He walked towards Anders with his chest puffed out, waving now and then to the bus stop kids. 'Get him, Sammy,' the Blonde said. He responded by showing his thumb, tilting his chin, smiling a smile that could be mistaken as arrogance if the rest of his face didn't appear so stupid and clueless. She slapped the steering wheel and pointed to Anders now shifting behind him, running faster than he had ever ran before. His eyes focused only on the gate and his bare feet flicking up dirt.

'No, no, he didn't,' Sammy said. He then removed his T-shirt and rubbed his brow with it. The bus stop kids cheered. He smiled and the cheers went up another notch. Then he did one press up. Again, they cheered for big Sammy. He did another one, and then another, again more cheers for Sammy. The Blonde placed the heel of her hand over her eye, she held it there and shook her head. Sammy was nodding at the cheers. He set off moving both hands over his six-pack. The woman in the turtleneck sweater watched and poked a finger towards her open mouth, pretending to vomit while all around her cheered for Sammy.

Anders kept running for the gate. It was becoming a fussy blur to him now. He blinked muddy sweat from his eyes and adjusted his spectacles. Focus cleared, seeing the gate as a gate again, he kept on pushing himself, focussed, ignoring the pain in his feet and not daring to look back. Run, run, running, heart pounding, genitals swinging. Suddenly he smelt onions and felt hot breath tickling his shoulders. A large shadow was looming as Sammy quickly gained on him. He saw the shadow but kept his focus on his feet. Never had he moved them so fast, and under different circumstances, he might have taken a moment to be impressed with himself. The gate was much closer now. Right there, he thought, only a few more strides.

'Sammy, you better run,' the Blonde hissed, 'or that's it.' She leaned over the car door and felt her breasts. 'They'll be no more of this for Sammy.'

Sammy watched them bounce in her hands. His teeth showed. He wore an insatiable expression. His eyes swelled. His jaw then clenched. It was an expression he held as he ran, and one he continued to hold as the tip of his foot met with a tree root, sending him forward, arms stretched out and skidding face down in the dirt. Anders guessed something had happened as the cheers turned to laughter. But he kept going, not daring to look back.

'Up, Sammy,' the Blonde screamed, but Sammy just lay there. She stepped out and slammed the car door. Her heels scratched on the pavement as she walked to the other side and pressed the steering wheel, three quick beeps. 'Sammy, he's escaping.'

'Jesus,' Sammy said. Then he got up rubbing his dirtied hands on his thighs.

The hot onion breath was gone, as was the shadow, Anders knew as he clattered into the gate, which suddenly seemed much bigger now he was close up. He pushed into it but nothing gave. It was solid and locked on both sides. He pushed again with his shoulder, nothing. He jumped high and gripped the top with his limp, floppy arms, struggling to lift his own weight, hands cut and bleeding. He dropped. He leaned on the wood breathing heavily and then turned watching Sammy set off again.

Meanwhile, across the road from his balcony, now stooping, now holding binoculars over his eyes and turning mechanically, far left, far right, then up and down, was the old brown-toothed man. He located Anders at the gate then paused, and swinging his bottle towards his open lips, wet his tongue with a drop of bourbon. He grinned now showing mashed beans on his gums, and of course, that one brown tooth. He let go of his binoculars. They hung around his skinny, chicken like neck on a piece of tattered string. He then kicked a can of cigarette ends across the decking. Then he danced in them barefooted, rubbing his toes into them.

'So I see now,' he said. 'I see what I've been missing.' He picked up his beans and topped them with more bourbon. Then suddenly he was fist pumping the air, fist pumping and chanting Aussie rules, and then leaning on the balcony edge, pecking the wooden beam with his singular tooth. He took some beans, took some bourbon. Then he straightened up to perform an Irish jig in his open dressing gown, which revealed a sunken and pale chest, patched with curly grey hairs. He quickly lost balance, staggered across the balcony and leaned over the wooden beam, opening and closing his eyes. 'This is good stuff,' he said. 'I'm into this.'

Anders was on one knee. He got up now and tried again. This time he hitched a foot up into a dinted horseshoe mark in the wood. It took his weight while he pulled himself higher, managing to curve an arm over the other side. He rested there, shoulder dug into the wood, taking splinters, taking his weight. Then he swung a leg over.

'Ohhhh!' People winced as Anders's legs opened and his backside parted.

'Drumstick,' the old man yelled, lowering his binoculars and pointing the bottle, pointing it at Anders's genitals. 'Don't let him snare you that way. That's a drumstick he's showing you.' He laughed. His scraggy hair parted and dropped to one side revealing a bald middle, which was blotchy with different shades of brown, and had a crack where his skin had dried over and burnt again in the sun. 'Up, big fella,' he said. 'Up and after him, and don't let him snare you that way, he's using tactics.'

Sammy smiled at the bus stop kids. He held it long, held it until his jaw vibrated. Then he was swaggering over to the gate, taking his time and nodding as the cheers began again. With one hand over his six-pack, he paused now and then pretending to be out of breath and tired.

'Get him!' the Blonde screamed.

'I'm in agreement with the hooker,' the old man yelled. 'This is a contact sport, go full chicken wing on that weasel.' He sat on a stool then stood again. He kept standing and sitting, eating beans and drinking bourbon. He saluted Sammy. Then he turned to the Blonde outside the cafe and saluted her. 'Aussie rules,' he said. 'What a man lives for.'

Anders hung on, panting heavily like a dog with a thirst on a hot day, hair wet and muddy, pasted across his forehead. His arms and legs were either side of the gate. He wanted to swing them over to escape. But he felt drained, for now he just dangled, dangled there looking spent. Sammy laughed taking his ankle. He tugged it. He held it up to the crowd, tugging and grinning as Anders struggled to hold on. There was only laughter now, no more cheering. Sammy's smile faded. He glanced towards his car to see the Blonde keying numbers into her mobile phone. He raised one arm, nothing. He flexed his six-pack, still no cheering.

'I want action,' the old man yelled. 'You can bask in your glory after you big cunt, now fix that chicken wing.' He pinched the curls on his chest, twisting them with his fingers. 'Yes, yesssss. Get him!'

Sammy tugged again. Anders leaned one way, arching as much weight as possible to the other side of the gate. Both resembled a pair of wrestlers duelling in a steel cage match and the resilience of Anders seemed to change the crowd's attitude. Ponytail stamped on his cigarette, curved a hand over his top lip, began booing.

'Let him go you muscle clad, jock,' one voice said. 'Yeah, you're twice his size,' said another from the street below the old man's balcony.

'That's plenty down there,' the old man said leaning over his wooden beam, his thick eyebrows and baldhead giving him the appearance of a prehistoric bird. 'I'm into this. This is good stuff.' He thrust the bottle out pointing his forefinger towards Sammy and Anders. 'Good stuff I said.' He poured bourbon into his mouth and then turned the bottle, bringing the label close to his eyes. 'This is good stuff too.'

'Go take your weekly shit, old man,' someone shouted without looking up, thumbs hooked inside their belt, staring forward.

The old man ignored him. He laughed, he put down the bourbon and rubbed both hands together. 'We're coming to a good bit,' he said.

'Now, how about that chicken wing, I want him pissing in the dirt, you hear me, pissing. He snared you and he snared me, and I can't let that go, I won't.'

Traffic moved on. A bus pulled up on the street kerb and Sammy's fans, the bus stop kids, slowly and reluctantly boarded it, while the girl in the turtleneck sweater watched them leave. The Blonde also made her move, marching off down an alleyway swinging her handbag. Two waitresses stacked empty cups outside the cafe, watching her dramatic exit. Then the man with the German Shepherd appeared. Again he staggered past, tugging the dog's lead as it pounced at Anders for another sniff. There was no cheering now, no laughter, just boos and protest toward Sammy's treatment of Anders.

'Let the poor bastard go,' Ponytail yelled tapping out another cigarette from its pack.

Sammy kicked the gate. It wobbled but Anders clung on. He scrunched his eyes, felt the sandpaper like wood chafing his groin. 'Why don't you climb down?' Sammy said to him. 'I got you, it's over, climb down.' Anders twisted his foot trying to pull away from Sammy's grip but nothing gave. He tried again, this time dragging his foot across Sammy's face as he spoke, rubbing it back and forth over his lips, muffling his words. 'Com... dow... fro... up... ther...' Sammy turned. He spat out dirt. 'Come down from up there I said.' Then making a claw shape with his spare hand, he raked his fingers down his tongue and wiped his forearm over his lips. 'Come down.' He spat again.

People began cheering for Anders. Sammy looked across the road at them, his face crumpled, his upper lip twitching and coming high to show big, white teeth. Now with both hands on the ankle, Sammy was tug-tug-tugging again and rocking that gate. Tears sprung to Anders's eyes, wood tore into his armpit, chest and groin. He moved slightly seeking comfort, and seeing opportunity, Sammy yanked him completely away from the gate. Anders was loose now, loose and falling backwards with the sun blinding his eyes.

'Boo!' People protested as he hit the deck, body vanishing in a mist of powdery dirt.

The booing continued. Everyone seemed disappointed that the underdog had been caught, all apart from the old man on the balcony. He leaned with his chest on the edge, on the wooden beam, his perch. He spat beans. He swore. A man below took off his cowboy hat and looking down on it, saw splatters of badly chewed up beans. Angrily, he picked something from the floor, pulled an arm back and took aim.

'Behave down there,' the old man yelled. 'That was a fair take down. This is Aussie rules and that means full contact.' He sniffed, he looked around. 'After him,' he said, seeing through his binoculars that Anders was crawling back towards the bushes. 'After him you dopey square headed tool.' He waved his mess tin, took a few beans.

There were more boos as Sammy walked slowly behind Anders, then suddenly launched himself through the air like a missile, directing his muscular shoulder into Anders's back. Anders felt pain from head to toe. He felt his spine vibrating, his teeth and jaw locked. Now he was pinned. Sammy was over him, digging an uncompromising knee into his kidney.

'Good work,' the old man said, 'now there's still time for that chicken wing.' He looked ready to say more when a brick struck him between his eyes. For a moment he rocked, bottle turning over in hand, liquor spilling on the decking. He staggered back sway-swaying, moving heel-toe, heel-toe, then forward to collapse across his perch. A trickle of blood marked his brow. His eyes had crisscrossed in opposite directions. 'A little help,' he wheezed slowly, but nobody paid any attention.

Anders was fighting back. He kicked out and pushed off the ground. An astonishing amount of dust rose around them and both coughed

84

while Sammy got back on top. Then cupping a hand over Anders's mouth, he dug his knee further into the kidney. Anders started to cry. He cried into Sammy's wet fingers and they smelt funny, smelt fishy, he thought, as Sammy rubbed them over his face, same way Anders got him earlier with the foot treatment. He moved them up and down. Then he moved them in circles. 'Hold still,' he said. But Anders kept spitting, turning his face from the rancid smell. Soon there was vomit shooting out both sides of his mouth. Sammy got up leaving Anders facedown in vomit and dirt. In the sunlight, he lifted his hand and studied the warm milky, brown frothy substance dripping from his fingers. Then his face darkened and the sunlight was gone, for now two men dressed in thorn coloured uniforms and Stetson hats had appeared in front of him, blocking its glare. Anders lifted himself resting on one elbow, but with tears and dirt in his eyes, he saw only blurred images. And before he could clear his view, gloved hands were grabbing his ankles and dragging him away.

Chapter eight

Andrew knelt over an open suitcase, his hands sifting through a pile of unwashed clothes. 'Hang on. Are you saying he suddenly jumped off the balcony?' He paused now to look at John. 'Is that what you're saying?' He sifted through clothing again, some he bunched together, some he brought to his nose for a sniff. 'You saw that, did you?'

John didn't look at him. He sat edge of his bunk, head down, pillow over his knees, picking at fragments of eggshell with his thumbnail. 'That's what I keep saying, lad. One minute he's playing guitar and singing Blue Bayou, badly, as per, and then he's springing off the balcony like something from a science fiction film.'

'Was he okay?'

'I think he was.'

'But did you check?'

'No. Why should I leave my bed for something like that?'

'He might've got hurt?'

'Well if he did he didn't sound it. I heard him laughing and speaking Swedish, sounded fine to me.' John pinched the pillowcase in his fingers. He lifted it. 'Damn you, Andy. Why egg?'

'Forget that,' Andrew said, changing his bloodstained vest for another white one. 'Why did he jump?'

'God knows,' John said coming down his bunk ladder. 'Think they took stuff. I smelt weed a few times.'

'Don't think weed makes you jump off balconies, John.' Andrew closed a flap over his suitcase and stood watching John drink from the water tap.

'I remember him with those guys,' John went on. He stayed by the sink now resting his arms on it, staring forward, water dripping from his chin. 'Bastards kept me up.'

'Stop talking soft. What happened?' Andrew sat on his suitcase, elbows on his knees, looking up at John. Then he glanced round the room, pausing on the bloodied tea towel on a chair outside. 'Then what happened?'

'I drifted in and out of sleep, was lucky to grab an hour or two, bastards.'

'I'm not bothered about your sleep,' Andrew said. 'What happened to Anders?'

'I'm not sure. Seemed weird to me, the way they acted, you know.' John turned. He stood in front of Andrew and leaned forward, picking brown pants off the floor. 'I woke again just before it happened,' he said stepping into his pants, pulling the zipper. 'I heard him doing his Roy Orbison act, heard Steve's chair legs going on the decking. The pratt kept rocking in it. And both mentioned something about crayon, that everything looked normal but as though drawn in crayon.'

'I never heard such bullshit. Is that the best you got, lad?'

'I don't know,' John said. He began walking up and down the room, slowly. 'What do you want from me?' He put a hand on each shoulder, he too now looking at the bloodied tea towel. 'I'm saying it as it was.'

'Okay, forget Anders for a second. What about Steve?'

'What about him? He's bald and crazy as fuck as far as I'm concerned.'

'Where did he go?'

John shrugged. He stepped into his shoes and did up their laces. He went outside on the decking, peered over the balcony's edge. His belly pressed on the wood causing it to creak. He backed up and kicked through empty beer cans. Andrew watched, then stood and joined him. The beer puddles had dried in the hot sun and ash and cigarette ends covered the table. Andrew touched the dinner plate, looked at his stained fingers and rubbed them over his thigh, leaving a line of black ash on his jeans. 'You're breathing like a pig,' he then said with his back to John.

'That ain't me,' John said, 'it's coming from that spare bunk.'

They went silent. They listened to grunts and snorts, and began pushing each other towards the animal like sound.

'Go on soft lad,' John said nudging a fist into Andrew's back. 'Go on, go see what it is.'

'Okay, I'm going,' Andrew said creeping forward, stepping on the cans and wincing as they crushed under his bare feet. 'I'm going, fuck off with your fist.'

Leaning over the spare bunk, he saw the profile of the snorer's face, now covered with a bed sheet and where cloth, dampened with saliva, moved in and out near the snorer's lips. He lifted a piece of sheet and turning to John, said quietly. 'It might be Anders.'

'Yes, yes, possibly,' John said clasping both hands behind his neck. 'Now get on with it.'

Andrew's fingers disappeared under the sheet, patting the snorer's head slightly. 'It's not Anders.'

'Well who the hell is it?' John dropped his hands and frowned. He came behind Andrew, nudging him again with his fist. 'Who is it?'

'I can feel a baldhead.'

'Get under there, get a proper look.'

Andrew took a breath. He lifted more bedding.

'Bloody hell,' John said bobbing down, putting his hands over his knees, craning his neck. 'Right, I see, cover him up again.'

'What shall we do?' Andrew covered the snorer's face, placing the bed sheet as it was. Now he stood side by side with John, looking down on the hidden, snoring, grunting body.

'I don't know, let him be I guess.'

'Maybe we could wake him.'

'I'm not waking him, we need to go soon.'

'He might know about Anders.'

'I'm not waking him.'

Both paused suddenly. They moved their eyes towards the door, kept still and listened now as a key turned harshly in the rusty lock.

'No need,' John said, 'sounds like he's back.'

The door opened but no one entered. There was heavy breathing in the corridor for a while, and they listened to it looking at each other suspiciously. Then a small, dwarf like man swayed in wearing a vest and slippers, clutching his chest with four stubby fingers. He wheezed in front of them like an overfed Bulldog, sweat bubbling on his chimp like forehead, dripping from his mutton-chop sideburns, from his fat red cheeks, from his thick bushy eyebrows. He puffed on a cigar, marched round the room showing damp patches front and back of his vest. His neck and shoulders were very wide, grey hairs curled on them and down both arms too. His potbelly moved as he marched, and his belt lay hidden beneath it, holding up his baggy jeans, which sagged at the back showing arse crack, more hairs, more damp patches.

'I don't believe this,' he said wheezing between words. 'Naked, running around town naked.' He flicked ash everywhere as he spoke. 'This is a wind up? A prank?'

'What's up with you?' John and Andrew asked simultaneously.

'Someone's winding me up, that's what's up.' Dickie puffed on his cigar blowing smoke out his mouth and nostrils. Then he looked around the room. His thick eyebrows drew inward, staring over cans and cigarette ends on the balcony.

'Slow down, Dickie,' Andrew said. 'What are you saying, what's up?'

'Babs just received a call from the cop shop,' Dickie said coughing, and then slapping ash from his belly with the flat of his hand he added. 'This is not good. They got Anders. They're holding him for indecent exposure.' He took more cigar. He blew smoke in their faces and watched them turn away as though trying to find cleaner air.

'The dirty sod,' John said, coughing, looking up at the ceiling.

'Listen boys,' Dickie went on. 'If he wants to show his frank n furter, that's his life, but I'm not running a charity here. I need my rent. He's no good to me behind bars.'

Both nodded.

'We'll fetch him,' John assured Dickie. 'We'll have him back by tonight.'

'Dang right you will,' Dickie said. 'And you'll go right now.'

'We'll go now,' John repeated.

'Right, that's what I said, you'll go now. Both of you will.'

Again they nodded.

'Go now and bring back that kraut. I need him working and earning, you hear me? All of you, all working, all earning.'

'He's Swedish,' Andrew said.

'Who you say,' Dickie said rubbing each sideburn in turn with the back of his thumb. 'What you say?' He angled his cigar, looked down at the glowing ash.

'Anders, he's Swedish,' Andrew said. 'You called him a kraut.'

'You think I give a rats what he is?' Dickie jabbed his cigar in front of their faces. 'If he ain't paying me rent, he's nothing to me.' Jab, jab, jab, ash fell to the floor, jab, jab. 'Bring him back.'

John and Andrew stood flinching. Their chins tilted, their arched hands wafting smoke, then stepping backwards and nodding.

'Relax, Dick,' John said. 'Just give us the address, we'll deal with it?'

Dickie reached into his back pocket, his trousers slid further down showing more crack. He pulled a beer mat with an address scribbled across it in pencil, handed it to John.

'Fifty dollars,' Andrew said, reading it over John's shoulder.

'What you pay in this town for flashing,' Dickie said. 'He better realise, flashing your tackle don't come cheap, not in this town.' Dickie spoke slowly and paused for a moment as though speaking from experience. Both stared at him, mouths open.

'What?' he asked, cigar wedged between his lips.

'We don't have that money,' Andrew said. 'We don't have a bean.'

Dickie brought both hands up to his forehead. He held them there. Then he dragged them down his face. Then he eyed sweat on his palms. 'You three are taking the piss,' he said almost biting his cigar.

'Just think of it as an investment,' John said folding the beer mat between his fingers. 'We get vaccinated today, we'll be earning soon.'

Dickie paused, he looked at the beer cans again on the balcony.

'Something tells me I'll regret this,' he said flicking ash, watching it settle on his slippers. 'Go downstairs and see Babs.' More sweat rolled down his cheeks. 'I'm subbing you the fifty. Now go.'

'Sure thing, Dick,' John said.

'And in the meantime,' Dickie yelled, bending to scoop something off the floor. 'I'm holding this guitar as collateral, and, one more thing.' Both were pushing past him now, shuffling out into the corridor. Andrew barefooted, pumps in hand. 'I want interest on my fifty, you hearing me?'

Neither answered him, they were heading down the corridor now at a slow jog, discussing how they'd tell Babs that Dickie had agreed to sub them sixty dollars, then discussing if sixty each was a stretch too far.

Dickie stayed in the room, now slumped on a bunk ladder to hold up his weight, puffing on his cigar. 'I run a steady ship,' he said to himself cheerfully. Then he sniffed up, scrunching his nose at the scent, looking again on the table and decking. 'Wait a minute,' he shouted. 'Who's been smoking pot and partying in my barracks?'

He threw his cigar into the sink, watched as it hissed extinguishing in the water. Then sitting down edge of the spare bunk, with an arm and a leg beneath him he looked down, lifted the bed sheet and hunched forward over Steve's face.

'Wake up, you,' he said. 'Get up. This is not your room. Get up now you. Get up.'

When Steve didn't answer, Dickie swayed to the sink. 'Ignore me in my own place, eh. I'll wake you up one way or another.' The tap was running now and it seemed, as he filled a bowl with water, that Dickie had another tactic in mind. 'Piece of shit ignoring me, ignoring me in my barracks.'

Chapter nine

Anders sat on the floor of his cell. His head dropped forward resting on his knees, his arms hugging himself, his body trembling. Around him crumpled in heaps, were baby wipes stained bloody and brown with earthy like colours. He was clean now and without the camouflage of dirt, his cuts and scratches appeared much redder, like raked markings on pale skin, which came mostly down the sides of his arms and legs. That bush, he kept thinking, that bloody bush. He cursed the bush, he cursed Sammy too, the big bastard had left him bruised with a nice purple patch across his lower back, of good size, the size of the big bastard's knee, he thought, running his puffy fingers over it. His feet were puffy too, swelled and puffy as though he'd had an allergic reaction to the thorns and the splinters, and to Sammy's fishy hands.

He lifted his head facing forward, facing a red brick wall. For a short while he just sat there, staring. Then he began bunching together the dirty wipes. Then, with wipes in hand, he crawled to a dark place underneath a wooden board. The board hung from the wall by two chains. This was his bed, and across it lay a mattress encased in plastic, which was hard, flat and without pillow. Underneath the bed was a tin bucket and that's where he disposed of the wipes. At the back of the cell, facing a thick and heavy looking door was an old-fashioned toilet, with a water tank above and a long chain dangling on one side for flushing. But that was all. The rest of the cell was empty, and he was thankful not to be sharing with anyone else.

He got up now and resembling an old man with vertigo, slowly eased himself onto the mattress. The plastic coating stuck to his skin. He clenched both fists. He felt the saltiness of other peoples sweat burning into his wounds. Then he paused. He listened now. There was fighting in the corridor outside and he listened. Guards seemed to clatter into his door, as though grappling with someone, pulling and pushing some feisty character into the cell beside his. There was the sound of a body hitting the deck, boots retreating, a door slamming and then keys jangling and twisting in the lock. The scuffle over, Anders thought, hearing the guards breathlessly moving on, some mumbling about what they had to deal with, too old for this shit, aren't paid enough for this shit, stuff like that.

'Bastards,' the feisty one yelled, sounding very angry. 'No one boots Maniac in the gut and gets away with it,' he added referring to himself.

Maniac was a small man with muscles, stocky, with the neck of a pit-bull-terrier and a spiky Mohawk haircut, shaved at the sides showing scars, and a tattoo of some barcode on his forehead. Picking himself off the floor, he began bouncing round his cell as though he had springs on

97

his feet. He shadowboxed, threw jabs, and held his fists out in front of himself as he walked. He jabbed Anders's wall, two jabs, hissing with each jab. 'Hey, hey, is someone in there?' he asked slapping both hands on the wall. Then he was jabbing again, hiss, hiss.

'Relax, cell four. Or we'll go again,' a guard yelled from the corridor.

'One doesn't obtain the name Maniac by taking orders,' Maniac yelled back. 'Who's next door to me?' He put his face on the wall. 'What you in for, neighbour, fighting?'

Anders stayed on his mattress, silently facing the smoky coloured ceiling and its cobwebs above him.

'Don't hold your tongue, answer me.' Maniac was jabbing and hissing again. 'Answer me. I've cracked heads for less.'

'No, not for fighting,' Anders said sullenly. 'I'm no fighter.'

'No problem,' Maniac said. 'That's why God invented cherry-bombs. We can't all succeed with our fists. Lucky for me, I'm good with both.' There was a period of silence before he continued. 'You got a name?' he asked, but again there was silence. 'Don't leave me waiting, neighbour.' Maniac began jabbing again, jabbing and hissing.

'Apologies, my name is...'

'Shush,' Maniac said. 'You shush now.' Maniac squatted by his cell door. His ear was on the keyhole. 'Those bastards are saying stuff,' he said. 'Stuff about me.' No one was speaking. It was silent. 'Okay, sounds okay, I bet the bastards knew I was listening. Now, where were we?'

'My name,' Anders said, 'call me Lindsay.'

'That won't do,' Maniac said. 'That's a shitty name, a girly name. From now on you're called Disciple, understand that? Now repeat it to me, you're Disciple, yes?'

'I'm Disciple,' Anders whispered.

'Louder!' Maniac commanded, crisscrossing his hands behind his back.

'Disciple, my name is Disciple,' Anders sat up and shouted.

'Your name will be Daffy Duck in the loony bin if you speak like that again, cell five,' a guard yelled tapping his baton across Anders's door. 'Now pipe down.'

'Ignore them,' Maniac said. 'Explain now, what you in for?'

There was silence. Then Maniac reminded Anders about his tendency to crack heads.

'Not sure,' Anders said. 'I blanked out, had too much beer.'

'I appreciate that, we all been there and done that.'

'Yeah, sure, you know what it's like,' Anders said.

'Well you seem pretty eager to know why I'm in, guess a guy has no secrets in here, so I'll go right out and say it, shall I?'

There was a pause, silence. Anders was thinking about the guard, the one that brought him in. He wondered where he'd gone. He was supposed to be fetching him some spare clothes, but that was over an hour ago. Now he wondered how long he'd been naked for, actually how long, half a day?

'You guessed it,' Maniac said without cue. 'I got agitated. I smashed a bottle of Tooheys over some hotshot's head. And yes before you judge me, the prick deserved it. No one asks Maniac if it's hot outside, not when they can clearly see, they knew, they saw my nose and forehead were sunburnt.'

'Sounds like he were asking for some,' Anders said.

'Yeah,' Maniac agreed, 'and he got some too.' Then he laughed.

Anders peeled his body away from the mattress, turning onto his side, facing the red bricks. For a while he listened to Maniac shadowbox round his cell, jabbing, hissing. Then there was silence, then heavy breathing. He was at the wall again. 'Where's home, Disciple?' he asked. 'You sound different, you sound Irish to me.'

'Donegal,' Anders said. 'Ireland, as you guessed.'

'Ah, yes, Ireland,' Maniac smiled. 'They enjoy a drink and a fight, my kinda place. Maybe there's hope for you yet, Disciple,' Maniac said, crouching, scuttling near to his door. 'Shush now. They're coming.'

Anders made no sound.

'I said shush, damn it.'

Boots trod down the corridor. Keys swung. Both sounds grew closer. Anders stood pulling his bare skin off the mattress. It peeled away like wet dough on a baker's board. Then he cupped his hands over his penis and sat back down again. The sound of boots and keys stopped suddenly. A guard appeared outside his cell. He was a broad shouldered and muscular man, tall and neat. His hair was dark, slicked back, wet and shiny. His uniform of trousers and shirt were thorn coloured and his sleeves were turned over showing tanned arms. On Anders's cell door was a piece of square glass, and suddenly the guards face appeared there chewing gum. He watched Anders through his Aviator sunglasses, stubbly chin pressed on the glass, breathing on it. Then he entered.

'Dress,' he said chucking a balled up T-shirt on Anders's lap, dropping flip-flops by his feet and standing over him with thumbs hooked on belt buckle, showing chewing gum between his teeth.

'Who's that?' Maniac asked facing the wall. 'Talk to me, Disciple.'

Anders brought one hand up, plugged both nostrils with his fingers. The T-shirt reeked of sick and seriously strong body odour. The armpits had crusted over, giving it a different texture to the rest of the T-shirt, which had relatively soft linen. On the front, seeming rather pleased with himself was a faded print of Jason Donavon. Anders took solace in that, was happy it had faded, was also happy that the T-shirt was extra-extra-large, since the guard had not brought any pants. He imagined a woman of real size wearing it during the eighties, front row, screaming over Donavon's lyrics, and somewhere between then and now, various tramps had wore it in cells like this one, pissed on it, sweated on it, possibly wiped their arses dry on it. And judging by the smug look on Donavon's face, Anders could see a temptation in that.

'What's going on in there?' Maniac asked.

'Shut it,' a random guard said striding past the cells, tapping his baton on Maniac's door.

'I'm just warming up,' Maniac replied, and ragging his mattress from its wooden board, he began flipping it round his cell, repeatedly, then propping it up on the wall and using it as a punch bag. Hiss, hiss, hiss.

'You want breakie?' the Guard asked Anders over the sound of Maniac hitting the mattress, hiss, hiss.

'I think so,' Anders said looking at the T-shirt. 'What do we have on the menu?'

'This isn't the Ritz, fella,' The Guard said. Then he rested a foot on the brick wall behind Anders's shoulder.

Anders laughed. 'I guess not. I think the beds and the stinky toilet gave that away.'

The Guard yawned on the back of his wrist. He looked at Anders and lowered his Aviators. Anders saw now that he was bogeyed and wasn't sure where he was looking, though it seemed to be near his crotch. He checked his hands, smiled at the Guard. The Guard took his foot away from the brick. He came closer, took a set of keys and choosing one, began combing his moustache with it. Anders laughed, nervously. The Guard nodded a while. Then he cracked a smile and laughed too.

'Better not be laughing at me,' Maniac said. He left the mattress, came back to the wall. 'Update me, Disciple,' he said. 'If you're part of this, they'll be trouble.' He waited by the wall, breathless from his mini workout.

'What's so funny?' the Guard asked with a smile that showed all his teeth.

Anders returned his eyes to the T-shirt and shrugged.

'You laughed, was there a joke?' the Guard asked again, smile fading.

'Nothing,' Anders said. 'It was nothing.'

'You laughed though, why was that?' the Guard said pushing his Aviators back over his eyes, chewing gum.

'Don't answer that, Disciple,' Maniac said other side of the wall. 'That's a trick question, be careful now.'

'Not sure.' Anders shrugged again. 'It was nothing.'

'Nice,' Maniac said encouragingly.

The Guard walked up and down the cell. Then he stopped. He looked over his boots, both black and shiny, like his hair. 'Okay look now, slugger, it's like this,' he said. 'We got eggs, eggs, and more eggs. Now do you want some or not, because you and that clown next door are beginning to test me.'

'There's a clown next door, huh,' Maniac said moving his fingers one side of his face. 'That's good,' he said. 'Disciple, make contact with this Clown. We may be able to recruit him.' He paused for a second as though thinking, fingers now stopped on his chin. 'But don't get excited,' he said, 'a new recruit doesn't guarantee your promotion.'

Both Anders and the Guard ignored him.

'So, eggs then?' the Guard asked.

'Yesh,' Anders agreed, sounding more Swedish than usual.

'You sure about that,' the Guard said. 'You don't sound very pleased, rather ungrateful if you ask me, and what's with this "yesh" shit? Has Sean Connery turned up or something?'

'Sorry, yes, I would much appreciate some eggs.'

'Ah, being sarcastic now, eh,' the Guard said. 'Go on then, how does double-O-seven like his eggs?'

'Fried, runny yolk, pinch of salt.' Anders spoke fast. He didn't care much about the eggs, he just wanted the Guard gone so he could dress into the awful smelling T-shirt without the Guard's wondering eyes all over him.

'Boy, you know your eggs,' the Guard laughed.

'Don't take them eggs, Disciple,' Maniac said slapping the wall. 'That's an order.'

'Look, we only do scramby,' the Guard said, both choosing to ignore Maniac again.

Anders shuffled his feet on the concrete floor. He looked at the T-shirt and messed with a string of fabric. 'What's scramby?' he then asked.

'Jesus Christ.' Palm to his forehead, the Guard disappeared into the corridor. 'Lance, take note, we got a moron in cell five.' Anders read the number five on his cell door. He shook his head and looked away.

105

'Copy that, Big Dee.' Lance yelled back, sat end of the corridor, bits of paperwork across his long legs, tuna fish sandwich in hand.

'Leave him be, you bunch of piggy bastards,' Maniac shouted, now standing and pulling up his shorts.

Two guards marched towards Maniac's door but then stopped abruptly, as though meeting a cliff edge and were now reconsidering their destination. They stepped back slowly, hands open, wafting them rapidly in front of their faces while Maniac laughed and danced in circles around something he had done, something brown, something he seemed very proud of, something he was careful not to step in.

'Where you going?' he said pausing a moment, noticing the guards were retreating. 'Get me out!' He put his face on the glass peephole. 'It stinks in here.'

Big D stayed in the corridor nodding at the retreating guards. Two backed away while another keeled forward, retching. Lance laughed at him showing mouthfuls of tuna fish and bread. Then he dipped his fingers into a leather knapsack by his feet and pulled out a flask. 'Rookies, hey, Dee. Rookies got a lot to learn.' He said tipping coffee into a small cup. 'They just don't have the stomach for it, do they, Dee?'

Big D nodded then shouted through the cell door to Anders. 'Scrambled,' he said, 'scramby means scrambled.'

'I see,' Anders said blinking. 'In that case I'll take scrambled.' He spread the T-shirt over his thighs as though it was a napkin, smoothed out the creases with his palms and checked it was hiding his penis.

'Okay,' Big D said coming back into the cell. 'Okay then.'

He'd been there over ten minutes now, clothes dropped off, breakfast ordered, so why, Anders thought, why was he still hanging round like a bad fart under the bedding, doing laps, hands crossed behind his back, watching him on that clammy mattress. A mattress Anders had to be careful on, to move on as slow as possible. But some noises escaped him, and now and then his bottom would get hot, and squelch on the plastic. Big D turned sharply hearing such a squelch. He stared vigorously from behind his Aviators, began grinning.

'We do fine scramby eggs here, slugger?' he said taking a big step forward.

'Oh,' Anders said. 'That's nice. Will you be ordering them soon?' Anders thought the question might prompt Big D to leave, but he was silent, poking his finger between two bricks, messing with a loose chunk of mortar.

'I'm ready for them, I think,' Anders went on, but Big D did not engage in conversation, so he smiled and kept talking. 'I remember putting one in the microwave once.' He wasn't even sure what he was saying now, but he continued regardless. 'I'd not removed the shell, made a fabulous explosion.'

A chunk of mortar fell. It bounced across the concrete, broke in two pieces and clinked on the tin can under the bed. Big D squatted, as before he lowered his Aviators, and as before, Anders guessed where those wonky eyes of his were staring, he felt for the T-shirt.

'Are you dressing or what?' Big D said.

'Shush!' Maniac said jabbing the wall. 'I'm interested in the egg story. Disciple, you mentioned an explosion.'

'You can talk eggs day and night where you're going, cell four,' Lance laughed in the corridor. 'And as for explosions, you'll be doing plenty, plenty in your shorts.'

Big D poked his head into the corridor, watched a team far end. Soon Maniac would have visitors. Lance looked up from his papers, smiled with thin lips, raked a hand through his thinning hair and took some coffee.

Now fed up with Big D bobbing in and out of the cell, Anders decided to take action. Besides, many people, most of the town at least had already seen him naked, so one more was okay, no harm in one more, he thought, this was obviously what Big D wanted, give the pervert what he wanted, he thought, take action, let him have it.

He stood up ready for him. His T-shirt dropped. With his hands on his hips, he began thrusting his pelvis forward and back, his penis swinging between his thighs like a pendulum, thrusting back forth, back forth. But Big D was still head and shoulders in the corridor. He saw nothing. Then, low on water, dizzy and hung over and reconsidering his whole life, Anders found he was staggering back, and just as quickly as he was up, he was now back down again, falling onto the mattress in a panic.

'Need to go,' Big D said, 'need to take a leak.' He came back inside, unzipped over the bowl.

Anders put the T-shirt back as it was, eyes scanning the cell for CCTV cameras, suddenly worried a double case of indecent exposure could be heading his way. His cheeks reddened. He gasped, took a breath, assured himself there were no cameras. No one had seen him. He was okay. He hoped.

'Hey, what's the idea?' Big D said. He zipped up and swung round.

Anders felt both cheeks burning, his mouth was dry and hung open. Now Big D was thrusting, thrusting a boot towards the toilet bowl. 'That a pathetic dirty protest, eh,' he said. 'That the idea?'

109

'Good work, Disciple,' Maniac said jumping on his mattress. 'Now pass word to the Clown, he can lay a third, three in a row,' Maniac chanted, 'three in a row.' Then he paused, he tapped his teeth with his knuckles. 'Hang on. What is he saying is pathetic?' Maniac ran to one end of his mattress and jumped off, bare feet trampling in his own shit. 'What you done in there, Disciple? What you done?'

'I've not used the toilet,' Anders said. 'I guess the previous occupier dropped it there.'

Big D ignored him, now tugging the long chain side of the water tank. He sweated, damp patches showed on his shirt. Another tug, there was a flushing sound. Fresh water came down. He watched the turd spin, nodding as it sank. Then he walked up and down the cell shaking his head. 'It's back,' he said with a hint of disbelief. 'It's only resurfaced.'

'Maybe there's a blockage,' Anders said.

'I bet,' Big D said looking down into the bowl. 'And you did it.'

'Nothing a few cherry bombs wouldn't sort,' Maniac added wiping his toes dry on the brickwork.

'Are you and that idiot plumbing experts now?' Big D said, waiting for the water tank to top up, feet almost dancing on the concrete.

'I was being helpful,' Anders said.

110

'Be helpful by shutting up.' Big D held the chain double handed, shoulders dropped slightly, ear to the water tank. 'Your dropping has gotten us into this mess.'

Yank. Big D was yanking the chain. Yank, yank. Nothing came, no water, no flush. He yanked harder. The chain snapped in two pieces. He looked at it. One-half swinging side of the tank, the other hung either side of his closed fist. He opened his hand, worked the chewing gum with his teeth, squatted and peered over the bowl. 'Stone the crows,' he then said taking big strides out of the cell.

A moment later, he returned with his sleeves almost up to his shoulders and a toilet plunger in hand. He stood over the bowl watching it, his legs far apart.

'Need any help?' Anders asked.

'No,' Big D said pointing the plunger at him. 'You stay back, you've done enough damage.'

He faced side to side, moved his chin up and down, neck muscles cracking with each turn. Then he removed his Aviators and put them inside his top pocket ready for business. Anders stayed seated and watched him, his shoulders were going now and suddenly he began jabbing with the plunger.

'Huh, huh, huh,' he said thrusting the plunger in and out of the water. 'Huh, get some, huh, huh, huh, Get some. Get some.'

Water splashed over the sides of the bowl. Chewing gum dropped from Big D's mouth as he jabbed the turd, mashing it good. 'Huh, get some. Huh, huh,' he went on, repeating himself that way, sounding like an over enthusiastic trigger-happy Yank in a Vietnam War film.

'What's going on in there?' Maniac asked slapping both hands on the wall. 'I have a right to know.' A baton tapped the glass on his door and Lance faced him other side of the peephole, pointing the tip of his baton towards Maniac's face.

Maniac grinned showing small teeth. 'Got something for me, you pasty faced bitch?' he asked.

'Last warning,' Lance said, 'keep it shut or we'll drag you over to the penthouse suite with the rest of the fruitcakes, there you'll be in the hands of the white coats, so shut it.'

'Step inside,' Maniac said holding his grin. 'I'll put that stick up your arse, sideways.'

Lance faced away. He watched a group of guards chatting in a small side room, stepping into plastic suits and rubber boots. Then he faced back again wearing a ratty grin. 'Reckon you could do that to four

112

people at the same time?' he laughed walking away, running the baton across each door he passed, whistling.

Meanwhile Big D stood breathing heavily. He had one arm rested on the brickwork and his other by his side, plunger swaying between fingertips. More damp patches marked his shirt, a mixture of sweat and toilet water. Anders listened to the baton and the whistling outside his cell, then to Maniac asking what was going on in cell five. Big D then straightened himself, was going again for round two. 'Get some, get some.'

Suddenly the water came high and erupted spilling over the bowl like a volcano of shit and piss. Big D stepped back and fell over, then began shuffling backwards on the floor, pushing away on his palms, dragging his backside over the concrete. Just before puddles of waste touched his boots, he sprung up and staggered out of the cell pushing the door shut. Then, dipping a hand to his pocket, he grabbed his keys and locked Anders in with the waste and the stench. Anders lifted his feet and stayed on his mattress, eyes on the floor, seeing all kinds of nasty stuff swishing below him. Quickly his eyes formed tears and he curled up with one hand over his mouth, the other was wafting, just wafting in front of him.

Maniac was clapping now. He ran to the door glass pressing his face on it. He watched the raw sewage passing along the corridor. 'Yeah, yeah,' he said stepping onto his mattress. 'Not pathetic now,' he laughed. 'You showed 'em, Disciple. You did good.' Then he was coughing, running to the corner of his cell, covering his face with his hands. 'Strewth,' he said watching sewage flow in through a gap under his door. 'What you been eating?'

'Final warning, cell four, I mean it.' Lance shouted, now stood on his plastic chair with his fingers pressed to his nostrils, watching the corridor turn into a brown canal.

Anders rolled side to side on his mattress, as though being suffocated by an invisible man. 'Dress.' He heard Big D saying from somewhere. 'Get dressed.'

Anders looked around through his hazy, steamed up lenses. He cleared them with his thumbs, gagged at the horrid smells, which was like a combination of sour cabbage and ammonia. 'Let me out!' he shouted.

No one answered him. He picked up the T-shirt that smelt nearly as bad as the sewage and still gagging, brought it down over his head. In his rush, he accidently caught his head in one of the sleeves, which tightened to his face and nudged his spectacles up above his forehead.

114

'You're making that look hard work, slugger,' Big D grinned through the glass peephole. Anders heard him but could not see anything. He whipped his head one way, then another. The linen of the sleeve pressed tight over his nose and lips, was as though he was wearing a gimp mask. Keeping one hand on his testicles, he used the other to work the sleeve with his fingers, pinching and pulling it.

'Want any help?' Big D asked, nose touching the peephole.

'No!' Anders answered as fast as he could, sounding muffled. 'Go away, please.'

'Give me an update, Disciple,' Maniac said, mattress between his arms, using it to push shit and piss back under his door. 'What's the Clown doing, he gone quiet on us?'

'I'm gonna fetch your eggs now,' Big D said.

'I don't want them,' Anders said ducking out of the sleeve. 'I'm not hungry.'

'That's good,' Maniac said. 'Don't dare, don't take anything. These bastards will lace your food. Back in O two they got me good, kept me nine weeks at some facility. Was in the outback somewhere, I reckon. Some crazy scientist worked there, name was Buggberd, I think, Dr Buggberd, was one crazy bastard-bitch he was, did all sorts of tests on me, especially on my arse. God knows what he put up there, but boy oh boy it was bad, he had me crapping computer parts, toy cars, flying-willards and plastic whistles for a whole week. Then I blew the place up and made my escape, you know, still crapping an all that, crapping that shit out for weeks. I tell you, and that all began with a spoonful of porridge, so don't trust 'em, you hear me?'

The team was dressed now. They marched down the corridor. Their rubber boots swished through sewage water as they passed a gaunt-faced man with a stooped back, dragging his mop and his bucket. They lined up, side of Maniac's cell. Four men, all wearing plastic suits with hoods up, goggles and facemasks on. They spoke to each other in low voices. They made gestures with their gloved hands.

Anders put on his T-shirt correctly and listened to Maniac who had not stopped ranting. He spoke of conspiracy theories, of explosions, of Dr Buggberd and of the things he had put in him.

'I want out,' Maniac said punching the glass on the door. 'I can handle my own, but God damn Disciple had to blow a gasket.' He paced round in circles, shadowboxed, fists clenched. 'I want an Uzi nine millimetre,' he demanded. 'I want my boom sticks back.' He kept pacing, now punching his face, cheeks turning a patchy red colour. 'Disciple and Clown, be ready now, the both of you.'

His door swung inward and crashed on the brick wall. One after the other, the team in plastic suits rushed in. He backed up. Then he came forward, fists clenched, hissing and throwing hooks and jabs. He got one against the wall, pulling on his goggles and mask. One guard stayed in the doorway looking everywhere and doing nothing, another grabbed the back of Maniac's wrists and helped set his partner free, who now, with goggles and mask below his chin, grabbed Maniac at the legs. The forth guard watched for a while, calmly. He held something in each hand and pointed to Maniac's pants. Then coming up beside Maniac, began taser gunning him in the arm. Almost instantly, Maniac's body was in spasms on the wet floor. The man by the door, who until now had done nothing, kneeled beside Maniac, tugged down his shorts and signalled with his finger to the man with the taser, who looked at the needle in his other hand, nodded, and then bent forward and moved it towards Maniac's lower-half. Once he'd been injected, the four men stepped back and waited for Maniac's body to go still. This took only seconds, and within a few more seconds, they had strapped him to a metal trolley and were wheeling him down the corridor. The wheels passed over the brown water almost soundlessly. The gaunt-faced man nodded at the team of guards and made room for them by pushing his

117

bucket with the end of his mop, then looking up and seeing Big D striding towards him, stepped to one side and got out of his way.

'You done?' Big D asked tapping his keys on the square of glass.

'Yes,' Anders answered sharply, not bothering to turn or look up at him.

'Good. I'd better get those eggs then,' Big D said. 'You ordered scrambled, right?'

Anders didn't answer, he knew the man was either stupid, insane, or winding him up, he guessed stupid and stared blankly at the raw sewage that surrounded him, and when he faced up again, Big D was gone.

'Wait,' he said quickly. 'Can someone get me out, put me in another cell?'

'You did it, fella,' the gaunt-faced man yelled. 'I'd rather be doing better things with my day,' he said. 'That Cuban missile you launched, that brick, it messed up the whole block. All cells are shitty thanks to you.'

Chapter ten

The spectacled clerk sat opposite Anders, behind a large glass window and wooden desk. He was a short, slim, feeble looking man with limp hands. His skin was an unhealthy grey colour. His moustache was wiry and long and dangled over his jutted front teeth. Greasy perspiration shined on his baldhead, and often he rubbed it with a napkin. But no matter how often he did this, the perspiration, grease and shine would reappear again almost instantly.

On his desk were papers, a plate of toast, a pot of vegemite and a butter knife half submerged in thick, brown extract. There was also a cup of hot tea, chamomile, Anders guessed, smelling its scent through tiny holes in the window that separated them. Suddenly he felt very hungry and thirsty. He looked at the tea, then at the clerk who was reading the papers, nodding now and then, taking toast now and then, biting it and moving his lips slowly underneath his moustache. Then, with nose twitching, the clerk looked up and through the window, staring at Anders. 'Hmm,' he said now, looking down again to scan his papers. 'You bring me some characters, Big Dee.'

Big D stood tall, smiling with his muscular arms folded behind Anders. 'I keep you in a job,' he said, 'It's what I do, Shiny.'

From his desk, Shiny smiled back at him. 'Indeed,' He said picking up a ballpoint pen, clicking it vigorously with his thumb. 'Is this the one that caused a disturbance this morning, with the toilets?'

Anders looked up, then down at his flip-flops and bare toes still dirty with toilet water.

'Yep,' Big D said. 'But he's been educated now, we advised he add some fibre to his diet, some grapes perhaps.'

'Hmm,' Shiny said. 'Indeed, indeed, I had to do my morning special across the road, not happy, had to use the market toilets.' He looked at Anders. 'Did you take note about the grapes?'

Anders didn't answer, he kept looking down, moving his flip-flops on the carpet.

'Hmm.' Shiny drank tea, his moustache dipped in the hot water leaving toast crumbs on the surface. 'Hmm, what is your name?'

Anders pointed to the papers on Shiny's desk. 'My name is there,' he said, 'on your report.'

Shiny grumbled as though he had something stuck in his throat, possibly a toast crumb. He touched his spectacles and looked at Big D.

'Just answer his questions, slugger,' Big D said stooping towards Anders's ear, 'unless you wanna be here all day.'

'Anders, my name is Anders.'

'Full name, please,' Shiny said click-clicking his pen, rocking in his chair with an air of supreme authority, like a high court judge or school headmaster. Guessing he was like this with everyone, Anders took no offence.

'Anderson,' he said facing the papers, as though reading from the report. 'Anders Anderson.'

'Anderson, ah, we have a Scotsman, do we?' Shiny slumped low in his chair. He clicked his pen raising an eyebrow to Big D, cueing him in.

'Well,' Big D laughed rocking on his heels. 'If he is, he's wearing the worst kilt I've ever seen.'

Shiny began laughing like an imbecile, jerking his head and shoulders. His knees were going. His eyes were bulging. Anders listened to the high-pitched laughter. He kept his head down. He felt the hem of his T-shirt with his fingers and waited patiently for the moment to pass.

'Good one, Dee,' Shiny said. 'That's a good one.' He began applauding, tapping his twiggy fingers on his palm while Big D tilted his head back, grinning. 'Well then,' Shiny went on, his face now straight and serious, 'Mr Anderson, I presume you know why we detained you this morning.'

Anders nodded. He waited for Shiny to continue.

'Indecent exposure is not acceptable, not acceptable at all.' As he spoke, Shiny began pointing his pen at Anders's lower half, moving it in circles. 'You're very lucky that that young lady you flashed will not be pressing charges.' Now his arms were on the desk, he looked over the report, eyes on a certain paragraph. Then he closed it. He pushed away the pages and stared at Anders. 'I would keep you a while longer,' he continued, he stood up and felt his moustache with both hands. 'Maybe you could think about the distress you have caused everyone. Honestly, it chills me to think about it, to think you and your perverted mind will be out there soon, out on those streets.' Suddenly he paused. He reached into his shirt pocket bringing out fresh napkins, dabbing them over his nose and baldhead. 'What if we made the law, hey, Dee?'

'That's a thought,' Big D said stepping back, looking down on Anders's bare legs, squeezing his bottom lip between his teeth and holding it there tightly. 'I'd like that.' He came forward again, close behind Anders. Anders then felt something, a prodding feeling on the back of his thigh. Sometimes it stayed there a moment, then it was prodding again. He tensed up. He swallowed slowly. 'I really would,' Big D said, 'I'd like that.'

'I'd like that too,' Shiny agreed as he sat corner of his desk, arms folded. 'Look at him. He's probably thinking about sex right now. Perverts like him never stop. They're insatiable. Personally I blame a lack of hobbies for it.' He unfolded his arms. There were toast crumbs on his fingers and he looked at them. 'That's the problem with the younger ones, isn't it?' Perspiration appeared on his baldhead. He stood up, began walking about in front of the glass. 'You're bored, bored all the time, and it's always somebody's fault, never your own, oh no. You refuse to work hard for anything. You want everything instantly, instant kicks is what you're about, instant kicks.' He took crumpled napkins from his desk and rubbed them all over his face and baldness like a gerbil giving itself a bath.

'In my day we'd take a girl out, treat her right,' he said. 'I'd wait patiently for weeks,' he said, 'months sometimes, months and months before any hanky-panky or slap and tickle.' He picked up the chamomile tea and stared at it before putting it back on the table. 'But you, you,' he said. 'I guess you're too important to wait.' He came to the glass. 'You can't wait for anything, can you, can you boy?'

His voice rose at the end of each sentence. The words "can you" bouncing off the walls of his box like office. He went on that way for some time, like a headmaster scolding his pupil, pausing only to dab

123

sweat, click pen, sip tea. There was no accent in his tone, no life. It was just plain, dull, boring.

'Now,' Shiny said tapping his pen on the glass, tapping it until Anders looked up at him. 'You will be leaving our pleasant guesthouse soon, but before you do, we'll swab you, we'll photograph you, we'll take your fingerprints and we'll do whatever it takes to stop you showing yourself again.' For a moment it seemed Shiny had more to say, more to talk out. But he didn't, he just opened and closed his mouth. Then he stared round his office and went back to his chair.

Anders thought it wise to say nothing, to face the carpet, to nod now and then, and to ignore the prodding feeling on the back of his thigh. He chose to appear repentant. Best way, he thought, for who knew what happened during that acid trip, in those early hours. Certainly not him, he may have flashed more victims, more people, he only remembered the morning and being in that bush, naked. What mischief had he caused before that point? What gardens or farm fields had he paraded through? There were at least, he thought, four hours missing from his memory, nothing but a complete blank patch, and pondering that, and taking account of the drugs and the nakedness, a fifty dollars penalty and a scolding from Mr slap and tickle seemed, at that moment, a fine outcome.

Chapter eleven

Outside was hot and bright, noisy with traffic and conversation. Suddenly he felt more vulnerable, felt an urge to return inside and ask for his cell back. If Shiny was so concerned with him flashing his bits, then why, why had they let him go pantless? He imagined bumping into the Blonde, imagined a gust of wind striking him, and puff, his T-shirt was up and over his head. He thought about that and about Sammy chasing him again, dragging him back to cell five with his putrid, fishy hands, and then bunking him up with Maniac in the penthouse suite. Thinking that, thinking about sudden gusts of wind, Anders kept one hand on his T-shirt and stepped towards an area shaded by the police station wall, which led to some steps, which he made his way down awkwardly, flip-flops slapping on each one.

Nearing the bottom steps, he saw John and Andrew sat on the street kerb with cars whizzing past them as they argued about the night before. They were shouting back at each other. He heard John's voice.

'No, no, no,' John was saying. 'You cracked an egg on my head, you deserved that beating.'

'Yeah, but I wasn't ready,' Andrew said. 'I'd have you now. I'd have you now, you fat jabber.'

Neither noticed Anders coming. He jumped off the last step and stood over them smiling. 'Still arguing, are we?'

John stood up rubbing his hands together, staring at Anders in his ridiculously sized T-shirt. Andrew stayed on the kerb. He looked at the flip-flops and leaned back slightly.

'Glad to see you both,' Anders said stepping closer.

'Wow, not that close,' John said, 'you stink like shit.'

Andrew got up now. He stood behind John and lifted his vest over his nose, pinning it there with the back of his wrist. 'What the hell happened to you?' he asked. 'Your legs and arms look as though they've been through a pencil sharpener, and,' he paused, lowered his vest to speak more clearly, 'don't get me started on your outfit.' He paused again. His mouth closed. He blinked rapidly. 'Or that stench,' he added quickly.

Anders was laughing as they set off. He walked behind them making sure his T-shirt covered his privates, pulling on it with both hands. 'I've had an awful morning. My cell stunk worse than me,' he said trying to catch up. 'What an awful thing, what an awful thing to be locked up.' He glanced back over his shoulder, looked at the grey stone building behind him and hoped he'd never have to see it again.

'Take it easy, Mandela,' John said marching on. 'You've only been locked up a few hours.'

Not speaking, they crossed a road heading for another street. Cars were beeping and a stationary bus had its windows open and when Anders passed, someone sprung up from their seat yelling the word "freak" at him. At the next street, he began to jog. 'Wait,' he said, 'slow down,' he said, and the three of them stood with space between them, forming the shape of a triangle. Meanwhile the cars kept beeping.

'This is embarrassing,' John said looking at the traffic, and then at Anders.

'You think so,' Anders said, 'try being me.' Then turning, he saw a man in a thorn coloured uniform. It wasn't Big D, he thought with relief, watching him cross the road and wondering what he was carrying. He was closer now, and without saying a word the officer reached out, stuffed a paper plate into Anders's hand, turned, and headed back towards the station.

Looking down at the plate Anders moved his eyebrows and felt his lips with his fingers, as though in deep thought, as though deciphering a cryptic code or something. 'Big Dee said they only do scramby,' he spoke at a whisper, still looking down.

'What's that then?' John asked facing Andrew. 'What did he just say?'

'Scramby, something about scramby.'

'Scramby,' John said, 'you still pissed, lad?'

'Ask him,' Andrew shrugged his shoulders, 'he said it.'

John turned looking ready to query the word "scramby", then, looking down on the plate, he paused. 'Strange,' he said pointing a finger.

'What is?' Andrew asked. 'What you getting at?'

'There's no ketchup.'

Andrew glanced up at the sky as though a bird had done a dropping on his forehead. 'It's not that strange,' he said clicking his fingers in John's face, motioning a hand towards Anders. 'See the state of him, he looks ready for an eighties slumber party, and you find no ketchup strange.'

'I don't much like ketchup,' Anders said. 'Well, not with egg at least.'

'What's he gonna do with it though?' John asked. 'There's no fork.'

Andrew broke the triangle and stepped between them. He was frowning. His mouth opened ready to speak but John was already swiping with his big arms, pushing him out of the way. Then he was pointing and he stuck his finger so close to the egg that he almost popped the yolk.

'No fork,' he said. 'Andy, run back,' he said, 'ask that officer for a fork.'

Anders picked up the egg, held it between thumb and forefinger and smiled.

'No!' John said reaching out. 'Not like that you bastard.'

Yolk dribbled either side of Anders's lips. The cars beeped at him and sometimes comments followed – 'Freak! Tosser! Homo!' Feeling toughened by the day's events, he blocked them from his mind and continued eating the fried egg. This was nothing, he thought, not after what he had been through, and anyway, none of these people knew him. Now he laughed showing his yolk-stained teeth. He began to enjoy the feeling of not caring and the look of embarrassment on John and Andrew's face. Beeping cars and nasty comments are nothing, he thought again. 'This isn't humiliation,' he said eating more egg. 'They can only get you if you let them.' He smiled at his comment. He reminded himself to jot that one down later, his new philosophy.

'He needs to get a grip,' John said. 'We still have an appointment to keep.'

'We do,' Andrew said. 'But why's he half-naked?'

A car slowed down. A voice spoke. 'Put some pants on, kid.' Beep! Beep! It was gone again. John turned his back to the traffic. He stared through a shop window. It was an electronics shop and the TVs were going. 'Anders why are you naked,' he said folding his arms, watching the TVs.

Anders said nothing. He bit more egg and looked at the yolk on his fingers.

Beep! Beep! Beep! 'Where's your pants?' a driver yelled extending an arm from his car window, holding his Stetson and waving it.

'I second that question,' John said. 'Where are they?' He turned from the TVs. 'Where are your clothes?'

Anders paused, and looking at John with an eerie grin, cleaned his lips with his tongue, tasting weed and vomit.

'Come on now.' John showed Anders the face of his watch. 'We have an appointment. What happened?'

'I can't remember,' Anders laughed. He took more egg.

'I'm done with him,' John said looking at Andrew. 'If he wants to fuck everything up he can, but I'm going to the appointment.' And without hanging around any longer, John set off.

'Don't go,' Anders said with egg flopping between his fingers. 'I need my clothes.'

John stopped but refused to turn round, keeping away from the embarrassment and stench. Andrew stared at Anders, then at the egg and the dripping yolk. Then he stared at the back of John's head.

'My clothes,' Anders said, 'You brought spares, yes.' He smiled. He pulled a mocking face at the T-shirt he wore then pointed at the face on the front. 'I need to change.'

John turned. Andrew was about half way between them and they stared at each other silently for a moment before Andrew spoke. 'We might have forgotten,' he laughed, 'completely forgot,' he laughed again, 'I mean, you know, we left in a hurry.'

Anders pointed eggy fingers at him. 'Enough,' he said smiling, 'hand them over.' He waved the plate. Having fallen for one pre-rehearsed joke already, the kilt gag, set up by Shiny and executed by Big D, Anders refused to fall for another. He waited, anticipating the crescendo, the punch line due any moment, he thought. But nothing happened. Both just stared at each other and the cars kept beeping. 'You brought them, yes,' he said again, tongue working the corners of his mouth, mopping up yolk. 'Fetch them please, the joke is over.'

Beep! Beep! Beep! 'Jason Donovan sucks!' A driver yelled, arm rested on the truck's open window, knuckles tapping the door.

Anders nodded and waved as he passed. 'You,' he then said turning back to John and Andrew. 'One of you, doesn't matter who, just go fetch my clothes. We have an appointment to keep. I'd like to attend wearing pants.'

'We messed up, we've got nothing,' John said straight-faced. 'Now stop acting the pratt, we need to go.'

Anders was barely listening. He bit more egg. 'Yummy,' he said, 'this egg tastes good, or should I say yumbo, just a word I learned today, that and scramby of course.' He waved the egg above his head. 'Wonder why it's fried,' he laughed, 'they only do scramby.'

John came back, was leaning over Andrew's shoulder now, whispering, nudging his body into him. 'We'll miss the appointment at this rate,' he said, 'have a word.'

With a hand covering his nose, Andrew swayed over to Anders, grabbed him by his T-shirt and pulled him forward so they were face-to-face. He shook him slightly. He spoke clear and loud. 'Honestly now we don't have them, okay.' He pushed him back and pulled him forward. Anders staggered unsteadily on his feet. His flip-flops slapped on the pavement and he kept stooping forward with his mouth open and tongue extended, trying to eat more egg. But then he was pulled and pushed again, forward and back. He kept missing his mouth, skimming the egg across his cheeks, leaving streaks of yolk.

'Get a grip now. We don't have your clothes. Are you listening?' There was no response. Andrew began slapping him a little, front hand, backhand, repeat, pull, pull, push, push. Anders's face stretched as though he was cueing a yawn and he began burping loudly. Andrew backed up waving his hands, puffing his cheeks, blowing air through them and staring at Anders as he ran towards the shop window, where John now stood. Taking long strides, John sprung out of Anders's way and looked back at him over his shoulder. Anders threw down the plate. Then he threw down the egg. It splattered on the pavement. Finally, he threw down himself. Now on his knees, he stooped, arching his body over the plate, clutching his stomach with both hands. Nothing but retching sounds came from him. John and Andrew crouched behind, getting an angle on what was going on. They saw blobs, frothy orange blobs coming from his mouth, fizzing as though someone had dropped a Berocca inside him. He caught the blobs on the plate and sat on the pavement with eggy bile dripping on his chin.

'And that's that,' John said kicking a small rock, 'that is without doubt that.' He set off marching. Cars beeped. Drivers laughed at Anders, pointing at him as he stared forward now on his hands and

133

knees. He looked at Andrew for help, but he was following John and he watched them disappear round a corner. Then crawling, he moved under the shop doorway and felt cold in its shade. He began shivering, tugged his T-shirt over his knees and held it there securely with a hug, rocking in the darkness, like a man suddenly gone insane.

Chapter twelve

'Your friends, the two you just described, yes, they went through earlier.'

'And me?'

'I'm sorry. Not you, not like that. I'm very sorry.'

'But I had an accident,' Anders stepped forward, looking at the young girl to study her reaction. She turned in her chair to face him. Her computer was on and she typed on her keyboard. 'Well that's unfortunate,' she said, blushing. 'It is and I'm sorry.'

'Very unfortunate,' he said. 'That's why I have no pants. It was my guts.'

'Your guts?' she said pulling her keyboard closer.

'Yes,' he said. 'I fear needles you see. I fear them badly.' He shuffled on his feet and peered around the reception area making sure only he was there. 'In truth I'm terrified of them.'

'I see,' she said, her eyes fluttering between him and her computer screen. 'I want to help you, but I also want to keep my job.' She spoke sincerely now. 'I've not been here long. I don't want any trouble.' She leaned over the countertop on her elbows, moving her pen between her lips, watching him. He rubbed his forehead with his fingers. His headache was getting worse, his stomach felt sickly, and fear, he knew, was getting the better of him.

'Bea,' he said reading her nametag, noticing it pinned to her breast pocket. 'Listen, without this vaccination I can't work. I have no money left, nothing for rent, nothing for food. I have nothing.' He licked his lips, moved his fingers in circles on his temple. 'My trip,' he said, 'would be over.'

'You're a backpacker?' she said.

'Yes I am.' He nodded. 'I've been dreaming of seeing Australia for years, always wanted to travel here, though,' he paused and looked at her, checked he still had her attention. 'My luck recently has been awful, things not working out, you know, nothing going a plan.'

She took the pen from her mouth, smiling now, touching her neck with her fingers and nodding as he spoke.

'I want to see your beautiful country,' he went on, 'I want to experience all its wonderful wildlife.'

Bea watched him and kept smiling.

'I want to go to the places I read about in school, see crocodiles and kangaroos, observe them in their natural habitat, get a photo at Ayers Rock and snorkel The Great Barrier Reef.' He paused again, happy she was still smiling. He thought whether to continue or quit while ahead,

136

he chose to continue. 'What a joke it would be,' he said. 'What a laughing stock I would be. Picture me now, returning home to speak of my travels.' Anders came onto his tiptoes. He puffed out his chest speaking in a grandeur manner. 'Gather round everyone while I speak of my tales of Rockhampton,' he spoke with fake laughter. 'Gather, gather, all will be told of the wooden buildings and the Stetson wearing arseholes, the touchy-feely police officers and the smelly meat factories.'

Bea had folded her arms, her smile was gone, her pretty face was now twisted and sour looking. 'Hang about,' she said, 'what's wrong with Rockhampton? I've lived here my whole life. My uncle wears a Stetson.'

Anders stepped back as though sucker-punched, caught off guard, stunned on the ropes. His plan was to win her over, not insult her hometown. He went to speak but nothing came. He stuttered. He fake laughed again as though he was joking.

'Nothing at all,' he said. 'I love Rockhampton, a lot, a lot, a lot. I bloody love it.' For some reason the word "bloody" came out in an Australian accent. He blushed holding his cheeks with both hands. 'I'm sorry I didn't mean it like that.' He looked at her and saw she was smiling. 'I'm sorry I said that, Bea.'

'Just stay here,' she said, 'and don't speak to anyone okay?' He nodded and watched her take keys from her desk. She entered a side door and through a pane of frosted glass he saw her silhouette. 'I may have something.' She was giggling on the other side of the door. 'Teddy stayed over last night.' He listened to her fumble round what seemed like a small closet. 'This might actually work.' There was excitement in her voice. 'Yes,' she giggled again, 'this might do it.'

Dressed in Bea's black tights and Teddy's Thomas the Tank Engine underpants with small grey socks, Anders entered the L-shaped waiting room, clattered over a wet floor sign, dodged a coffee table covered with magazines and leaflets, and seated himself opposite John and Andrew.

Only they waited and like in the police cell, he was thankful. Ignoring their smirks, he surveyed the sky blue walls laden with the same healthcare promoting posters he'd seen in every hospital, doctor's office, and clinic he'd ever been in. Though one in particular caught his eye. It was a grumpy looking gorilla with muscles the size of watermelons and a banana in each hand. Underneath a caption read – *Try telling him fruits and vegetables are for wimps.* Anders smiled. He kept his eyes on the poster and stared forward trying to block out John and Andrew's laughter.

138

'Bloody hell, Anders,' John said crossing his feet on the table, 'you looked better before.'

Anders said nothing. He then blinked lowering his eyes a little, staring at his new socks.

'He's right, you know,' Andrew laughed, he pointed to the socks and tights. 'Before you looked accidental, any fuck-wit can lose their pants. But this,' he moved his finger near Anders's legs, 'this all looks pre-planned, as though picked from your own wardrobe. It's more disturbing in a way, it is you know.'

Anders continued to ignore them. He needed to gather his thoughts, to prepare for the needle, to keep calm and relax his mind.

'Jesus he looks pale,' John said, 'those lips,' he said, 'as blue as death.'

'He's worrying about the needle,' Andrew added. 'Matron will have him touching his toes soon.'

There was silence after that. Anders kept staring at the poster, gulping, tasting bile on his tongue and its acidity burning on his throat. He sniffed up. The room smelt strongly of disinfectant and the scents from the recently mopped floor made his head feel worse, as though the air was thickening around him. Hang on in there, he told himself, be strong, strong like the gorilla.

'I'm not a fan of needles either,' John said picking his teeth with his thumbnail.

'Nor me,' Andrew said, 'have you ever given blood?'

Anders kept silent. He was beginning to sweat now and his armpits became damp, turning the crusty T-shirt soft again, as though rehydrating it, releasing new odours of rotten meat and foul cheese, and this, mixed with the scent of disinfectant, made him want to vomit. He plugged his air holes with his fingers, but soon he felt dizzy. The tight underpants were not helping his situation, he thought, *they are tight as hell.* He then thought about Teddy. He wondered how old he was.

'I've never given blood,' John said. 'I'm not much into that, that's for lonely do-gooders chasing a free biscuit.'

'I gave it once,' Andrew said. 'I won't bother again.'

'Why?' John asked.

Anders looked at them quickly then licked his lips and returned his gaze to the poster.

'The nurse messed up,' Andrew said feeling his arm. 'She couldn't find my vein, tried twice, missed twice.'

'What a waste of time that was,' John said. 'Why twice, why not have another go?'

'Because,' Andrew said, 'if they miss twice that's it. They don't attempt a third.'

'What a shitty experience for you,' John said.

'It got worse,' Andrew said, frowning.

'How,' John said, 'how did it get worse than that?'

'Well,' Andrew said stretching his legs out to meet with the table. 'I gave no blood, right, so I got no biscuit, no Hobnob, not even a Rich Tea. The bastards made sure, they sent me down another lane, the failures lane, the lane that led straight to an emergency exit. They stabbed me up twice and I left with no Scooby snack. I was pretty upset. I was almost as pale as Anders.'

They stopped talking now. A door opened and a nurse with slippered feet appeared holding a clipboard. She was small and stumpy, her hips wide and her arms short and fat. She had a man's haircut, spiky and trimmed short at the back and sides.

'I have John next,' she said looking round the room. 'John Moore.'

As John entered her room, she lifted her spectacles and glared at Anders. He felt bad vibes from her. He wondered if she knew about his indecent exposure incident. It was a small town after all, he thought, maybe word had spread quickly. He closed his eyes, waiting, breathing very slowly. When he opened them again, she was gone.

A man and a woman entered the waiting room. He looked as sickly as Anders. He was tall and thin and beanpole like, with chalky skin and a receding hairline. His wife was much shorter and she looked up at him as he stooped over her in discussion, pestering her for tissues, saying people should be careful where they leave their stuff. He pointed to his shoe, lifted his foot, hopping awkwardly one way then another. 'Hurry up,' he said clicking his fingers. 'Find the tissues, Tracey.'

Head down and still hopping, the man nearly tripped over Anders's foot. He jittered backwards as though an electric pulse was running through his knees and shoulders. 'Find them, Tracey,' he spoke fast, he hopped away from Anders. 'Find those tissues.'

'Be quiet, Simon,' she said, now sat down with her handbag on her lap, rummaging both hands through it. 'There, take them and stop whining. You're always whining.'

'No I'm not,' Simon said scrunching the tissues in hand, 'just people leaving their stuff in doorways. What was it anyway?' She ignored him. He looked at her for a moment then dropped to one knee and tilted his shoe, rubbing its tread with tissues, cleaning away egg and vomit. When he finished, he got up and stood centre of the room with a gorping expression. Again, he looked at Tracey, showing her the soiled tissue on his open hand, looking vacant, lost, as though someone had just wiped his memory and dumped him there.

'Over there in the corner.' Tracey pointed with her finger and following her direction, he tottered over to a bin and disposed of the tissues. 'Sit down, Simon!'

He sat down. He stretched his long legs under the table and stared gloomily at his feet as they appeared on the other side between two stacks of magazines. But his stillness lasted only seconds, soon his head was going in all directions. John crossed the room and the nurse began calling her next victim. Andrew stood up laughing. 'Won't be long now, Anders, you'll be next.' He followed the nurse's call with Anders and Simon watching him, both looking as pale as each other.

John held a paper towel over his upper arm. He was looking a bit pasty himself now, not saying much either. He looked underneath the paper towel and then left through a side door, which led to a toilet. Anders continued to watch the gorilla poster, listening to Simon argue with Tracey, questioning why she had picked a holiday to somewhere that involved three vaccination shots. 'I don't like needles,' he said. 'I'm not looking forward to this holiday now.'

'Oh shut up,' she said, and she grabbed the first magazine from the table. 'Here read this,' she said. 'It's good for taking your mind off it.'

'Take my mind off my holiday,' Simon said. 'I thought one is supposed to look forward to a holiday. Though I admit, I'm certainly reserved about this one.'

'I don't mean the holiday you imbecile. I mean the injection.'

Simon said nothing. He just dangled the magazine before his face and stared vacantly at the tanned bodybuilder on the front cover, all buffed up with oiled skin, dressed in underpants that were almost as tight as Anders's and showing teeth so big and so white, one may assume they were piano keys.

Two doors opened, John and Andrew met centre of the room, and again Simon's head was going. 'Bloody hurt that, lad,' Andrew said. 'You could've told me.' John looked down at the needle mark, the little red dot, the white puffiness around it. 'Yeah,' he said. 'Tell me about it.'

Chapter thirteen

'Anders Frisk,' the nurse was calling again. 'Mr Frisk,' she yelled.
Anders ignored John and Andrew who were now laughing. He got up
and moving his jelly like legs, left the waiting room.

'Shut the door, please, Mr Frisk,' the nurse said, 'and wait on the bed,
there.' She stood behind her desk pointing her clipboard to where she
wanted him.

The bed had a long paper towel over it, still crumpled, still warm
from where John and Andrew had sat on it. He sat there hugging
himself, rocking his body forward and back, like a crack addict gone
cold turkey. His foot began tapping the bedpost. His eyes flickered to
all corners of the room. She watched him, rubbing her nose on the back
of her hand, her other hand moving her nurse's cap, adjusting it top of
her head. Still watching him, she stuffed her big bottom and big hips
into her chair and rode it from one filing cabinet to another, collecting
papers.

Just above her head was a square window. Anders looked through it
seeing trees and the town hall. He watched people entering and leaving,
going up and down its steps, and taxis pulling up and beeping at each
other. 'You're Anders, yes?' He looked away from the window and
nodded. When he breathed in he smelt a combination of antiseptic gels,

and garlic coming from a food container doing spins in a microwave. He stared at the microwave as though in a trance. Then he stared at her desk and the rest of her lunch, a banana and two oatcakes wrapped in tissue paper, and beside them in the shape of a kidney, was a small tray that held both the syringe and the needle. He moved his hand up to his chest, his heart had more beat than an Ibiza nightclub, he thought, feeling very strange, as though hot, dizzy and freezing cold all at the same time.

He sucked in his lips. He held both knees to stop them shaking. To Anders, the room seemed to be shrinking smaller and smaller, as though everything was intruding on his space, taking his breath and squeezing him tightly. A man in a small box, he thought, a small box filling with toxic gas.

'Stop tapping that foot, please,' the nurse said, interrupting his deluded mind. She lowered her clipboard, 'I've asked you to stop, please.' Her forehead had darkened. Her eyebrows drew in. He had weighed her up earlier and guessed she was old school, no nonsense, the last of the matrons. He knew she saw him as a wimp, just another needle fearing wimp that needed to get on board with her program and man up. He remembered going to the doctors as a kid, remembered getting a superhero plaster on his boo-boo, or a lollipop for being a

146

brave little boy. But not from this one, he thought, if anything he got the impression she enjoyed dishing pain out, a real dominatrix, maybe seeing him cry would be an achievement in her book.

'I won't keep saying it, your feet, keep them still,' she said.

'Apologies, matron,' Anders said tightening his grip on his knees, trying to control his erratic body.

'No need for matron, thank you,' she said. 'My name is nurse Fudge.'

'Yes, nurse Fudge.'

'You're tapping your foot again.' She came close to him, her wide build taking his space. The squeezing feeling went up a notch. He was sweating badly. 'You're a nervous boy,' she said. 'Are you nervous?'

He didn't answer. He moved his eyes to the window and thought about jumping through it. Then looking above the trees, he saw a darkening sky and thought even the clouds were moving in on him. He puckered his lips, rapidly blowing air threw them like a woman having contractions during childbirth.

'I can't have you sweating that way,' she said.

When he ignored her, she ragged shut the curtains and pushed her fist through a cardboard box.

'Here,' she said stuffing a wad of paper towels into his hand. 'Use them, dry yourself.'

147

Leaning back, resting and enjoying the coolness of the wall, he ran

the paper towels over his damp skin, neck, arms and face. It felt nice

against the wall. Eyes now closed, he relaxed his arms and lowered his

tensed shoulders. Then he opened them again feeling pain. There was

prodding and for a moment, he thought the bitch was injecting him.

Another prod, then another, both on the upper arm, prod, prod, prod. He

came forward slowly with widened eyes, gasping for breath.

'Here,' she said prodding with her pen again. She pinched his wrist,

stuffed more paper towels into his hand.

'Jesus,' he said. 'I thought you had started.'

'Nonsense,' she said walking back to her desk, hips swaying. 'I just

need you to calm down and dry off.'

Again he ran the towels everywhere, arms, face, neck. He raked his

fringe to one side with his fingers, and then felt his thudding heart with

the thought that he was dying. He kept some towels in one hand,

squeezing them tightly. He was sure the room was now half the size it

had been, everything seemed smaller, everything but the nurse and the

needle.

He gasped again and reaching out with eyes closed, relaxed his elbow

on something hard and cool. He kept it there, squeezing paper towels in

hand, listening now as rain patted softly on the window. The sound

148

became soothing, but only for a short while. *Jesus Christ*, he was screaming inside his mind, *she's prodding me again. What a bitch. My heart. My heart will explode.*

'Keep away from that,' she said tapping a plastic box with her pen, returning to her tray of doom.

Anders coiled back from the box as though it had breathed hot steam into his face. He leaned, almost lay, propped up on one elbow, staring at the bright yellow box covered with red and white hazard signs, warning of its contents, a deposit box for used needles. He checked his hands for marks, then his wrists, then all over.

'Take these,' nurse Fudge said dropping more paper towels onto the bed. 'You're sweating again.'

'I don't feel good,' he said.

'It will be fine,' she said. 'Now remove that T-shirt, Mr Frisk. It will all be over very soon.'

Anders arched his head and shoulders, shuffled out of the T-shirt and sat bare-chested, rubbing his arms, shivering. Thunder clapped in the sky. The pleasant patter of rain changed instantly, was now bouncing bullishly on the window, as if it was trying to get in. Nurse Fudge put the tray down beside him and checked its contents. He felt the thudding everywhere now, not just his head and heart, every pulse, his veins, his feet, his hands.

'Mr Frisk, you need to calm yourself.' There was no reply. 'Mr Frisk, settle down.' She clicked her fingers in front of his eyes. He stared at them, blinking.

'My name,' he said pointing a finger at the clipboard on her desk. 'You have my name wrong.'

'What do you mean,' she said. She went behind her desk, squeezing down into her seat. 'Anders Frisk,' she read out, finger on the paper on her clipboard. 'Same as the famous football referee, yes.' She came back to him with his information sheet in front of his face.

'It's all correct,' he said panting, foot tapping again, flip-flop slapping on the metal bedpost. 'But you have my last name wrong.'

'Please, please, stop that,' she said putting her hands over her ears. 'We run a nursing practise, not a skiffle group.' He held his knees, the slapping stopped. 'You're an odd one,' she went on. 'You're acting very odd.'

'I've had a rough day,' he said tasting dry saltiness on his lips. He knew he needed water but he wasn't sure if his body would take it, worried that whatever went in, might come straight back out again, with vengeance.

'What is it then,' she asked, eyeing the needle. 'What is it if you're not Frisk?'

'Anderson,' he said. 'Anders Anderson.' *And no, I'm not a Scott.*

'Here,' she huffed handing him her pen, throwing the clipboard on to the bed. 'Correct it and we'll move on. I have lots more people to see, you know.'

He leaned over the information sheet, pen pinched in his trembling fingers. It took nearly a minute to correct it but finally he managed, putting a black squiggle through the name Frisk, forming some scruffy looking letters beneath it. Then as he handed the pen back, lightning flickered at the curtain lighting up the room, lighting up nurse Fudge's face like a baddy on a TV screen. She had the syringe now, moving it in front of his face. He wanted to shuffle back, but there was no more space, only hard wall, needle box on one side, curtain-covered window on the other, then her, the bitch ready to jab him. More lightning flashed in. Rain pelted the window. He imagined a swarm of killer wasps outside, thrusting their stings into the glass, trying to get in and pump him full of Q fever antibodies.

'Relax your arm.' He heard her say. 'Stop tapping that foot.'

She held the syringe in the air, squeezed the plunger, clear fluid dribbled from the needle. There was another flash of lighting. Then the rain stopped. There was total silence now and he closed his eyes looking like a gulping, squinting, sweating, pale mess. The tip of the needle touched his skin. He pulled away, tensed up.

'Hold still,' she said, tracking his movements with the syringe, 'relax.'

Pop! She got him. It went in and he opened his eyes, and looking down he began screaming.

Meanwhile, other side of nurse Fudge's door, having heard the screams, Simon was pacing the waiting room and jumping with his arms so straight by his side that he looked like a giant pencil. Then he began whipping his head side to side like an alerted dog, one that had woken suddenly by its own fart, now ultra aware.

Nurse Fudge acted in a similar way, she moved up and down the bed, her small, stumpy body trying to get to the needle, her short, fat arms flapping by her sides. Anders had turned, now holding the bed rails tightly like a drunken sailor, pressing his forehead on them. He felt damp, cold and warm all over. Then everything seemed to go dark, and then there was nothingness.

'Please, keep still, Mr Frisk,' she said crawling onto the bed. 'I need to locate the needle.'

He was still, curled up like a fetus, completely still. She was over him, her breasts on his face, clicking her fingers and slapping his cheeks. She rolled off, tottered behind her desk and made a phone call. 'Some assistance, please, my room, it's nurse Fudge.' She hung up quickly and poured herself some water from a jug on her desk. She drank while watching him. He groaned, rolled over, raised his arm. 'It's there,' she said. 'I see it.' She reached for it hanging there deep in his flesh. But he moved suddenly, springing forward as though to grab her. She screamed, she backed up watching him with his head down between his knees.

'There he goes again,' Andrew laughed as two members of staff passed through the waiting room. They opened nurse Fudge's door and then entered. Still laughing, he craned his neck trying to see inside, but they closed it swiftly behind them. 'He's screamed twice now,' Andrew said showing John two fingers.

John nodded sullenly and looked at his own needle mark. 'That,' he said, 'is because he's a bloody soft arse.'

The two staff members held Anders up by his arms. He arched forward, speaking in short bursts as though badly out of breath. 'Are... we... done... M'm'matron...'

153

'Not quite,' he heard a voice say, and when he opened his eyes he saw two blurred faces either side of him. *Angels,* he thought, *come to carry me away.* To him, the room was spinning and everything in it disappeared and then reappeared in blurry images, as though on a playground roundabout with three faces watching him. 'We're almost there,' another voice said, 'we just need to inject.' He stopped trying to sit up. He leaned to one side and the nurses assisted him, allowing him to rest there with his cheek on the bed. Then staring forward and seeing things more clearly, he glanced at himself in a mirror on the other side of the room, and seeing the needle hanging from his arm, he screamed with his mouth open so wide that his lips cracked.

'I think he's gone again,' one nurse said, stooping, looking into his eyes. 'I think he's urinated too,' said the other.

Chapter fourteen

It was nice under his covers. He felt warm and rested and wanted to stay there. His headache had gone. His cuts and sores now had that slight burning feeling, that wasn't so sharp or painful anymore. He drifted in and out of sleep for as long as he could, ignoring John's feet stomping heavily on the floor. Often he'd pass telling him to wake, or stop and pull his toes or his ankle. Then for moments it was nice again, and Anders lifted his knees up high and slept.

'Am I the only one awake?' John said from the balcony, drinking coffee. 'Today is our first day. We got a twelve hour shift in the kill room.'

Anders peeked from his covers. Behind John's blurry image, he saw the dark sky was getting lighter. He closed his eyes again and listened to the sounds of a new day, of voices outside, of car engines ticking, of birds chirping and fluttering in the trees. A minute passed, then another. John seemed to have given up, but then his feet began stomping again.

'Up, up, up,' he said now, charging, almost running into the room. 'No one is listening to me.' He leaned over Anders, spraying him with coffee breath. 'You're not sleeping in. You're not spoiling this for me.' He pulled the covers. 'Get up now, boy! Hands off your cock! Feed on this sock!'

He stuffed a dirty sock inside Anders's mouth and stood up, watching him cough and splutter. 'You're not listening to me so you deserved that.' He walked away but came straight back again. 'Why is no one listening to me?'

Anders spat out the sock. He looked at it on the floor, face squinting like a woken gerbil. Then John's hands were over him, grabbing his blanket, snatching it away. Soon it was on the floor. He tried grabbing the sheets but Anders had twisted them round him, looking like a crocodile doing a death roll. 'This is our first day,' John said. 'I'm not turning up late.' He stuck a thumb between Anders's ribs and held it there, moving it vigorously until Anders's body untwisted, letting go of the bedding. John backed away dragging two sheets with him. He dumped them outside and stood on the decking drinking more coffee, watching Anders curl up in his underpants, hugging his pillow. 'Don't you dare go back to sleep,' he said. 'I'll take that too.' He folded his arms and kept talking. 'This coffee is good. I'm enjoying it where I am. But it won't stop me. I'll sort you again if needs must.'

He waited a few moments, standing the same way, finishing his coffee. Then with shoes in hand, he strode across the room and opened the door heading out into the corridor. 'Get up you lazy bastards.' He ran back in. 'Get up!' Quickly he staggered out again, leaving the door wide open. 'Get up!' he screamed.

'What was that,' Andrew said under his covers. 'What just happened?'

Anders said nothing. He lay on his mattress for a while, gently moving his fingers over his upper arm, feeling the sticking plaster. Nurse Fudge got him good, he thought, trying to forget the image of the needle hanging from his arm. Now he rolled over, stood wearily and wandered to the kitchen top. Yawning and moving his hand over the side of his face, he smiled seeing two steaming mugs beside the sink. Both dark and thick, as John always made it, like molasses. He smelt the coffee wearing the expression of an anguished child, one tasked with eating stewed cabbage or lumpy potatoes. Then, regretfully, he tasted some. Rabbit droppings and cigar ash was not a flavour he was familiar with, nor did he intend to be, though if he was, he thought, the combination would be similar, or pretty damn close at least, to John's coffee.

Ditching the coffee for a glass of water, he went to the willow tree and glanced up, as he did every morning hoping to see the Possum. It wasn't there. He drank from the glass and sat down leaning forward, seeing the fading darkness in the sky, no moon, no clouds in sight now, just blue sky and over the distant hills, the orange glow of sunrise.

He glanced at the road. It had rained during the night and was not yet dusty. Workers walked on it looking tired and gloomy, heading towards the meat factory's gates, their heads down, their knapsacks over their shoulder. Some men came the other way, walking sluggishly after a long night shift, their stooped, worn out bodies dragging themselves home, some holding bottles of beer to their lips, drinking it slow.

Andrew watched him watching the workers. He leaned out of bed, his hair stuck up, his blanket across one shoulder. 'How you going to cope today,' he said. 'You know, being a veggie bollocks an' all that?'

'Cope,' Anders said standing up in his underpants, turning to him. 'I always cope. I coped yesterday. I coped fine.'

'Well,' Andrew said rubbing his eyes. 'You did scream three times.'

'It wasn't three.'

'It bloody was,' Andrew laughed.

'It bloody was not,' Anders said coming into the room.

'Okay, okay,' Andrew smiled, he yawned, sat up, placed a pillow behind his back. 'Pass me that brew and I won't mention it again.'

Anders took the other mug from the sink, held it down for him. 'So,' Andrew said taking it, cupping it with both hands, 'what happened the other night?'

'I can't remember.' Anders picked up his combat shorts and stepped into them. 'It began with that Steve, I blame you for that.'

'I'm sure if you asked nicely he would've left.'

'I tried that. That bit I do remember.'

Both then paused. Noises came from under the spare bunk. They listened to something rolling like a glass bottle.

'What was that?' Andrew sat up straighter. He put down his mug.

'God knows,' Anders said, now both looking at each other, 'probably rats knowing this place, rats or giant cockroaches.'

'I agree, could be anything like that knowing this place.' Andrew threw back his covers and sat forward, both feet touching the floor. 'It could be anything like that,' he said, still wearing yesterday's jeans that he'd slept in all night, as he often did, and was now reaching into an open suitcase, moving his hands roughly through heaps of crumpled clothes. 'There's something you're not telling me though,' he said, selecting a worn T-shirt.

'There's really nothing to tell,' Anders brushed past him. He bent near the sink and washed his dirty hair with both hands. 'We drank

159

beer,' he spoke over the sound of the tap. 'We smoked weed. Henry left after that and it got weird, that's when he did what he did.'

'Did what?'

'Put LSD in my drink, sent me on a major trip.' Anders walked up and down the room rubbing a towel over his head. On his bedpost, he found a chequered shirt and shook out its creases.

'Right,' Andrew said, 'the nakedness makes sense now. Bet you did all kinds of crazy stuff.'

'Possibly,' Anders said wearing the shirt, messing with its buttons. 'But I can't remember, well, there's the odd hallucination, but that's it.'

'First trip was it?'

'Yes, was my first and will be my last, and before you ask me, flying elephants are no cliché. There was fucking hundreds of them. There was...' Anders went quiet. He stared downwards holding his pumps by their laces. Then he was kneeling, kneeling beside the spare bunk and moving John's dirty socks out of the way. He then frowned and touched the floor with his fingers, kept touching the same patch.

'What do you think did that?' Andrew said coming close, sitting beside him. 'Have they always been there?'

'Can't say I've noticed, there's always so much stuff on the floor.' Anders said, now feeling the marks with his thumb, 'creepy though, very creepy.'

'What do you think made them?'

'Not sure. Rats?'

'Be some big bloody rats. Big scratch marks them. Look how deep they go.'

'Odd,' Anders said, 'odd marks aren't they,' and though he guessed Andrew was thinking the same thing, he just couldn't seem to say it, though he was sure they were, to him, they really did look human.

A thin woman with grey hair stood outside their room, as though she'd been listening at the door. Her skin was blotchy and marked with red and white dots, like she'd had many years of sun exposure, and her cardigan sagged on her small shoulders, smelling badly of cigarettes, urine and cat food. They moved away from her and she dipped her head, crying, rubbing her eyes with tissues. Her hands, Anders noticed, were like the rest of her, old and frail, with purple veins going in all directions, like roots of a tree. Often he wondered if Dickie had named The Old Crow after her, maybe it was her wedding present.

'Boys,' she said, stuttering and staring, eyes redder than a badger's arsehole. 'Boys,' but before she could say anymore, Andrew cut in.

'Babs, please, we're already late.'

'But it's my Dickie,' she said carrying on regardless. 'Have either of you seen him?'

They looked at each other shaking their heads. 'Why?' Andrew asked.

'He's missing,' she said. 'I haven't seen him since yesterday morning, just before I subbed you that hundred and twenty dollars for him.' She pointed at Anders. 'I heard what you did,' she said. 'Don't worry, I don't judge.'

Andrew looked at the carpet, then either side of the corridor. 'Maybe he stopped out,' he said. 'You know, stayed with a friend.'

'He never does that.' She dabbed her eyes with a tissue. 'He would've told me.'

'Well,' Andrew said. 'Just wait a bit longer.' But it was as though she didn't hear him, she'd taken a cigarette from its carton and was staring at it between her trembling fingers. Anders stared at it too. He was thinking about the hundred and twenty dollars, and the fact that John and Andrew had used him to make a nice profit. 'If he doesn't show by tonight,' Andrew said, 'we'll go search for him, okay.'

There was no response. She now held the cigarette in her mouth and felt her pockets for matches. When she took them out, they rattled in their box and she struggled to select one. Andrew took one for her, he

162

struck it edge of the box and held it while she bobbed her head down, nodding, taking quick drags on the cigarette. Grey smoke appeared through her tensed nostrils, matching the colour of her hair and cardigan. Then she stared forward not looking at either of them. 'I'm terrified,' she said. 'Apparently there's a mad man in town.'

Chapter fifteen

Inside the factory walls, John had been pacing up and down for nearly thirty minutes. Near to him, constantly checking his watch stood their supervisor, Pat Patanga. A short, South African man with light brown skin, thick eyebrows and a smoothed, perfectly rounded baldhead. 'Over here quick,' he said dressed head to toe in a white uniform and rubber boots, watching Anders and Andrew pass through the gate-lodge doors, rushing, almost falling as they ran and skidded down some steps.

'We made it,' Andrew said, pausing to catch his breath. 'Six o'clock on the nose.'

They stood now with John. Patanga checked his watch again and looked over them, showing deep creases between his eyebrows. 'Your friend,' he said to John, 'he not understanding something. Is he special?'

'Apologies, Mr Patanga,' John said. 'This won't happen again.'

'Well for ginger's benefit and to make sure I'm not waiting like an idiot every morning, I'll say this.' Patanga tucked his hands inside his immaculately white overalls and stepped forward. 'You're no good to me here at six o'clock, at six o'clock I want you ready, working in the kill room, each day, not here, not outside these bleddy factory gates fingering each other's bleddy arseholes. Understand?'

164

He extended a finger. He pointed behind himself and they nodded. 'Up there and ready,' he said. 'You all got that.' They agreed they understood. 'What about you, ginger, you got that?'

Patanga didn't wait for an answer, he had set off and they followed, lagging behind, with John and Andrew arguing with each other over the start time. Anders got further in front. He tried to catch up with Patanga who was now looking up, in the shadows of a tall grey building, which reminded Anders of a workhouse in a Dickens novel. 'Kill room is up there,' he said. 'Place used to be a mental asylum back in the eighteen-fifties.'

'That's very interesting, Mr Patanga,' Anders said, now side by side with him.

'Don't be so bleddy formal, boy. Call me Pat.'

'Pat Patanga?' Andrew sniggered.

'Don't get funny, ginger,' Patanga said looking over his shoulder. 'Pat will do.'

He set off again, leading them down a tarmac path to the entrance of the grey building.

'Pat.' Anders was beside him again. 'I was wondering about the other options here. I'm squeamish with blood and was wondering about work on the loading bay?'

'Does he not mean squeamish with bled?' Andrew said copying Patanga's accent, kicking John's heel.

'There's no work there,' Patanga said touching a button with his key card. He opened a door, held it with his foot while they passed. 'But I'll keep you in mind. If something comes up, you'll be the first one to know, how's that?'

'Is there anywhere other than the kill room?' Anders said, almost on Patanga's shoulder now as they climbed up a stairwell, John and Andrew still lagging back.

'Yes,' Patanga said, 'but not today.'

They reached the top of the stairs and shuffled past a few laundry baskets. Linen hung from them, crumpled, smeared with blood. They came onto a corridor, a long one with brown walls and small windows on one side. It reminded Anders of a hospital. He touched his spectacles slowly with his fingers and sniffed up smelling an unpleasant smell, something between a butchers shop and mop-bucket water. It grew stronger as they followed Patanga.

'Today,' Patanga went on, 'as with most days, we're short staffed on the kill room floor.' He used his key card again, held another door. 'We need two for spinal cord duty, and a slops guy.'

'Slops?' Anders said.

'Yeah,' Patanga said kicking through some double doors. 'You see some workers take out the shit we don't eat, stuff like innards and organs, and they dump all that shit into a bucket, a slops bucket.' Patanga was laughing now. They took a turn, came onto a new corridor. This one had no windows, but the smell was the same. 'You'll know when you get there,' Patanga went on. 'Those buckets fill up fast. Can be a dangerous place to work in a kill room, slops guy plays an important role, keeps the place tidy and less shitty.'

He stopped at a vending machine. He fed the slot a dollar. 'My friend, you're our new slops guy.' He glanced up at Anders, reached under a plastic flap for his can of Coke. 'You'll do us proud, yes?'

They went down another corridor, one as plain and as white as Patanga's overalls. They dodged more laundry baskets, passed a glum-faced porter arguing with his set of keys, selecting one and tut-tutting as it refused to turn in the lock. Through another door, they turned left and entered the changing rooms.

'I'll fetch your stuff,' Patanga said without looking at them, disappearing through a door-less hatch.

Anders moved away from John and Andrew. He sat on a wooden bench and looked around. There were shirts above him bunched on pegs, shoes on the floor stuffed with socks, puddles everywhere. He smelt body odour, cheap aftershave, cigarettes, urine. He heard taps hissing, saw steam clouds drifting in from the shower block and noticed a naked man wearing one sock, moaning to a porter, saying it was the same every day, every fucking day was the same, some bastard was always taking his sock.

'Come now, boys,' Patanga said suddenly appearing, dropping rubber boots on the floor, handing out tops and bottoms. 'Take off your clothes, strip.' He stood on a bench holding his Coke. 'Hurry up.'

Everything Patanga gave them was white apart from one thing, Anders thought, holding the top in his hands. 'My top is red,' he said while John and Andrew pulled their jeans down to their ankles. 'Why is that?'

'Is that not obvious, slops guy?' Patanga laughed and sipped Coke. 'Actually,' he said, 'let me swap that for you, you'll want a long sleeved one to cover those wounds.' Patanga disappeared and returned with a red top with long sleeves. He passed it to Anders and handed out three facemasks.

'Don't worry about us, Patanga lad,' Andrew said handing back the facemask. 'We were vaccinated yesterday.'

'True, ginger, very true,' Mr Patanga said. 'But it can take a week or two for immunity to kick in. As a precaution, and as your supervisor, I insist you wear a mask.'

'Fantastic,' Anders said staring at John, 'all that yesterday was for nothing.'

'What's got slops guy agitated?' Patanga asked.

'The vaccination shot,' John said, 'he thinks it was for nothing.'

'Not necessarily,' Patanga said sipping more Coke. 'Two week from now he'll be immune, won't need a mask then.'

'And if I'm on the loading bay?' Anders said.

'Then you won't have to worry,' Patanga laughed. 'There's no catching Q fever down there, not unless Gollum pays you a visit.'

'Who is Gollum?' Andrew asked.

All three looked at Patanga.

'You'll find out soon enough,' Patanga said, 'Come now, best not keep him waiting.'

They followed him through a canal of pink foamy water. It swished over their boots and stepping out on the other side, Patanga lifted a hosepipe and waved it in front of their faces. Then he sprayed it over and under his boots. Hot steam came up around them. 'Keep this away from your skin,' he yelled passing the hose to John. 'Use it like I did,' he yelled, 'then come here.' He stood by a long stretch of sink. 'Get under your nails like this.' He put his hands in more soapy water and scrubbed his fingernails with a brush. 'Get between your fingers, pump that soap on, wash everywhere,' he kept yelling, 'go all the way up to your elbows, wash 'em good.'

Anders sighed. He felt silly watching Patanga's demo, as though he was revisiting his potty training years. Suddenly he saw his mother's face superimposed on Patanga's. 'More soap, ginger,' Patanga yelled over the sound of splashing water. 'That's it, slops guy, very good, but be careful near those wounds.'

They left through a haze of steam. Patanga brought them to another room, where metal armour hung from shelves and hooks and nails, there were boxes on the floor, overflowing, all holding more metal armour, enough to suit a Saxon army. The door closed behind them and for a moment, the only noise was the thud of machinery coming from behind another door, behind which was the kill room, and Gollum.

They patted their hands and arms dry with paper towels while Patanga went on. 'You need to wash that way each time you come in and out, okay?' He waved his hands, showed them his nails, pointed to each wrist. 'We can't have any cross contamination here, you all got that?'

He got up on a stool, reached for two butcher's aprons and pulled them from a hook. With his other hand, he tapped Andrew on the shoulder. 'Lower yourself,' he said. 'I need to dress you.' He hosted a strap over Andrew's head and then fixed two more, one to his shoulder, one round his waist. Then he grabbed a mesh glove and told Andrew to stick his hand inside it. 'You next,' he said calling John, repeating the process with him. 'Do yours like that too, ginger,' he said pointing to a chain on John's glove, fixing it to the apron. Finally, he went round giving everything a final tug. 'Does that feel okay?'

'I feel like King Arthur,' Andrew said facing the glove. 'What will we be doing?'

'Well,' Patanga said messing with John's waist strap. 'You'll have this suction gun right, a powerful, dangerous suction gun. You'll take it and when the cows come along one by one, you'll press a button, and you'll run the gun right down the spinal cord sucking it out, all in one go.' He paused for a moment. 'You'll be happy I dressed you like King Arthur once you start.' He opened up his overalls, stuck his thumb inside a deep hole near his hip. 'Be careful, ginger, you don't wanna miss.'

171

He yanked another strap on John's apron, then, stepping back and placing an arm on Anders's shoulder, began laughing. 'Ah, check them out, slops guy,' he said. 'Two Knights of the realm, eh.'

Anders glanced down at his red top and his white pants. 'What about me. I want some gear?'

'Sure,' Patanga said dipping his hand into a cardboard box, 'put these latex gloves on, cover up those wounds.

Chapter sixteen

The kill room had brick walls. There were no windows, no ventilation. It was dank, hot, humid, noisy, dimly lit. It was cramped everywhere. No space for anything. There was thudding machinery, yelling workers, mooing cows. Down the middle of the room, at long tables, butchers sorted meat on thick wooden blocks, with flesh, bone and skin all around them. Every worker had a bucket, but some slops made it to the floor, puddles of blood, tongues and hearts, eyes and stomachs. From a conveyer belt line, round the edges of the room, cows dangled by their hoofs, now cut in half, and that way they came, one half cow at a time, just as Patanga had said. One brushed against Anders's arm. It still felt warm and he moved back seeing another with snot and blood dangling from its muzzle. Their eyes, he noticed, though very dead, were still moving, pulsating, as though winking at him, staring at the vegetarian, as though he'd come to save them.

Steam was on his lenses. He cleaned them using his top. Then he dodged another cow and ducked under its outstretched leg. 'Stop being so jumpy,' Patanga said leading them down some metal steps. 'They're dead.'

At the end of the room was daylight. It was open down there, and there, a group of men hung round, dressed in rubber gloves and rubber

173

aprons. One of them wore a Stetson. He stood looking mean with his bolt pistol in hand. 'That's where they kill 'em,' Patanga said. Anders saw the cattle coming in off the wagons, running up the ramps, trodding through their own dung, then waiting, always waiting for the man with the pistol, stepping away from the daylight, into the darkness.

When the cows dropped, the men in the rubber aprons stepped back while a dripping red saw came down. The saw ran through the cow's middle cutting it in half. Then someone attached a clamp to its hoof, and up it went, hoisted along, just another half cow on the conveyer belt line. The workers had to move fast, digging in with knifes, or saws, or tools, or pieces of machinery, removing stomach, heart, bladder, skin, spinal cord, bone, sinew, fat, all sorts, all of it wet, all of it shiny and dripping with blood, and again as Patanga had warned, the buckets filled fast.

'Next one,' yelled the man in the Stetson. 'Next one! Next one! Next one!'

They followed Pat Patanga. They stepped on hearts, livers, eyeballs and other bits, all wet and slippery, still warm, still pumping, still alive. The foul smell began to disturb Anders, began to play on his mind. It wasn't the cow shit, though there was plenty of that. It was something else, something he could not label, something he'd smelt long ago, when his uncle Victor had died. Then he realised, the smell was just the same, death was death, cow or human.

Now they passed a line of dishevelled, dark-eyed, under-slept workers, ripping into cows like a bunch of insane surgeons, reaching in with their tools, coming out with something dripping and then adding it to their bucket. There was a "moo", then a thud as another one hit the deck, huge beast flattened by a tiny pistol. Patanga looked round with his hands on his hips. When he looked down, a bucket of eyeballs was skidding towards him. 'Need an empty,' a boy shouted, 'Where's Gollum,' said an older voice. 'Hey, Patanga,' a bearded man then said, arm rested on a metal rail, blood dripping from his fingertips. 'Are we getting another slops guy or what?'

'I'm dealing with it,' Patanga said continuing to look round.

Another bucket skidded towards them, this one packed with intestines. More voices yelled asking about Gollum. Patanga was asking for him too. He climbed up on a step, asking passing workers if they'd seen him. Another bucket skidded along.

'They spotted your red top now,' Andrew laughed, was laughing hard until a hot loin slapped his cheek from somewhere above. He began looking round the room, shiny blood trickling down his pale skin.

Anders then noticed a crouched figure watching them, hidden in the shadows of the machinery. 'Patanga,' he said, 'Patanga over here.'

'Ah!' Patanga rubbed both hands together. 'There you are, come on out of there, meet your new apprentice.'

The figure crept out, very small and skinny, his body childlike, his face like that of an old man but with big bulbous eyes. As he moved slowly, Anders saw he was wearing a red top like his. He moved low to the ground, arms swaying like a chimps but without any muscles, knuckles almost grazing the factory floor. His beard was scraggy, clotted with blood and bone, and more bone tangled in his hair net, which was pasted thick with blood, hanging to one side like a beret.

'Ah, Gollum,' Patanga said, smiling, jumping off the step. 'Now boys, this, you see this, this is a bleddy hard worker.' Patanga took a latex glove from his pocket. He put it on. Then he put his gloved hand on Gollum's head. 'He's a good worker.' Still smiling, he looked at Anders.

Anders understood now what Patanga had mentioned earlier, how you couldn't catch Q fever on the loading bay, not unless Gollum paid you a visit. The man looked as though he used the buckets for something else, as though he bathed in them, bathed in blood and guts. There was something twitching in his pocket, too, possibly an eyeball, Anders thought.

'Teach him well,' Patanga said leading John and Andrew up some steps to the conveyer belt area. He stopped at the top, chest pressed on a metal rail, shouting over the thud of the machinery and tools. 'Teach him the way. Get a day's work out of him.' He laughed and moved on with John and Andrew lagging behind, then, all three disappeared behind a line of swinging cows. Anders only saw their faces now and then, because the cows kept coming, blocking his view.

'So,' Anders said turning to Gollum. 'Where would you like me? Where should I start?'

Gollum showed him something. He held it up, pinching it in his fingers. It was a fair sized piece of sinew, about the size of a fat slug. 'What are you doing with that?' Anders asked, then, 'No, you don't, do you, oh, you are doing.' He watched Gollum dangle the sinew over his lips. His tongue stuck out, long, thin, black, like a reptiles. 'Is that what you do?' Anders asked. The sinew was in Gollum's mouth now. He was chewing it, moving it from one side to the other. Then he took the bucket of eyeballs and the bucket of intestines. He took them away, dragging them, creeping under a low arch, disappearing back into the darkness, behind the machinery.

'Hey you, red top, slops guy,' a voice said suddenly. Anders looked up. There was a man with muscular arms and he yelled from the conveyer beltline, his face was red and twisted with anger. He pointed a knife down at his boots, showing them, covered with what looked like pink sago coming up over his ankles. Then a cow swung past blocking his angry face. Then he appeared again, swearing, holding the cow by one horn and moving his knife inside it. More pink stuff spilled out around him, over his boots. Letting go, he looked again at Anders. 'I need more buckets. Get me more fucking buckets!'

'I don't know what to do,' Anders said back, lifting his arms in the air.

'You're a disgrace to that red top,' a voice said, but Anders wasn't sure who had said it, the cows kept blocking their faces.

'Where's Gollum?' another voice said.

Anders held his hands up again. 'I don't know.'

An empty bucket struck Anders's chest. Gollum was back now. He pointed at the floor, pointed at the bones and the skin and the tongues, tongues that people had trod on, flattened with their boot marks. He spat sinew into Anders's bucket and pointed with his wet fingers to more empty buckets stacked in the corner, where a boy stood rinsing them, spraying them down with a hose. Anders blinked watching

178

Gollum leave him again, dragging another bucket, this one filled with a peachy coloured froth. He passed under a small gap in the machinery. He seemed to know all the little gaps, Anders thought, seemed to fit through them all too.

Chapter seventeen

Anders had had his face under the tap for almost ten minutes, arms
trembling, elbows resting on the sink as water splashed over him.
Beneath the sink, by his feet sodden with cow's blood, were his top and
his gloves. He kicked them as he stood. Then dragging a paper towel
down his face, he followed a line of bodies into the pink canal, blinded
by steam, touching the damp bodies in front of him and apologising as
he passed, then feeling the sides of the canal with his boots, seeking a
way out.

The steam began clear. He rubbed the lenses of his spectacles with his
thumb, watching naked bodies wander the dimly lit changing room.
Men were towelling themselves dry, talking over each other,
dominating the room with their deep voices, strong accents, overbearing
laughter. Some stood smoking cigarettes, some sat on benches half-
dressed, and some strolled up and down, hands in pockets as though
waiting for someone.

Again Anders touched his face with the paper towel. He walked on
past a bench, past a man smelling a damp sock, past another man eating
a beef sandwich, his fingers still bloody from the kill room. Then there
was a man dressed like a pimp, selling x-rated videos from an open
duffle bag, cigarettes and wine. Near to the pimp were younger ones,

kids of college age, still in their work gear, punching and kicking each other through what they called the tunnel of death.

Moving on he came now to his clothes peg and sat down underneath it, kicking off each boot, leaning forward and watching as they skidded into a dirty puddle.

'Your first day, nipper?' an old man asked cheerily, foot rested on the bench, rubbing himself, dragging a towel over his grey pubes.

Anders ignored him, but then felt bad because the man was old and cheerful.

'You'll get there, nipper,' the old man said, now stepping into his shorts. 'I been here since forty-nine me, right from school. I been here so long my retirement is coming up,' he laughed. He looked one way then the other, then behind himself, slowly, as though he was reminiscing. His jaw clenched when he saw the pimp, then he was speaking again. 'Was a mental asylum back in the day, they put my great granddaddy in here.' His hair was grey and thinning, he brushed it with a comb. 'I believe this was the ward,' he said tapping his foot on the floor, folding his towel. 'Scary stuff, huh, scary, scary.' He stared at Anders for a moment. Then he picked up a bottle of aftershave and disappeared through the naked bodies.

181

Anders pulled down his bottoms and moved them under the bench with his foot. Suddenly he heard cheering. He jumped a little, thinking he was back in town being chased by Sammy. But the cheering was not for him. It was the younger ones, for a boy he now saw escaping the tunnel of death, holding himself and smiling with tears in his eyes, trying, Anders thought, to seem unhurt.

'Jesus,' Andrew said to John, both appearing in front of Anders. 'That armour takes ages to get off.'

'Yeah,' John said, 'it does. But I see slops guy made it through. '

Anders took his shirt and shorts off the peg. 'Don't call me that,' he said. 'It was horrible in there.' His fingers were still trembling, he pulled up his shorts and struggled with the zipper. 'That bastard,' he said. 'That Pat Patanga,' he said. 'He better get me on that loading bay, he better you know, I'll quit if he doesn't. I'm not doing that every day.'

'Stop talking so soft,' John said getting onto his knees to peer under the bench for his shoes. 'You can't quit after one day.'

'Watch me,' Anders said.

'It's not that bad, you're being wet. Andy, back me up, isn't he being wet?'

'Piss off, John,' Anders said. He picked up his pumps. He began slapping them hard on the bench. 'Just piss off.'

'Will you both calm it,' Andrew said.

'I am calm,' John yelled red in the cheeks.

'You bastards had it easy,' Anders said. 'For twelve hours I've been crawling round that kill room floor, was covered in all sorts, and what about that Gollum chasing me everywhere?' He looked at them but they said nothing. 'What about him threatening me for missing an eyeball.' Anders paused. He noticed people staring, shaking their heads in his direction. 'And,' he spoke now at a whisper, 'and, making up rules about sinew, all of them, that all pieces of sinew are to be split equally, fairly, evenly and shared out, shared at the end of each day.' He glanced round, brought a hand over his mouth and spoke behind it. 'He eats them.'

'Chews 'em,' the old man corrected, now smelling like Old Spice aftershave. 'He only chews 'em.'

Anders kept silent. He sat down and waited while the old man packed up his bag and left. That's when he thought about his outburst and reminded himself to be careful. To get work on the loading bay, he thought, Patanga was a man he needed on side. Maybe yelling "that bastard Pat Patanga" in public was not a wise move.

183

'What about those eyeballs though,' Andrew said. 'Guys, did you see how twitchy they were?'

'I bet slops guy noticed,' John said in a huffy tone.

'Yes,' Anders said, 'Most of it was twitchy and warm and horrible.' He had stood. He had one foot on the bench lacing his pumps. From behind, John nudged into him leaning slightly on his shoulder. 'They call it hard work,' he said speaking close to his ear. 'What would you know? All you do is moan. You moaned in the fields when it was hot, you moaned picking cabbages when your legs hurt, and you're moaning now, moan, moan, moan. It's all you do.'

The changing room was emptying. Just the younger ones hung round now, playing, messing in the showers, dashing about in their wet underpants, spraying hosepipes, laughing, stuffing tissue paper into plugholes, kicking water at each other. Then there was the pimp, still there, looking shifty in the corner, stashing his gear inside a tall locker and glancing over his shoulder.

'Moan, moan, moan,' John went on, dropping more weight onto Anders's stooped body, pressing down on him. 'Well guess what,' he said, 'my legs hurt, my back hurts too, those spinal cords were hard work but I carried on. I'm not moaning, am I?'

Anders shrugged him off and straightening their bodies, they came face to face with their eyes twitching as badly as the cows. 'I'm sick of babysitting you,' John said, 'sick of wiping your arsehole, wiping it while you moan and moan and moan.'

'Guys, enough now,' Andrew spoke but they ignored him.

'You,' Anders said fake laughing, 'you babysitting me.' He came up onto his tiptoes craning his neck, trying to get level with John. 'You forget whose money got us here, don't you? Don't you, Mr babysitter. If not for me, you would be slumming still in Brisbane. Both of you would be, if not for me. Have a think about that, Mr babysitter. Think about it.' Anders picked up his shirt. 'I can work as hard as anyone,' he said. 'You think I can't, but I can. I can work and suffer. I can take it. Now fuck off!'

Chapter eighteen

The factory gates were behind him now. His shirt was open and a soft breeze soothed his body in the late afternoon sun. He felt good to be outside, he felt free and enjoyed the sound of gravel crunching underneath his feet on the roadside. It was moments like this that he felt hope and happiness. He pushed back his shoulders continuing to The Old Crow, thinking about John's words, and about tomorrow. He would be back, he decided, kill room or not, he would be back not only to prove John wrong, but to earn and save up for a ticket somewhere. Four weeks, maybe five, he guessed. That would do, enough to get out of Rockhampton, enough to move on alone.

Further on he noticed flashing lights coming from police cars and ambulances, all parked on the roadside. There was a big truck too. Its doors were open showing scuba diving equipment and snorkels lay on the path. Through the trees, he saw people gathering before the Fitzroy River. The Fitzroy ran behind the meat factory. He knew that area well and went there often. When he first arrived, some old timer, who had had a few too many, Anders thought, sat at the bar telling him tales. He told him about bull sharks and crocodiles and how they swam the Fitzroy, how the sharks and the crocs lingered there for blood, cow blood, pumped into the river each night from the meat factory. True or not, Anders wasn't sure, but the idea had excited him and he'd sit there sometimes for hours, watching dark green water, hoping for a bull or a croc. But he never saw a thing, not even a stickleback or a newt, nothing.

He turned off the road stumbling through waist high grass. A slope of dirt appeared and he sledged down it on his bottom. Then he got up, came onto a gritty path, a path he recognised, a path that led to the riverbank. He passed through stinging nettles and pink-bamboo, through a patch of soft mud, through thick weeds, and moved carefully across a plank of old wood, which lay across an empty pond. He turned sideways and shuffled between some bushes. The floor suddenly became soft. He trod through the sooty black sand. The river was there, and so were the police officers. All stood in a line before it, their arms locked together like a human chain, facing a mob of people, trying to hold them back. Two more officers were putting crime tape around trees, shutting off the area behind them. Anders studied the scene. He saw Babs looking hysterical, crying into the arms of a white haired police officer with tanned skin, her feeble fists drumming on his back. 'No,' she screamed. 'I want to see, let me through.'

The people made noises simultaneously, gasping, oohing and aahing, watching something float about on the dark water, something big and fleshy. Two divers swam either side of it, shaded by a canopy of trees. Anders jumped up and down. He moved closer but it was no good, there were too many people blocking his view. They swayed as one unit, stepping back and then advancing forward to the bank, charging almost. Those further behind pushed others forward. Some people fell on the sand, staying there while shadows moved over them. The police officers held their line and ordered them back, shouting and pointing their fingers. One of them had a speakerphone. He spoke into it and his voice was blunt and stern. 'This is a crime scene,' he said. 'Move back! Move back! Move back! This is a crime scene.'

Babs continued to spill tears. She walked through the crowd, repeatedly rubbing her eyes with her fingers, rubbing them vigorously, was as though she was trying to rub them away, as though seeing was believing, and she didn't want to believe. The mob parted for her. Maybe they sensed she was an important character to the plot unfolding before them. They yelled for her. They ordered people in front of them to move for her. 'Let her through', the voices said.

The white haired officer followed as the gap began to close, blocking his way. He pushed through, but the people were absorbing him on all sides. He stumbled. He flapped his arms resembling a man in an infinite struggle, a man wading through thick treacle. He sunk into them,

188

became stuck, squished, face wedged between two round bellies. He broke through feeling blindly for her cardigan. She was gone.

Anders began climbing a tree, he shuffled along a branch patting leaves from his face, then, with his feet dangling over one side, he straightened up and watched Babs. He saw her stooping under the crime tape. She ran a short distance, screaming. Her hands were either side of her face, clasping her cheeks. Tears trickled down them. Her lined skin tightened turning a dull grey, turning the same shade as her hair. The white haired officer caught up. The flaps of his shirt hung over his pants, he was missing a few buttons, and his shoes were scuffed and dirty. He held her shoulders. Someone handed him a blanket. He put it around her. Everyone watched the water. Everyone saw it now, the blue face, the swelled cheeks, the strained expression and the bulging eyes with slimy river creatures feeding on them, like tiny slugs or leeches.

The two divers climbed into their dinghy and paddled to the bloated body. One took its arm. The other took its feet. On the count of three they began tugging, heaving it into the dinghy with them. A whistle blew. A third diver appeared out of the water. He removed his goggles, began waving to an officer on the riverbank. The officer on the bank wore a Stetson. His dog barked excitedly by his side, circling his legs, biting the rope. The officer pulled, he pulled and he pulled until the

189

dinghy touched the bank. The divers then gave a signal to a group of paramedics in green uniforms, who looked at each other and backed away as though no longer needed. Babs stepped forward with the white haired officer following closely. She stood a little in the water. She lifted her dress showing varicose veined legs. Her eyes were the colour of ash, red around the edges. She dropped tear sodden tissues in the cold water and fell against a big rock, still crying. Both divers watched as she reached out, like she wanted to help the man in the dingy. But it was no good. Her Dickie was dead.

Chapter nineteen

'So he's dead. That is what you're telling us, isn't it?' John put three mugs of coffee on the table. Anders didn't answer him at first. He watched the sun setting and the sky turning a beautiful red and yellow, like the colour of peaches, he thought.

'I guess so,' Anders said, 'Who else could it be? She did say he was missing.'

'This is very strange,' John said clasping his hands behind his neck. 'He didn't strike me as a wild swimmer.'

'No, I agree.' Anders took his coffee, tasting it slowly as though by force. 'I wouldn't put him as a swimmer at all, or a skinny-dipper.'

'What,' John said, 'was he naked?'

'Yes, they pulled him out naked.'

'It must be sinister then. Dickie didn't take that vest off for anyone or anything.'

Anders nodded. Then he looked at Andrew sitting next to him and thought about the marks they had discovered earlier. Joking or not, he believed John was on to something. He had been thinking about the marks on and off all day. Now they bothered him even more. The more he thought about them, the more he realised other things, like his key was missing and had been since he met Steve. Also, the creamed corn

191

had vanished, and when they arrived back to their room, it smelt rotten, rancid, almost as though something had died in there, eat creamed corn, then died. Sinister was the right word, he thought, something wasn't right. He sat forward. He blew air upwards, moving his fringe away from his eyes. 'What time did Steve go the other night?' he asked.

'He didn't,' John said walking back to the kettle, putting water on for another brew.

'What do you mean, he didn't?' Anders asked removing his spectacles, putting the earpiece between his teeth and biting it slowly, like a stiff detective in a stuffy TV drama. When they answered, he kept drawing his eyes together, and pulling an astonished expression, as though each word was a new clue, another piece of the jigsaw.

'He stayed over,' Andrew said, 'He slept in the spare bed, the one you sleep in when John puts the fan on. The one you slept in last night.'

'Okay, this is getting interesting,' Anders said.

'Why?' John asked rejoining them at the table.

'Well, this morning, Andrew told Babs that you hadn't seen Dickie since yesterday, when he told you about me.'

'Yep, it was,' Andrew said laying out some playing cards on the table. 'He was pissed off about everything.'

'Yeah,' John added lifting his mug. 'We left after that. He was still in the room. He was going on about other stuff. We just left him there.'

'This is extremely interesting,' Anders said pinching his lip with his fingers, nodding, watching Andrew leaf through the playing cards, pausing on the ten of clubs before tasting John's coffee.

'This tastes shitty. You make it shitty.'

'That's how you take it,' John said, 'You gotta take it thick to kill the hunger pains. It's all we got.'

Anders studied them both. 'Be serious for a minute, can you confirm that Dickie was in this room when you left, just him, alone with Steve?' He took the earpiece from his mouth and looked at it.

'We already have,' Andrew said.

'He was,' John said tasting his fresh brew.

'This is all quite interesting.' Anders was nodding again, nodding and stroking fluff patches of early beard growth on his young chin, not quite stubble, just awkward fluff, and he reminded himself to shave and shower later. 'Rather, wouldn't you say, all rather interesting?'

'Does he always talk this way?' Andrew said to John, 'I've never noticed before. He's getting on my nerves with it.'

'What's so interesting, Anders?' John said. 'Spit it out.'

'Yeah,' Andrew said, 'and stop biting that earpiece, it's annoying. Just tell us what you're getting at?'

'What are you getting at, Anders?' John asked. Then Andrew asked him again, the same question.

'I have a theory,' Anders said standing up.

'Sit down,' Andrew said, 'John, make him stop now, he's gonna make a twat out of himself.'

'Shush,' Anders said stamping his feet on the decking, walking up and down past the table. 'You both left Dickie here, yesh.'

'Yesh, Andersh, thash ish correct.' John and Andrew laughed. 'Yesh, for the fourth time, yesh.'

'Right then,' Anders said. He eyed the scratch marks on the floor and began fastening his shirt buttons. 'Dickie turns up, okay. Bad timing right, awful, awful timing.'

'Sit down,' John said. 'You look like a gay detective.'

Anders ran across the decking trampling over empty beer cans. 'John, please, please, please, please be quiet. I want to get this out. I have a theory.' He crossed both hands behind his back and walked like a pigeon. 'I have a theory,' he said.

'I have a headache,' Andrew said.

'Where is this going, Anders?' John asked.

'You not been listening?' Andrew said. 'He has a theory.'

'He does, doesn't he,' John laughed. 'He has a theory that involves Dickie getting butt-fucked I reckon.

'I want to draw my verdict,' Anders said pressing himself between them. 'The scratch marks on the floor,' he said. 'You saw them too right.' He looked eagerly at Andrew.

'That's right,' Andrew said, 'from when he got butt-fucked, think we're all on to something. He has a theory, we have a theory too.'

Anders disappeared into the room. He threw himself face down on the spare bunk. Springs squeaked on the mattress. 'I have a theory,' he screamed into a pillow.

'That's right, Anders,' John said. 'Sounds like we all do.'

There was movement on the bedsprings. Anders sat up now and then reappeared in the doorway. 'Will you let me finish?' he said. But they kept on talking as though he wasn't there. Mentioning more and more outrages theories, more and more juvenile out comes. Things about Steve riding Dickie on the river, using him like a dingy. Anders just ignored them; he stayed near the door thinking about the marks, the creamed corn, the missing key.

Chapter twenty

Anders sat on the worn carpet outside their room in the corridor. He needed to escape John and Andrew for a while, escape their daft behaviour. He held his knees, resting his chin on them. He faced a door. It was door number eight. It was the only door to have a number, and the room belonged to Babs.

Outside another room, further down the corridor near the stairs, he noticed two suitcases, and there, behind the suitcases and behind a half open door was an argument going on. He heard two very different voices, a man and a girl. The man spoke with a strong German accent. He spoke with hardness and anger, with sordidness and bite, while the girl yelled back in softer, weaker tones. Struggling on her words, she spoke with long gasps, as though her throat was imploding on her vocal cords. But somehow she managed. She got out her complaints about dead cockroaches and brown pillowcases, about green fungus on the walls and yellow bedding. This made Anders chuckle. He related to her feelings, she reminded him of himself when he had first arrived.

'That,' the girl said. 'There see, see it on the lightshade, hanging there? That thing, it's a used condom.' Then she went silent. When she spoke again, she was asking to go home.

196

'What did you expect, bitch?' the German yelled. 'What did you expect?'

The girl stepped into the corridor and looked at Anders. Her eyes had tears in them. She had picked up her suitcase and was now stumbling with it. She fell and got back up again, her thin arms dragging her suitcase laboriously down each step, as though it carried bricks.

'Bitch!' the German said following her, watching from the landing and then turning to Anders, thrusting an open hand in her direction. 'What a bitch, huh,' he said. Anders raised both arms and lifted his eyebrows, he looked at the German as if saying - *yeah, but what can you do about it, brother?* The German stayed there a moment, his hair was blonde and parted down the middle, it came long down both sides of his face, his skin was bronze, his stomach was flat and muscular. At six-foot-six, he reminded Anders of a Norse god.

Then the white haired officer appeared. It was the one from the Fitzroy. His shirt was open and white curls showed on his tanned chest. He and the German looked at each other for a moment. Strange expressions came over their faces, as though they were two time travellers caught in the continuum, and their meeting could put the world in jeopardy. The German shook his head and returned to his room. The white haired officer carried on now towards Anders. When he spoke, his voice was hoarse and raspy, like a heavy smokers.

'I'm Geoff Buttle,' he said flashing his police badge. 'I'm an officer with Rockhampton police. Not sure you've heard this, but we pulled your landlord from the river earlier.' He smiled showing the whitest teeth Anders had ever seen, and now he was closer, Buttle's skin looked almost orange. Anders got up and wiped his hands on the back of his shorts. Buttle continued. 'We're taking statements,' he said. 'I'll send my guys up to you, yes? To speak with you and your friends, yes? That okay?' Anders looked down the corridor, he saw Babs tottering towards them, crying. She pressed her face on Buttle's shirtsleeve. He patted her grey head. He held her.

'Me and my friends will be happy to help,' Anders said, he wanted to say more, something comforting for Babs, but nothing came and his mouth just hung there, open.

'Okay then,' Buttle said holding a smile.

'You can send them now.' Anders opened the door. He waited there while they walked away, side by side. Then he noticed Buttle's arm, which had been on her shoulder. It began to move. It slid down her back, his hand moved slowly, stroking her up and down, disappearing under the hem of her cardigan and then stroking her hips. When he glanced back at Anders, he was still smiling, showing those white teeth. They stopped on the landing. Babs settled beside the banister while Buttle lit two cigarettes. He smoked one and held the other for Babs, putting it to her lips each time she wanted a drag. Hazy blue smoke surrounded them. Two officers appeared, both dressed in thorn coloured uniforms. They spoke with Buttle and he pointed now and then to Anders with his cigarette. One of the men wore a peculiar expression, as though his eyes were viewing one-hundred places at once. Anders recognised it, he recognised his partner too.

'We meet again, slugger.' Big D grinned as he put on his Aviators.

'Almost didn't recognise the kid,' Lance added swaying in behind his partner. 'He looks different in those clothes, doesn't he? Doesn't he look different?'

The officers entered the narrow room throwing strange looks at each other, wafting their hands before their faces, pinching their nose. 'Someone die in here?' Lance asked kicking a dirty sock from his shoe. 'What a pigsty,' he said. 'Been partying here too, I see.' He went onto the balcony. He lifted the dinner plate. Burnt-out spliffs, dirty ash piles, and flattened snus bags spilled onto the table. He watched them. 'This is filth,' he said, 'This is pure filth.'

199

John and Andrew sat at the table, their eyes following Anders as though they were anticipating an explanation. But nothing came. He simply stood corner of the balcony. He turned his face away from their glances and watched the treetops across the road, watched them swaying in the night breeze. It was dark now. The road was empty and no noise came from the bar, which by this hour was normally rather rowdy. Tonight was different. Tonight the atmosphere was sombre, and with the sun having set, and the breeze picking up, there was an unpleasant chill in the air.

John offered them a coffee, but they refused and so he sat there drinking his third mug of the evening, eyes rapidly flicking between Anders and Big D, who stood between the double doors now watching everyone apart from Lance. Lance was walking around the table like an over confident predator does when stalking prey. He touched their stuff. He ran his fingers over the used coffee mugs, wetting his fingers in their dregs. He tasted his fingers and looked at John. He kept sniffing his fingers, sniffing and tasting them. He picked up a snus bag and ripped it open, then picked up another and sniffed it. 'Filth!' he said kicking beer cans. 'You bring us filth.'

'I got this one, Lance. You relax.' Big D said pulling a chair into the doorway, turning it, straddling it with his long legs on each side.

'What's going on?' John asked.

Lance kicked a beer can and went over to him. 'We ask the questions,' he said. Then he put a snus bag in John's coffee and kept it submerged with his finger. 'We ask the questions.'

'Okay, Lance,' Big D said feeling his moustache with his fingers. 'I got this.'

'Make a start then, Dee,' Lance said. 'This place stinks. I don't wanna be here any longer than necessary,' He held John's chair and stood behind him.

'I'll jump right to it then,' Big D said. 'He was reported in town yesterday.'

'Was he?' John said taking the snus from his coffee. 'And who is he?' But before John could say more, Lance began kicking his chair and yelling from behind. 'We,' he said, kick, kick, 'we ask the questions,' kick, kick. 'We ask the questions.' He put his face near the side of John's cheek. He spat as he spoke. His feet parted, his body stooped. 'Big fella,' he said sounding like a drill sergeant, 'Big fella don't ask the questions. We ask them. We ask them.' John clutched his coffee mug, brought it close to his chest and sank further and further into his chair. 'We ask them.' Spittle appeared on John's cheek. He began to flinch. Then Lance put both hands on his shoulders, and though John wasn't moving, Lance acted as though he was, and he held him there, warning him to keep still.

'Relax, Lance,' Big D said. Then straightening himself, he gestured a hand towards the snus tin on the table. Anders looked at it too, worried for a moment that Steve might have done something stupid, like stashed the acid tabs in there. Lance unscrewed the lid. He peeked inside and sniffed, and to confirm that it was empty, lifted the tin high in the air, showing Big D.

'As I was saying,' Big D started again. 'He was reported here recently at a meat abattoir, but we struggled to pinpoint his exact location. We know he's a dangerous man. We know he's a killer and wanted in Adelaide for some pretty nasty stuff.'

'That's right,' Lance said. 'We're dealing with a bad kitty cat.'

'Thing is,' Big D said, 'this sick bastard crossed state line some weeks back now, and those dick-faces in the south, well, they lost track of him. He's in our town now. He's my problem.'

'And mine,' Lance said brushing past John, dropping the snus into his coffee again. 'The bastard killed a prostitute,' he went on, walking the balcony. 'Can you believe that?' He asked John, but John didn't answer. He just stared at the snus floating on his coffee. 'He killed a bathroom attendant too, in a nightclub in Sydney.' Lance paused for a moment as though noticing something. It was another used snus and he added it to John's coffee. 'Apparently this bathroom attendant, who sounds to me like a big dumb fuck, offered the Mad Man a spray. He reached out, somehow missing his neck, somehow spraying Dior Sauvage into his eye, or so the witnesses say.' Lance sniffed and kept walking.

'Was more like Dior Savage by the time the Mad Man was done,' Big D said.

'True that, Dee, true that.' Lanced sniffed again. He felt inside his shirt pocket.

Anders stayed in the corner. He thought about saying something. He wanted to help, for Dickie, for the others, like the prostitute and the bathroom attendant. But he feared, as he stood there watching Lance pour John's coffee over the side of the balcony, as he listened to it splash over someone's car bonnet. That if he were to speak up, or even attempt to, that Lance would be on to him the way he was on to John, spitting and raging in his face, and that image in his mind was enough to keep him silent. Then he thought about Buttle, maybe he could tell Buttle, but he, Anders thought, seemed one creepy bastard, especially with those teeth, especially the way he was with Babs. Babs, the widow of the hour and already she had that orange man with diabolical teeth

203

trying to feel her up. The more he thought about it, the creepier they all seemed.

'We think the same guy killed your landlord,' Big D added, pausing while he felt for something in his pants. He produced a photograph and continued. 'The murder of Dickie fits his profile, the strangle hold, the nakedness, the fifty-cent coin wedged between the victim's arse cheeks, don't ask why, we don't know and neither do the psychologists. But it all draws us to him, these things he does, they're his trademark, his calling card if you will, all typical of the Mad Man, Mad Man Garrison, that's for sure.'

'Copy that, Dee,' Lance said, 'it's textbook Mad Man. Though he only does the coin trick with the male victims, apart from that, the patterns are identical. And patterns are what brought us to you.' Lance put John's coffee mug down on the table, he was pointing at Andrew now.

'Witnesses saw the Mad Man here,' Big D said taking over, 'with you and some hippy-type. What can you tell us about that?'

'Well,' Andrew said moving in his chair, 'what do you wanna know?'

'We ask the questions,' Lance reminded.

'First confirm this is the man you where drinking with.' Big D got up. He placed the photograph centre of the table.

204

'That's Steve,' Andrew said leaning over the picture.

'No,' Lance said. 'That's the Mad Man, Gary the Mad Man Garrison.'

'Well he looks like Steve to me,' Andrew said. 'He told me his name was Steve, and that's the same guy, that's Steve.'

Anders came to the edge of the table. He picked up the picture and studied it. Instantly he noticed the Ned Kelly T-shirt, and apart from a few more hairs on his head, and the younger, clean-shaven face, it was, Anders thought, most definitely Steve, or the Mad Man, rather. He put the picture back where it was and returned to his position in the corner, holding his pockets.

'He probably gave you a fake name,' Big D said taking the photo, taking his seat again. 'It's another trait of his. He used the name Burt while he was in Brisbane, so it's not uncommon.'

'Yeah,' Lance said. 'We heard he fakes it, picks the names of his favourite actors, you know, Burt Young, Steven Seagal...'

'I get it,' Andrew said cutting him off. 'Look, we had a few beers together and that was that. That was it.'

'Make a habit of hanging with criminals, do we?' Lance smirked, holding John's chair but staring at Anders.

'How was I to know?' Andrew said. 'Maybe you and your boys should be more careful when letting psycho killers into your town?'

Lance drew his baton. He lifted it high in the air and holding it tightly with a double grip, brought it down striking the back of John's chair. John shot up as though something had nipped him on the ankles. He moved unsteadily and slowly, he moved with stuttering steps, like a drunken chicken, towards Anders.

'You okay, Lance,' Big D said with an air of calmness.

'I'm fine,' Lance said following John, 'just got rattled there for a moment. I don't like to be insulted while doing my duty and this place stinks. I wanna go. The big fella is getting on my nerves.'

'Relax, we won't be much longer,' Big D said. He smiled and faced Andrew. 'What my partner meant, what he said about hanging with criminals, well,' he paused, was pointing the front of his shoe at Anders, 'first there's the Mad Man, your drinking buddy, and now, now we find you here with him, and well, after yesterday, we all know what he's capable of, don't we?'

'Patterns,' Lance added, touching John's cheek with his baton, twisting it there like a screwdriver. 'That's what I'm suggesting.'

'A murderer and a flasher don't look good in our town,' Big D continued ignoring his partner, as though his behaviour was all rather normal, all by the book. 'You get the picture, yes?'

'I wouldn't class Anders as a criminal,' Andrew said.

Lance turned. 'I reckon the hot piece of tale he flashed yesterday would disagree with that statement,' he said. 'I reckon she would, I reckon she'd debate that.'

'I think you need to get off Anders's case,' Andrew said, 'I thought this was about Steve, or Gary, or the Mad Man, or whatever the fuck you keep calling him.'

'Hold that tongue, fella,' Lance said showing him the baton. 'Hold it steady.'

'He was already naked,' Andrew said. 'How can you flash someone if you're already naked? I thought people like that, you know, weird people like that, they wear big long coats and stuff.'

Lance began to laugh. His teeth were narrow and green. His thinning hair had dampened with sweat. It dangled, came forward over his eyes. 'Wow,' he said, 'wow, he done a real job on him, hey Dee?' Big D nodded. Lance turned back to Anders. 'You, you done a real job on him, you got him all wrapped around your finger, you're a regular manipulative piece of shit and don't dare deny it, I'll smash you if you deny it.'

Anders said nothing. He looked away, first at the treetops and then at the road. He watched a passing truck, watched a dog barking in the back seat.

'I wanna keep this neat and tidy,' Big D said, 'you hear me, Lance? Neat and tidy, yes, so don't let 'em rattle you. Can you do that for me? I'd appreciate it if you could do that for me.'

'That,' Lance said, 'is easier said than done.' His fingers fished inside his shirt pocket. 'I don't appreciate the smug look on worm-boy's face right now, ginger keeps pushing back, and well, as for big fella, just look at him, he looks ready to go tango with me.' He sniffed twice, began moving his shoulders and cocking back his head. 'I'm starting to get agitated.' Sniff, sniff, sniff. 'Real, real agitated.' With his baton, he struck the wall above John's head and paint cracked, falling in slices across his shoulders. He looked at Big D, pointed to the baton and to the marks above his head on the wall. More broken paint fell. Andrew got up and joined them, all three stood in a line, waiting for Big D to control his sadistic, seemingly drugged up sidekick.

'Yep, there it is,' Lance said, grinning with spittle on the corners of his mouth. 'I think they understand now,' he said. 'I think these bastards understand what might go down if they don't comply.' He paused, he looked at John. 'The big fella is catching on. He's a fast learner.' Lance then laughed. 'I don't think he wants to tango no more.' He went face to face with John. 'Gone off the idea, have we?'

'For god sake,' Anders said, 'Is this necessary?'

'Found your voice, have we, worm-shit?' Lance put his baton on Anders's face. 'Have we, decided to join the conversation, have we, worm-shit?'

Big D got up. He held his partner by his shirtsleeves and ushered him to the other side of the balcony. Both stopped there. They spoke in low voices and Anders tried his best to listen, but he couldn't hear too well, only now and then he picked out some swear words and guessed by the way that Lance kept shrugging Big D's hands off his shoulders, that Lance wasn't happy about things, about the situation or the way Big D was handling him. He seemed embarrassed, and for the whole time that they talked, Lance stared forward, he stared at Anders.

'Fine, I don't care,' he said swaying away, standing between the double doors, sniffing up and rubbing his nose. 'I was getting bored anyway.' He took something from his shirt pocket and held it in his fist. 'I'll take my hit and wait out in the corridor,' he said, 'tell those pussies to take it easy, or I'll sort them. The way I'm feeling right now I don't need much of a reason.'

　After the balcony doors had closed, it went silent and they listened to the clatter of mugs and crockery, as though Lance was throwing things into the sink. Then there were chopping sounds, dinky soft chopping sounds, like thin plastic tapping on wood, then big sniffs, growing sharper and faster. Then the tap was going and it became obvious that Lance was washing himself over the sink, over the mugs and the crockery. 'I'll wait in the corridor,' he yelled running both hands through his wet, thinning hair, pushing it all back. 'Holler if it gets messy,' he said. 'I don't need a reason.'

An hour later, once Big D had taken his statement from Andrew and left, Anders began to worry. Maybe he should've spoken up, he thought, told them his theory, told them about Steve having been there in their room and drinking and spiking his drink with LSD. But John had stayed silent too, he kept assuring himself with a feeling of guilt, they must've thought the same thing, they mustn't have trusted them either. John certainly seemed shaken by the experience, he thought, and then he had a little chuckle to himself, picturing him, and the jittery way in which he had taken himself to bed and lay there a while, bug-eyed and heavily dosed up on caffeine.

But he was asleep now, and Anders was envious of that as he faced the darkness listening to him snore. There was much keeping him awake and in no particular order, he ran through the day's events in his mind. There was Patanga, Gollum, Dickie and Steve. There was the meat factory and the kill room. There were the scratch marks, the Fitzroy, the bad smell in their room and the missing key, and then most of all, the thing that had really got to him struck just before bed, as he went to brush his teeth and found with a horrified expression, that the bristles of his toothbrush were now stained, as though used in a hideous way. There was, he knew, something very fishy going on at The Old Crow, he just hadn't managed to put the pieces together yet, and in trying to do so, he struggled to sleep.

He tried everything now, he tossed and he turned, he kicked back his covers and flipped over his pillow, again and again, hot side, cold side, hot side, cold side. Nothing worked. He listened to his breathing, he cleared his mind, nothing. He got up, opened the balcony doors and crossed his legs on the floor. He meditated for two minutes and then climbed back into bed. It had been three hours since he went to bed, way past midnight now and he lay there agitated and sweating. Suddenly he got up. He was on the floor again, this time pacing up and down the room. He picked up a mug, paused at the sink and drank

211

water from it while staring through the balcony doors at the moon. Then he stared at the kitchen top, at the white powdery marks of cocaine where Lance had taken his hit. Finally, he took his towel and left for a cold shower.

Chapter twenty-one

For a while, the only sound was John's erratic snoring. Then there was rustling underneath the spare bunk. Then, scratch, scratch, scratch as Steve's fork began to work the dregs of the almost empty creamed corn, scratch, scratch, scratch, up and down, inside the can, scratch, scratch. Above him was a mouldy mattress close to his face, and with little room for manoeuvre, and with cockroaches running all over him, he awkwardly brought the fork up to his lips, pushing through cobwebs and choking on dust, and then eating what was left of his supper.

He then put down the empty can with the fork still in it, and, with his leg, pushed away a suitcase and crawled out, coughing silently as he stood. The cockroaches had scattered but many ants crawled on his T-shirt, and his face was black and sooty looking. He looked over the two curled up bodies, John top bunk, Andrew below him, both in deep slumber. He timed the sound of the tap with John's snores, waiting until they were at their loudest, then twisting it slowly and ducking towards the trickles of water, which ran down his muddy beard and his dirty neck as he drank. Then, beard dripping, he studied the kitchen top as though looking for more food or more drink. He found some old coffee and drank it, squinting as the cold, sharp, bitter taste went down his throat. Then, near the sink, he found Anders's wash-bag and unzipped it. He removed the toothbrush and just as he had done earlier that day, pushed the bristle side into his underpants and scraped vigorously between his cheeks and under his scrotum, knees jerking as he did so. Then, using the key he had stolen from Anders, he unlocked their door and glanced each way of the corridor. Quietly he closed it again. He had to be careful now as he tiptoed across the room and onto the decking, fists clenching as rotten wood creaked under his step. Facing the moonlight, he urinated over the edge of the balcony for a long time. He was grinning. He zipped up and patted dust and sand from his jeans. He took off his T-shirt and shook away the ants, watching them with his dark eyes, watching them regroup before stepping on them, crushing them with the tip of his shoe.

He yawned and picked a cobweb from his baldhead. The Possum was there above him, on a branch in the willow tree, its tiny eyes glowing in the dark, its tale curled snug around its middle. It kept tilting its head and craning its neck, peering inside the room as though looking for Anders. Steve ignored it. He put his arms on the wooden beam at the edge of the balcony and stared into the distance, shushing the wood as it swayed, cracked and creaked under his weight. The Possum rustled through some leaves and dropped down beside him. It sniffed the T-shirt in his hand. It looked at him but he shoved it away with his palm.

It backed up and came onto its hind-legs. He kept his hand over its face and it pawed his fingers playfully, pinning his hand down on the wooden beam, licking beneath his fingernails with its soft tongue, licking dried bits of creamed corn.

'Dirty rat bastard,' he said, 'dirty scavenger ugly rat.'

He dropped one shoulder, angled his body as though ready to fight. He made a fist with his right hand, keeping the Possum distracted with his left. He was grinning again. The blow was hard and straight and now the Possum was flying through the air with nothing below but rock-hard concrete. Its mouth hung open. Its eyes were glaring, still glowing, like falling fireflies in the darkness. It made no sound, no cries, no yelps or squeals. It just stared, stared and flinched back its neck, as though chocking on creamed corn and fresh air.

Its body thumped on the concrete. It bounced high and came back down again, was bouncing and skidding and tumbling towards a patch of gravel. Then it sprung up and limping, it moved gingerly towards a heap of twigs and soil. There it fell on its side, its tiny body trembling in the shadow of a bush. It stayed there, curled, still, watery eyed, bleeding from its tiny nostrils, stomach moving up and down, up and down.

Steve tucked his T-shirt into his jeans. It hung out at the back like a tail. Then he swung one leg over the wooden beam, then his other. The wood swayed and creaked some more, but this didn't seem to bother him, was as though his mind was elsewhere and his eyes looked only for the Possum. To his left was a rusted drainpipe. He shuffled towards it, feet moving sideways on the lip of the balcony. He came to the drainpipe and climbed down. The car park floor was marked with blood dots and he followed them as a guide, leading him to the gravel patch. His grin had faded now and he kicked the twigs where it had lay. He dropped flat, belly to the floor, eyes scanning below the parked cars and then peering into the shrubbery. He got up and spat twice on the gravel. Again, he kicked the twigs. Then he just stood there a while, bare-chested, turning sharply to the rustle of a leaf, the scuttle of a stone, the snap of a twig. It was a beautiful night, and as Anders was taking his cold shower, he couldn't have imagined the horrors that his friend, the Possum, had just been through.

Chapter twenty-two

Surprisingly the weeks passed quicker than Anders had imagined and though he still hated it, after a while, he became a rather good slops collector. Then during his third week, Pat Patanga found Gollum a new slops-guy and thanking Anders for his dedication, moved him to the loading bay. After suppressing the urge to kiss Patanga's baldhead, Anders then realised something, that all paths are eventual and once one accepted their fate, once one relaxed and enjoyed their journey, that naturally, everything you wanted came to you. Now as the weeks progressed it seemed to him that the pendulum of luck was finally swinging his way, his plan to escape Rockhampton, to escape John and Andrew and regain his independence, was soon becoming a reality.

It was a Saturday. It was another hot one and the sun glared over his rosy shoulders. He sat now on the decking cross-legged and barefooted, in an old vest with his pants rolled up showing ankle. A wooden board was in front of him, and with a knife in hand he bent forward taking fruit from a bag. The fruit had warmed in the sun and felt soft as he chopped it into pieces. Inside their room the radio was playing. It was classical, it was Strauss II voices of spring and he hummed along, cutting mango, slicing papaya. He'd already scattered the banana, now he scattered the rest.

'I'm feeling hungry myself now,' he said, smiling up at the willow tree. 'We could have lunch together maybe.' He laughed and went inside. He washed fruit juices from the chopping board. He wiped his knife on a tea towel. 'It is hot,' he said now opening the fridge, leaning into it, welcoming its coolness. 'I'm sweating.'

There wasn't much in the fridge. Only John's plate of corned beef with sliced onions, some beers, a bottle of wine, and Anders's box of vegetables. He blinked. Vapours of onion got to him. He searched through the vegetables with tears in his eyes and kept blinking, using his vest now and then to dry his eyes. Then he selected a beetroot. It was dirty. He scrubbed it over the sink, peeled it, washed it again under the water tap. When he was done, he rubbed his dirty fingers on his grey pants, looked at them and then took the wine.

'Ah, alcohol from a mug,' he said popping the cork with his thumb, pouring a drop, 'so unsophisticated.' The wine was very chilled and very sweet. It was just how he liked it, especially on a day like this, when the weather was so hot, so stifling that even the most effortless task, like chopping fruit and washing beetroot, had left him sapped of energy and dripping with sweat.

Now and then, as he prepared his meal, Anders would stop and appear on the balcony, mug in one hand, bottle in the other, talking up at the willow tree as if the Possum was there with him, trying to coax it out of hiding. He swallowed wine, glanced at the untouched fruit along the wooden beam edge of the balcony. 'Come now, old friend,' he said raising his mug. 'It's been too long. Show yourself.' He kept talking. He put his mug on the floor and picked up his backpack, reaching into it, giggling, falling to one side, and then pulling the backpack over him and reaching towards the bottom. 'I won't tell, old friend,' he said waving a tin of sardines in the air. 'But will you?'

He drank from the mug, got up and poured another. Then on the kitchen top, he used the ring pull on the sardine tin, emptied fish onto a plate and looked at it in its tomato sauce. 'You see that,' he said. 'You see how easy that was, and without using that Neanderthal's stupid pocketknife.' He sucked his fingertips clean of fish juices and went on. 'A big man like him getting all excited over creamed corn. Well, too much brawn not enough brains, that's what I say.' He sipped more wine and felt the draws for a butter knife. 'Not wise like me and you, hey, old friend.' He giggled. 'Now, where did I put that rye?'

He made space on the table outside and lit a candle for ambiance. Warm bread sprung in the toaster. He checked it and pushed it down again. Then adding to the sardines, he grated the beetroot and dressed it with peppercorns and with some vinegar that he had saved from an old pickle jar. The toast sprung again. He spread it thick with butter and cut it. Then he gathered everything - plate, mug, bottle, and sat down at the table with them, staring into the willow tree.

Shortly after, there was rustling in the leaves and hearing this, he grinned with a mouthful of beetroot and fish and showed purple stained teeth. He watched it now as it dropped timidly onto the edge, limping slowly along the wooden beam, nose dipped, sniffing towards banana chunks. It seemed different, he thought, more wary and the glow in its eyes that he had loved so much was gone. It kept checking its surroundings, he noticed, checking almost every second, as though it could not settle to enjoy the feast he had spread out. Sometimes it paused staring at him with dark, drawn eyes. Other times it stared into the room, and strangely, Anders thought, under their bunks. He tried speaking to it with tenderness, assuring it that this was a safe place, and that it would never be hurt here. He saw its scars, saw it was hurt and frightened. He wanted to help, but then he reminded himself not to interfere, this was a wild animal, this was nature, no matter how cruel, this was how it was, and like Anders some weeks earlier, the Possum would have to wait for the pendulum to swing its way.

Both began to scoff now, both watched each other while doing so, Anders forking fish into his mouth and sipping wine, and the Possum

220

gnawing on mango, eating the skin and all, popping up now and then with yellow pulp around its whiskers.

A piece of classical reached the end of a long crescendo and drew to a quiet finish. Anders had forgotten the radio was even playing. He heard only the sound of soft fruit moving inside the Possum's mouth, steady, like a constantly dripping tap. It bobbed down for longer periods and seemed less bothered about Anders's presence or the surroundings. Suddenly the jockey began to speak on the radio, now introducing the next one. 'Okay, gang,' he said excitedly, his Australian accent was high-pitched and enthusiastic, too enthusiastic. Anders didn't listen. He stared forward in a trance like state. 'We got a real beauty for you now, gang,' the jockey said. 'We got the Ecstasy of Gold by the great Ennio Morricone,' he paused to let out a breath. 'I can tell you, gang, let me tell you, there ain't no bad or ugly about this one, just the good, just pure class.'

He sounded all out of breath and he stopped speaking. The fast sound of piano began, joined quickly by violin. In the darkness of the under-bunk, a shadowy figure was moving, was twisting and a turning slowly, was moving on its belly, like a snake, a serpent of death. The soprano's heavenly voice joined the other instruments. The music grew faster, louder, and then the Mad Man appeared. As he rose, dust puffed out

221

around him and cobwebs stuck to his dirty face, matted in his overgrown beard. He puffed out his chest and moving his head side to side, cracked his neck muscles. His clothes were tattered and torn. His baldhead had patches on it, bits of hair, dots of it, greyish dots here and there. He looked like a mix of something, somewhere between a tramp and a zombie. But he stood tall, and looking round the room with his hands trembling with aggression, he appeared as bullish and as menacing as ever.

He reached towards a shelf near Anders's bunk, pinching the volume dial on the radio with his dirty fingers. The pace of the music seemed to increase with the volume. Transfixed with the Possum, toast in mouth, wine in hand, forkful of fish in the other, Anders had no idea that the volume had increased, nor had he realised that the Mad Man was emerging behind him, shadowing him, with a pile of loose change in hand, one finger fishing through it, searching for that fifty-cent piece.

Anders took more toast and licked his buttery lips. Sunlight glistened over him, fading slowly. Darkness, he noticed taking his eyes away from the Possum for a moment, was gathering over the brown hills in the distance, dark, dark clouds. A storm was heading his way, he thought, and he was right, it was.

Chapter twenty-three

'You like banana,' Anders said, eyes back on the Possum. 'Don't you, old friend.'

'Yes, yes I do,' Steve whispered stepping closer.

The Possum kept eating without fear now. Its pink leathery nose moved along the wood, sniffing out chunks of mango and papaya. Orange fruit juices dripped from its white and grey chin. Mashed banana stuck to its paws. It carried on, found another banana piece, held it in its jaw, and suddenly turned full circle. It was staring beyond Anders's shoulder now, up on its hind legs. Its jaw fell open. The banana fell too, lost somewhere under the table. Anders smiled and nodded. He held a slice of toast between his fingers and bit it.

'Don't look so sad, old friend,' he said pointing with his toast. 'There's plenty of mango, get some mango.'

But its jaw stayed open. It neither moved nor blinked and seemed utterly concerned with the two clenched fists behind Anders's head, as though it recognised them, big and hairy on the outside, they were the ones, fists that break ribs, fists that send one through the air at night, fists of a Mad Man.

'Well it wasn't that bad,' Anders laughed watching the Possum back away. 'It was only a bit of banana, there's plenty of mango left.'

223

It was in the shade of the tree now, and had urinated on the wood. It brought its body down low, but arched its back and kept one claw extended in front of itself ready to strike. Its eyes were flickering, dividing their attention between Steve and the branch above its head. Steve's mouth twitched at the corners, his dried lips came together. There was no way he could take both of them, not now, he'd have to wait, and as he watched it jump to the branch, and scurry off into the foliage, his mouth twitched some more.

'What was it, old friend?' Anders spoke with a mouthful of fish and drank more wine. 'Not ripe enough for you?' He put the mug down and ran a napkin over his lips. 'Ah well, come back tomorrow,' he said wearing a tipsy grin. 'We'll have boiled eggs.'

He laughed gazing up at the tree and sank down in his chair. The heat, the wine, the food had left him lethargic. He poked at bits of fish with his fork. He drained his mug and refilled it. Then he lolled back, eyes closed. 'Ah, life,' he whispered still thinking about the Possum, 'provides such simple pleasures.'

'You and that rat seem to get along,' Steve said touching Anders's hair.

'That you John,' Anders laughed again, 'good job you came back, there's a storm brewing I think.'

224

Steve said nothing. He moved his fingers through Anders's hair, gently, as though giving him a head massage.

'There's rye on the side if you fancy a bite,' Anders continued, 'fix yourself a drop too, my treat.' He kept his eyes closed. He pointed to the bottle. 'It's cool, crisp, sweet, and all rather tasty,' he said. 'It's certainly got me on my way, does the job.' Then he laughed, but soon Steve's fingers were pinching and pulling. 'Stop that, please,' Anders said. 'Stop pulling my hair.' But it continued and became more aggressive, faster now, yank, yank, yank. 'Enough now please. I'm all relaxed.'

Steve's fingers locked. He grabbed a fistful of hair now and pulled Anders's head backwards and forwards repeatedly. He rocked in his chair and his legs came high off the floor. He flapped out his arms. He kicked out his feet. When he opened his eyes, he saw the dirty face of the Mad Man, glaring down on him. Although this was only in flashes, soon he was moving forward again, face-planting sardines, peppercorns and beetroot. The peppercorns burned in his nostrils. The fork had stabbed into his cheek. He reached for it, but missed, backwards and forwards he moved, Steve pulling him and planting him again, face down in the beetroot, laughing as he watched him sneeze out purple strings of snot. 'Are you a fucking unicorn or something?' Steve yelled. 'Are you a fucking unicorn? You'll be shitting out rainbows next.'

He whacked him over the head with the mug, then with the plate. It broke into two jagged pieces and keeping hold of one piece, Steve began cutting him up, running it down his bare shoulder. Anders yelped. Steve grabbed another fistful of hair, dragging him like a puppet, moving him in whichever direction he desired, laughing at the fish and the beetroot smeared across his face, then grinning sinisterly as he sliced the skin on Anders's forehead with the plate.

Blood trickled into his eyes and there was another yelp. Steve let go. He pocketed a clump of Anders's hair and watched him. In a daze, Anders fell sideways onto the decking and with blood and beetroot in his eyes, he crawled about in no particular direction, lost, sometimes going in circles. Steve left him a while, just watching, but then Anders screamed and yelled for someone to help. He quickly silenced him with a kick to the stomach, then grabbed a chair and levelled him with it, snapping it across his back. He grinned again as blood appeared through Anders's white vest and along his spine. Then taking the wine bottle, he drank from it and stood over Anders's flattened body. 'Cool and crisp and sweet,' He kept saying, laughing, pouring wine over him, watching his body jerk as the wine burned into his cuts. 'Does the job,' he said, 'Certainly does the job.'

Anders caught a little wine on his fingers using it to clean his eyes. He then crawled forward through the doorway, collapsed over a suitcase, shoulders and knees going, teeth chattering as though freezing cold. 'I'll be with you in a minute,' Steve said calmly fingering sardines into his mouth from the table. 'Fuck me, boy, these are spicy.' Then he saw the fork in Anders's cheek. 'That doesn't look comfortable,' he said. 'I'll take that in a minute. I'll put it somewhere else.' He laughed and licked his fingers. 'Not sure where yet.' Anders quickly brought his arm up, squeezed his eyes together and pulled out the fork. 'That was my job,' Steve said now approaching him again. 'You taking my jobs from me?' He kicked Anders's legs and stepped back laughing at him. 'You need more effort than that,' He said watching Anders swing the fork in an effort to protect himself. Then leaning on the kitchen top with his elbow and eating rye bread, he said, 'Want me to come closer for you?'

Anders dropped the fork. He lay sideways on the suitcase with a high-pitched ringing between his ears, watching in a blur of white haze, Steve eating rye. In intervals of chewing bread, Steve spoke to him but he struggled to hear, was like listening to someone speak under water, he thought. Then he saw him moving. Then he couldn't see him at all and he coughed hoping it was over. That's all he seemed able to do now, cough and feel pain, pain in his ribs, his jaw, his spine. But the candle got him going again. Steve was behind him suddenly, moving its flame up and down his arm and then tilting it, letting hot wax drip over his face. 'Still some fight left, eh,' Steve said following him with the candle as he rolled off the suitcase.

The music ended. The jockey was speaking again. 'I hate this shit you listen to,' Steve said marching over to the radio, ripping it from its wire, cutting short the giddy jockey. 'I'll bash your head with this for a bit,' he said coming back to Anders with the radio. 'If you don't mind that is. You don't mind, do you?' Anders looked up. Blinking and seeing more clearly, he saw the radio in Steve's hand and his grinning teeth and the saliva that was swaying on them, giving him the appearance of a rabid dog. Naturally, Anders raised an arm to protect himself, but Steve caught it and he knew instantly that he'd made a mistake. 'Oh, you do mind,' Steve said. 'Oh well, I'll just bash your arm for a bit instead.' And he did, he bashed it until the plastic shell of the radio was broken and its wires and batteries flew across the room.

Anders felt a sickening pain run through his body. His skin had gone white. He was crying and making sounds as though ready to vomit.

228

'I'm having fun,' Steve said. 'Are you?' There was barely anything left of the radio now. He dropped it and tugged him up by his injured arm, pulling him round the room while his feet dragged lifelessly on the floor. To Anders, listening to his cries was a strange experience. They sounded distant to him, as though they weren't his own. 'I think it's broken,' Steve said. 'Your arm I mean, not the radio.'

Suddenly he was on the decking again, face down in a puddle of wine. The clouds had made their way over. There was no light in the sky, only a dull grey and noises of thunder. Without resistance from Anders, Steve ripped his vest off him and lifted him up. They looked like man and boy as he turned with him, keeping him upright, holding one arm across his chest. 'Stand up,' he said. 'Keep still and stand up.' Then he told him to face the clouds, told him that if he'd been a good boy he'd soon be up there, too. The arm moved up to his throat, tightening now on his windpipe. With his free arm, Steve reached behind himself, dipped a hand into his back pocket and fumbled through a bunch of coins, pulling out a fifty-cent piece. 'Been keeping a nice shiny one for you,' he said, 'lovely.' But then he was frowning. He turned with Anders and looked into the room. 'You cunt,' he said. 'It seems we have a problem.' He dropped Anders where he was and told him to stay there.

'Anders,' a voice yelled. 'Are you okay in there?' It sounded like Henry. He banged and kicked the door. 'Anders, you sound hurt.' Now he was shouldering the door, kicking, punching, shouldering and shouting. 'Anders, I'm coming in.'

Anders set off towards the voice on his belly, using his one good arm as best he could while the other dragged limply beside him. But his progress was short. Soon he felt Steve's hands tightening around his ankle, pulling him back. 'You stay out here,' he said pressing his foot on Anders's broken arm. Anders's mouth opened wide, but no sound came, only tears, tears streaming down his face. He shivered feeling sickness and paleness over his whole body. Then he passed out.

Chapter twenty-four

Waking to darkness and rumbling thunder, Anders was unsure if he had slept for minutes, hours or days. The tears and the beetroot had dried on his face, and he thought he could hear voices arguing close by. He turned onto his back peering upwards, something was moving in the branches of the willow tree, the Possum, he thought, then he thought he could see it staring at him, and through the pain in his cheek, he forced a smile. Everything seemed to him more beautiful than ever, and through his blurry vision, the colours began to mix, coming together like a Jackson Pollock painting, and there in the middle of this painting, surrounded by dots of green, brown, grey, black and white, was the Possum.

The voices were still arguing. He listened to them. One was calm. The other was excitable and accusing.

'Relax, I was helping him.'

'You piece of shit, you done that. Look at him. Look at the state he's in.'

'He's just had a few.'

'No way, you've beaten him.'

'You know what the kid's like when he's had a few. The kid can't handle his source.'

The voices stopped suddenly. There was silence. A cold and horrible silence, Anders thought, and he turned from his imaginary Pollock painting and looked into the room. There he saw an expressionless Henry. His hands, Anders noticed, were covering something and beneath them and under his chequered shirt, was a red patch that seemed to be growing redder and damper, and when Henry brought his hands away, Anders saw the handle of Steve's pocketknife, stuck there in his stomach. He watched him tug it gently. Nothing gave. He tried again, forcefully this time, groaning as he did so, still, nothing gave. The blade had stuck.

'Shame. I actually liked you,' Steve said kicking the door shut. Then smiling and seeing Henry's knees bend, seeing him slide down slowly with his back on the wall, breathing faster and faster, eyes staring at the astonishing amount of blood he was producing. 'They'll get you for this,' Henry whispered. 'They will.'

'Possibly,' Steve said now turning, going back to Anders and looking over a heap of change on his palm. 'I'll need to break a note for you,' he said to Henry. Then he quickly lifted Anders and relocked the chokehold, both arms this time, proper Mad Man Garrison style. 'Best get this done fast,' he said. 'I was planning to enjoy this but I've been rudely disturbed.' Anders wheezed and shuffled his feet as though dancing. He faced Henry. Both held eye contact with each other, reaching toward each other with their trembling hands, blood dripping on Henry's fingers. It was as though they were trying to comfort one another, as though they knew they were dying and leaving this world together, and that was okay, because they had each other. They wouldn't be between worlds alone.

Then through the ever-growing blurriness in Anders's eyes, he saw two silhouettes appear beside Henry's body. Angels, he thought, come to end our suffering. He spilled more tears, some for himself, some for his mother and father back in Sweden. He began to accept his fate. He hadn't felt his arms or his legs for a while, and the blurry haze was no more. It was almost pure white now. That's all he could see, pure white, and the ringing had stopped too. This is it, he thought closing his eyes. This is it. It is time.

'Don't just stand there,' Andrew said dropping Henry's lifeless body in the corridor. 'Do something.'

'What? What shall I do?' John said.

Henry had left much blood on the floor. Andrew's feet skidded in it. He lost a flip-flop. He held the door. 'You help him. You fucking help him.'

'But what's Garrison doing here?' John asked. 'What's he doing with that fifty-cent piece?'

'Who cares what he's doing here.' Barefooted now, Andrew was back in the room. 'Look, he's going to kill him.'

'Okay, let's charge that fucker.'

'Yeah. Together then on three. We'll charge the fucker.'

'On three,' John said, 'I don't think he's got three left in him.'

There was a clap of thunder. A rumble followed. Rain hit the roads and rooftops hard, and a group of girls were screaming in it, watching Anders from the car park below, watching him in their wet football kits, watching him look dead in the Mad Man's arms. John and Andrew continued to debate their plan, but soon it was pointless. Anders was limp now, his body almost blue. Then more thunder, more screaming as the Possum jumped from its tree and sunk its paws into Steve's eyes. Steve ran crashing into the table. He dropped Anders and stumbled over his body, yelling that the Possum was blinding him.

He threw punches at it but like a mini ninja, the Possum dodged all attacks with ease, dropping side to side, scampering across his shoulders, coming back up, appearing on another side of his face, and returning to his baldhead, and there it would claw open flesh, penetrating skin and leaving it in tatters, like minced meat. It showed no sign of injury now. It moved with speed, precision and purpose, while Steve ran blind, tripping on chairs, thrusting his shoulders. He jumped. He ducked. He swung more punches, but nothing worked. He was too slow, too sluggish. His hooks, his jabs, his power-bombs were all mistimed, and those that did connect, connected only with himself, as though he was boxing his own face, a true madman.

Now backing up to the edge of the balcony, he leaned on the wooden beam, pressing his lower back against it. The barrier swayed, he swayed backwards with it, like a troubled boxer on the ropes. It was creaking and cracking, but still he pressed more weight on the barrier, continuing to swing punches, continuing to miss. Then the beam snapped inwards making a V shape, and still he leaned into it, looking round at the noises with his eyes all squinted and clogged up with blood. There was another snap, then another. The girls on the car park moved closer, yelling for him to lean forward. 'Lean forward. For god sake, lean forward,' they yelled. 'Get away from there it's breaking.' But he fell in further, as if trapped in a giant catapult. The Possum left him there, still swinging punches. Then suddenly the barrier broke completely, and Steve, surrounded by bits of wood, was falling backwards through the air. The football girls ran, screaming, ducking away from the timber and the falling body, looking back over their shoulders, watching Steve swinging his punches midair, watching him swing to the very end.

'He's breathing,' Andrew said standing over Anders, looking at John. 'Come on! Help me!'

They grabbed his legs. They dragged him inside and there was no movement from him. John stepped back. He filled a mug with water while Andrew folded a pillow, sliding it gently underneath Anders's head. He then took the mug from John, nodding, drinking from it. 'Cheers!' he said sipping water. 'I needed that.'

John reached out. Between them was Anders and they sat either side of him. 'That's for him,' John said, trying to take back the mug.

'Ah, I'm with you now,' Andrew said dipping his fingers into the mug, wetting them, putting them inside Anders's mouth and opening it further. 'Yuck,' he then said, 'what's all this shredded purple stuff?' He shook his hand. He looked at his fingers. 'What is it?'

John didn't answer. He was shrugging his shoulders and pointing to the water, telling him to use it. He did. He tilted it to Anders's lips, fed him some, waited, fed him some more. Still there was no movement from Anders, so Andrew kept putting the mug to his lips, feeding him trickles of water.

'Wet him with it,' John said, almost yelling.

Andrew dipped into the mug again, wetting Anders's forehead with his fingers, touching it softly as though applying ointment. It made no difference. His eyes stayed closed, his body lifeless.

'I said wet him.' John snatched the mug. He emptied it over Anders's face, watching beetroot and fish change colour before washing away. Anders began to groan. He brought his hand up slowly and felt where the fork had been in his cheek.

'You back with us, lad?' John asked now on his hands and knees, shadowing over him.

'I think he's coming round,' Andrew said, 'back up, give him space.' He pushed John's shoulder. He picked up the mug. 'Here, get more water.'

There was another groan. 'No,' Anders said roughly, as though he had gravel in his throat. 'No more wet.'

'Okay, water cancelled,' Andrew said. 'Are you okay?'

Anders gave a wan nod and licked his lips. 'The ringing,' he said, 'it's stopped.'

'Okay, that's good,' Andrew said, 'Try not to move though, you look well beaten up. What happened?'

'I was eating beetroot.'

'Yes, we can see that,' John said. 'Stay still.'

237

'I had a fork in my face at one point.'

'Okay then,' Andrew said now looking at John, silently mouthing the word "what". 'Well I suppose,' he said and then laughed, 'I suppose you need to work on your fork skills, hey lad?'

Anders chuckled. 'Indeed, indeed. Is John here?'

'Yep, I'm here, mate. Are you okay?'

'I'm good but I want to apologise,' Anders said. He closed his eyes then barely opened them again.

John was smiling. 'For what,' he said, 'Don't be silly. You don't need to apologise. What for?'

'For blaming you for the bad smells,' Anders said. John's smile was fading now and he looked at Andrew while Anders continued. 'I think the rotten ones were Steve's doing,' he said. 'I know I kept accusing you of dropping eggs here and there, and I'm sorry for that. I wanted to say an apology.' Both waited for Anders to say more, to explain himself better, but that was it. He looked peaceful. He was sleeping again and they said his name and clicked their fingers in front of his face. Nothing woke him. Not even the screaming voices in the corridor where the German stood topless in his doorway, watching his timid girlfriend run up and down, knocking on doors.

238

Soon appeared a short man too, in scraggy clothes, with a can of beer in hand and belly showing. A voice spoke to him from another room asking why there was screaming, but he didn't answer, he just pointed at Henry's body with his can. Then door number eight opened and Buttle staggered out half-dressed with his hair all stuck up, looking as though he'd just this moment woken. Angrily, he began marching around in his underpants, belt draped over his shoulder, sock half on and trailing his foot, shirt in one hand, police radio in the other. He started taking names and demanding to know what the cause of the fuss was. Then he stopped behind the short man and stared down at Henry on the carpet, with the knife in him. He turned. He saw Babs tottering towards the open door, doing up her baggy dressing gown over her wrinkled body. Quickly, he slammed the door in her face and told her to stay put. 'Don't come out here. Don't you dare.'

Other doors opened and more people stepped from their rooms. The timid girl had stopped screaming and was now packing her stuff, yelling at the German, yelling that dead cockroaches and soiled condoms were one thing, but a human body, a dead human body in the corridor was something else. He yawned into his fist and stayed in his doorway, eyes now on Buttle, watching him speak into his radio for backup. When Buttle had finished, he felt his hip where normally he'd

239

clip the radio to his belt, but crossing his eyebrows and glancing down, he noticed he was, in all the excitement, without pants. Suddenly he began shouting, ordering everyone out of the corridor. All but the German began to scatter, to return to their rooms and close their doors behind them. But he, he walked out of his doorway and stood near Henry, staring at Buttle strangely, as he always did.

'Maybe I stay,' the German said straight-faced.

'Oh yeah,' Buttle replied lighting up a cigarette, staring back confidently, his legs set apart with grey pubic hair showing from his underpants. 'And what makes you so special?'

Chapter twenty-five

The rain kept coming. It had done all week and turning awkwardly now in his bed, Anders watched it through the open balcony doors. He liked it. He liked the way it bounced on the decking, like an illusion, like raining upwards as well as down. Between watching the rain he would sleep or read. He read a lot that week, two Hemingway novels. He slept a lot too, and the TV was always going. But he didn't watch it much. It just flashed in the corner, as it was now, without volume, with Neighbours playing and with Dr Karl Kennedy's face changing expression, eyebrows crossed, mouth moving silently on the screen.

Anders laughed at Dr Kennedy while holding the side of his face where the fork had been. In his good hand, he clicked a pen and looked over the letter he'd just written to his parents. In the letter he explained that an invoice was coming to them from Rockhampton Infirmary. He apologised for this and told them not to worry. That he was fine and recovering well after falling from a tree whilst photographing a possum. He said he loved them very much. He repeated this many times. Then he wished them a merry Christmas, and finally, with his good hand, he added that he was looking forward to seeing them again in the coming spring.

He folded the letter and sat up with it. Bedding covered his legs and from his top half, he was naked. His face was puffy, dotted now with pink sticking plasters, and over his spine was padding, held together by strips of tape, and down his shoulder was stitching where Steve had slashed him with the glass. Keeping the letter in hand, he eased his plaster cast arm into its sling, which hung around his neck and gently he closed his eyes, waiting for the pain behind them to pass. Out of all his injuries, the headaches bothered him the most and the dizziness was often overwhelming. Always he'd be yawning and dozy. Always he'd be taking strong painkillers. But now he'd taken his last one. Now paracetamol would have to suffice.

In the corridor, he heard laughter and glass bottles clinking together. Then the door handle was going, rattling, turning. Andrew swayed in clumsily with two bottles of beer in hand. He drank one and smiled at Anders. Anders tried to smile back, but the pain in his face was too much. He showed only the fronts of his teeth, like a timid hamster unsure whether to nibble something or not. The pain got worse and so he gave up, mustering a slow nod instead.

'Thought you'd be there all night,' he said watching John shuffle past Andrew, feet going like a man in fetters.

'Me too,' Andrew said, 'but John's piles are playing up.'

'I see that,' Anders said, 'I see by the way he's walking,' and he watched John paw through a small bag in the light of the TV, with, and rather ironically, Anders thought, an extreme close up of Dr Kennedy's glaring eyes, as though horrified to see the Rectumoid cream-stick in John's hand. Then, as though the drama was too much for the Doctor to handle, the program suddenly ended, and the credits rolled.

'This will sort the scoundrels,' John said holding the cream-stick in the air.

'Are they bad?' Anders asked.

'Bad?' John said, 'Jesus, it's like having barbed wire between me cheeks.'

'He's had them ages,' Andrew laughed, 'they're like family to him, like his kids now.' He swigged beer and looked at Anders. 'There's a lot of mouths to feed in that arse.'

John went to the balcony doors. He studied the rain coming in sideways, almost spraying his shoes. He held his hand out to it, touching it. 'Kids,' he said, 'yeah I wish. Kids grow up, kids move on, these fuckers ain't going anywhere.'

'Tell the story, John.' Andrew looked up at Anders and laughed. 'Tell the story.'

John put the cream-stick in the rain. Water dripped from its long thin nozzle and he watched it. 'We're in Phuket,' he said. 'There was a bus journey coming up and I needed sorting.'

'Yes, yes,' Andrew said, 'just tell the story.'

'I'd spent an hour walking chemist to chemist,' John went on, 'walking like a cowboy in a Western. You know, 'cause of my arse, 'cause of the pain.'

'Tell him to tell the story now,' Andrew said to Anders.

'I think he's trying,' Anders said coming out of his bedding, swinging his legs over the bunk rails.'

'I find another chemist,' John said still facing the rain. 'My arse was stinging on the inside, like it is now as I tell it.'

'Tell it then,' Andrew yelled. He opened another beer.

'There's this Thai lady, yeah. She's about four-foot-nothing and old as hell, yeah. Her skin was like rippled sand and she had no eyes. Well if she did I didn't see them. She shuffled off her stool, toddled over, moving the same as me. Maybe she had piles too, either she did, or she'd shat herself.' John paused. No one said anything. 'Anyway,' he said, 'she stood there, her wrinkled lips moving as though she was chewing something, a noodle I think. "Wat yu wan?" she kept asking. But the question got me. I wasn't sure how to explain myself.'

'Maybe point,' Anders said, 'point and talk very slow.'

'Yeah, that's what I figured.' John turned facing Anders, cream-stick in hand, waving it as he spoke. 'But when I used the term "anal sores" she seemed to get angry.'

'It's true,' Andrew said, 'was as though he'd offended her in some way.'

'She began hitting the counter top with the flats of her hands,' John said mimicking her, slapping his hands on his knees. 'She kept saying it, "wat yu wan, wat yu wan", slapping the counter top with each syllable she spoke.'

'She was a right one,' Andrew said. 'He had disturbed her lunch I think.'

'That's probably right,' John said. 'Anyway, I spoke slow and pointed behind myself with my thumb. "Wat, wat yu meen?" she says waving a finger. I think she wanted to wave it in my face but she was too small, it only reached my belly. Then she poked me with it and hit the counter top with her fist. I saw her turn. She looked at this bowl of noodles with these dried chilli slices. I think she was frowning too. But it was hard to tell, you know, with her being so wrinkly.'

Anders looked at the clock and climbed down the bunk ladders in his underpants. There was cold toast on the side, he took some and eat it.

Then he dressed and began gathering his things together, damp towel, books, bin-bag filled with dirty clothes. Both John and Andrew watched him as John continued telling the story. '"I have anal sores," I said. "Tomoro," she said, "yu cum back tomoro."'

'I'd have given up,' Anders said stuffing a T-shirt inside his backpack, 'seems you were fighting a lost cause.'

'She closed her lips tightly,' John said. 'They made like a ducks bottom and I imagined no teeth behind them. She pointed to the door. She looked at her noodles again. "Tomoro," she kept saying, "Tomorrow," I said nodding back at her, as though we'd reached an understanding. "Yu go now," she said, shooing me away with her doughy hands, and we went, and for a moment I thought I saw this black hole, and it was her mouth, she was smiling.'

'Then what,' Anders said.

'Then we moved on,' John said. 'We came to a clinic called Dr Pornsak's.'

'Pornsak,' Anders said glancing round the room, feeling his pockets.

'Yeah,' John said. 'I ain't making this up. Pornsak was his name,' he said. 'This guy wore specs and had much eyebrow. His moustache was pencil thin, really neat and thin, like liner across his top lip. He seemed rushed. Maybe he was the only doctor there. He moved fast and spoke fast. He kept rushing me along, then pausing to peer through this frosted glass, tut-tutting at the queue of patients lining up on the street. He had this bell on his door,' John laughed. 'It rang whenever someone entered. It rang a lot.'

'Not much patient confidentiality,' Anders said, 'You know, with the frosted glass window.'

'I agree,' John said. 'The waiting room saw and heard everything. I knew this because I'd been on the other side. I'd watched Pornsak treat a guy for gonorrhoea, or "burning penis" as Pornsak put it.'

'I'd have found another place,' Anders said.

'I was in too much pain for that,' John said. 'And Pornsak was a man that got things done. Within a minute my shorts were down and he was pushing me onto a bed, and then pushing my knees up to my chest saying aggressively, "curl, curl, curl, like bay-bee, curl like bay-bee." His eyes widened when he said "baby", and he said it very slow, as if I didn't understand English.'

'It was gruesome,' Andrew said acting out the part of Pornsak, outstretching his fingers, curving them to make a claw. 'Pornsak got stuck in.'

'I don't care,' John said coming into the room with his cream-stick. 'He got me sorted.'

'Not exactly,' Andrew said, 'you still have them.'

'Yeah,' John said, 'yeah I still have them. You don't need to tell me.' Then he winced and his eyes closed for a second. 'Christ almighty, lad, you don't need to tell me.'

'Wrap up the story,' Anders said checking the clock again. 'My taxi will be here soon.'

'Well,' John said, 'Pornsak examined me. I could feel him touching them, and part of me was saying just rip 'em out, rip 'em out, like bay-bee. I had no idea what they were. It can scare a person that, not knowing. He made funny noises, like ugh, oh, ah. He began to prod. Then he came up and removed his gloves. "What's going on in there?" I heard people saying. Those bastards in the waiting room were probably sat there with popcorn on their laps. It didn't bother me though. I was in too much pain for it to bother me. I just pulled up my shorts and listened to my diagnosis, along with everyone else.'

'We did listen,' Andrew said. 'Everyone in the waiting room went silent, though some joker got up and started dancing, dancing round the room singing curl baby curl – disco inferno.'

'Haemorrhoids,' John said cutting Andrew off. 'I should've known really. My dad Albert has them, has done for years.' He paused, looked at the cream-stick and continued. 'After Pornsak had told me, the

248

people in the waiting room began talking again. Guess it was an anticlimax for them, but not for me, felt like a small victory for me, and I got up feeling refreshed, feeling confident of a future again.'

'You didn't look confident,' Andrew said.

John ignored him. 'Pornsak wrote me a prescription,' he said, 'gave me some cream, gave me some things the size of Nerf gun bullets, told me to deposit them up my rosebud twice daily. Then he handed me a packet. He said they were "Go to the toilet tablets." Not the technical term, but I knew what he meant. They worked too, came out like liquid-butter.'

'Yes,' Anders said, 'I remember. Andrew got me with them in Brisbane. He spiked my vodka. Liquid-butter is an understatement.'

John and Andrew laughed.

'Anyway,' John said, 'that's when I found out, and the red grapes have nested there ever since.' He paused. He looked at Anders. 'No need for concern, lad. They aren't contagious. I warm your pillow each night. You'd know by now.'

He winked at Anders and shuffled past almost limping. Now with the cream-stick in his back pocket, tip poking out, like a mini rocket ready to launch. Anders stared at it as he left the room. Then his gaze turned to the pillow, his pillow, crumpled near the wall, imprinted with body marks, looking as brown and as yellow as ever.

'So when do you leave?' Andrew asked, jumping onto the kitchen top.

'Soon,' Anders said, 'very soon.'

He dragged his backpack near to the door and clipped it shut. He left some things out, things that he needed - wallet, snus, paracetamol, phone, bus ticket to Cairns. He filled his pockets with these things. Then he opened cupboards and looked under bunks, checking to see if he'd missed anything.

Suddenly John was back in the room. 'That German bloke,' he yelled puffing out his cheeks, 'God damn him.' He jabbed toward the corridor with his cream-stick. 'God damn him. That bathroom is always locked. That cunt has ten showers a day.' He then marched onto the balcony. The rain had stopped and he stood there in a puddle. It was dark, misty and gloomy, and the moon was hidden behind lots of clouds. He looked down on the soaked road. Across from The Old Crow was a solitary car, parked in the shadows of some trees. He watched it for a while, standing near the broken wood where Steve had fallen, near the yellow cones and the yellow tape that surrounded it, dripping wet. Then with folded arms, he looked at Anders, staring at him.

'You'll struggle, lad. You'll struggle without me,' he said sullenly. 'Your arm is broken. Who's going to hire a one-armed fruit picker? You should wait two more weeks. We can go together, the three of us.' He took his wallet, slapped it across his knuckles. 'We'll have saved enough by then.'

'You don't need to worry about me,' Anders said. 'Me and Henry planned this some weeks back. We were going to stay with his friend rent-free. I wrote this guy. I told him about my arm and about Henry. It turns out he wants me there anyway, said the offer still stands, said it would be nice for him to have someone around that knew Henry.'

'That sounds well gay to me,' John said stepping out of his shoes, nudging them under the bunk with his foot. 'Personally I think you'll struggle. Personally I think you should wait for us.'

'Well, maybe I'll surprise you.' Anders raised a hand and patted John's cheek.

'Would've been nice though, eh,' Andrew said, 'the three of us on the road again.'

'Look, we've had a few laughs,' Anders said shifting his eyes between both their staring faces. 'But I need to go alone for a while, you know, find some independence, you know, do things my way.'

'Jesus, Anders, calm down.' John turned. He limped back to the balcony and leaned on his shoulder in the doorway. 'You sound like Frank Sinatra.'

'Look,' Anders said. 'I don't want you getting upset about it. I'm grateful of our time together, and Jesus guys, you saved my life. But now, I just want to go alone, just for a while.'

Andrew looked away. He began staring, holding the beer bottle to his eye, squinting inside, staring at the dregs and the froth, as though the answer to the meaning of life was in there somewhere. John was looking at the car again, in the dark trees. 'You better go,' he said, 'taxi will be waiting.'

Andrew jumped down from the kitchen top. He picked up Anders's backpack and held it for him while he eased his arms through the straps. Then he adjusted the straps, and Anders asked if he would be kind enough to fetch his shoes, and put them on for him. Andrew laughed and called him a demic. John stayed on the balcony.

'You okay, John?' Anders asked while Andrew messed with his laces.

'Yes,' John said. 'It's just my piles. I want them creamed sooner rather than later.'

'If he feeds them after midnight,' Andrew said, 'they multiply.'

'Oh, that reminds me,' Anders said. He thanked Andrew for tying his laces, then went to the fridge and opened it. Sour smells got to him, a carton of milk had gone bad, and there was an onion sandwich on the rack, dotted with grey fungus. Quickly he reached in for a cardboard box, checking on his mangos, grapes, pears, apples, hoping they hadn't spoiled.

'For the Possum,' he said handing the box to Andrew. Then he moved to the balcony. The rain had left the decking slimy. He slid a little, steadied himself on a chair. Then, below the dripping branches of the willow tree, with the water droplets splashing his forehead, he stared upwards hoping to see its wonderful cute face one last time.

'I'll chop this tomorrow,' Andrew said putting the box on the sink. 'Come in now, it's time.'

Anders caught a droplet on his tongue. He closed his eyes. He stood there for almost a minute. John began tugging his sleeve, showing him the face of his watch. Andrew came out to join them, and they wished each other well. They shook hands and reminded each other to keep in touch. Anders went inside. He wrote his email address on the back of a cornflakes box. They followed him. They shook hands again. Andrew hugged him and laughed as he winced, and then apologised.

'Guess this is it then,' Anders said.

253

Both agreed it was and they sat on Andrew's bunk waiting for him to leave. But Anders was walking up and down the room, tapping his thumb on his teeth as though he had forgotten something. Then he disappeared behind a bunk. There was a scraping sound and when he reappeared, he was holding his guitar. He slid the strap over his shoulder, spun round, tiptoed about in front of them and began to sing. 'I'm the candy coloured clown they call the sand man,' he said feeling the guitar strings with his fingers, strumming gently. 'And I tiptoe to your room every night,' he sang high-pitched and out of tune, same as he always did. He sang and he tiptoed. 'First I sprinkle stardust, and then I whisper.' He held the strings. There was silence. Then he opened his palm and leaned over it, lips pursed, pretending to blow imaginary stardust into their faces. Both watched him, expressionless now as he backed into the corridor, still bending, still blowing. 'Go to sleep,' he said, 'everything is alright.'

Chapter twenty-six

John's second trip to the bathroom was more successful. He returned with a slight spring in his step, striding, whistling, he put the cream-stick back in the small bag and closed the balcony doors. The TV continued in the corner, bringing different glows of light into the dark room, which faded near Andrew's bunk, where he now lay on top of his covers, still clothed.

'Don't tell Babs that Anders has gone,' John said dropping his pants in front of the flashing screen. 'She'll want this TV back.'

'Buttle runs this place now,' Andrew said. 'He'll be asking for it back in the morning. He's worse than Dickie.'

John put both hands on his hips. He stood there watching the TV. 'I saw you cringe before,' he said.

'Well it's embarrassing,' Andrew said.

'Ah, what difference does it make?'

'None, it's just a bit awkward.'

'We'll probably never see him again, who cares.'

'The Possum though. What it did for him, he'd have liked that.'

'Yeah, well, you go running after him, tell him all about it.'

There was silence for a while. Then John climbed his bunk ladder and got into bed.

'Look,' John said sitting up, 'only we know about the Possum. Steve's head splattered like a watermelon, the death report mentioned no signs of an animal attack. Everything is better left the way it is.'

'I'm not bothered,' Andrew said. 'It's just awkward when he speaks as though we rescued him.'

'Like I said, we'll never see him again. Now did you pack his parting gift?'

'I did,' Andrew laughed. 'I wrapped it too.'

'Good. Did you use the Thomas stuff I gave you?'

'Yeah. And you, did you sort his phone?'

'Yeah. I went to his contacts and switched my name to Lindsay's. I'll text him something daft in a minute.'

'Okay, show me when you're done.'

'I will, just giving him a few minutes before I send it. But you know what?'

'What?' Andrew said, both were whispering now.

'I don't think he'll make it very far. I mean, something is bothering me, something I saw earlier, from the balcony, and I just don't think he'll make it. To be honest, I don't think he'll get that far.'

Chapter twenty-seven

The rain had made the river muddy looking. It was high now and ran harsh over the rocks, crashing, drowning out the football commentator's voice on the radio. Two men sat in their car and trying to compete with the river, the driver turned up the volume dial. The other man was beside him in the passenger seat. He turned it down again. Then he sternly reminded his partner of a thing or two. Like they were on a stakeout, and this was how they did it, quietly, in a dark spot, and this roadside near the Fitzroy was perfect, and he was not, repeat not, to touch the volume dial again.

After scolding his partner, he blew steam and sipped coffee from a paper cup. Then in the darkness, he struggled to read his paper, which he'd spread over both knees. His partner, looking sullenly at the radio, was eating tuna fish from a can. He scratched the dregs with a fork and by his feet, sandwich wrappings were rustling under his shoes. Passenger side then yawned. He finished his drink, shook his evening paper and folded it. First he looked at his partner, then he looked across the road. 'Target locked and one-hundred percent located,' he said turning off the radio. 'We better move.'

The driver leaned forward jabbing a key into the ignition. The engine bleated and with headlights on full beam, the car moved from the darkness of the trees. They turned across the road slowly coming to him. In the middle of the car park, Anders stared and blinked as the lights gave him a dizzy spell. White dots appeared before him and he staggered back. Then the engine cut. The lights went out and it was silent. He kept blinking. He heard car doors opening and footsteps swishing through puddles. Still blinking and staring through the fading white dots, he saw them coming to greet him, smiling as though they were old friends.

'Going somewhere, slugger?' Big D asked, signalling him closer with a finger. Lance had stayed back. He watched near the car bonnet, his thinning hair lifting in the breeze like a slice of cling-film. Anders said nothing. His shoulders were going and he faced the dark, wet floor.

'Keeping quiet, is he,' Lance said now coming forward, standing beside Big D. 'Typical.'

Again, there was no answer. Anders faced the floor.

'Well, slugger,' Big D said. 'I must say this doesn't look good, us coming to collect you and you all packed up ready to leave town.'

'I wanna know what slice of shit tipped him off,' Lance said. 'That's what I wanna know.'

'Easy, Lance,' Big D said, 'we'll get there.' But before Big D had finished his sentence, Lance had already taken the backpack from

Anders, and was now holding him by the shirt collar, marching him towards the car, feet splashing through puddles, pumps squeaking on the wet tarmac.

'Easy with him, watch that arm,' Big D said as they passed, taking the backpack from Lance.

With both feet, Anders kicked the car door. He began swivelling and turning with Lance, holding him by the arms. Both pivoted like ballroom dancers. Lance then grabbed him by the shirt and tugged him close, brow to brow, with his fringe dangling between their eyes. He spoke fast, spraying him with hot breath, stale combinations, Anders thought, of coffee and fish.

'In now,' Lance said. 'Get in the car.'

He leaned his weight on Anders and gripped the back of his neck, forcing him through the open door. 'Get in now,' Lance said. 'Yield boy yield,' he spoke breathlessly then gave him another push. 'Get in I say.' Anders's knees bent. He nearly collapsed but Lance pulled on his shirt again, lifting him and pushing him forward, and then laughing as Anders landed facedown across the backseats.

He closed the door and rested with his elbows on the car, shirttail over his pants, sweating. Anders turned watching him through the back window, watching him run his grimy, long fingers through his thinning hair. Then he walked over to where Big D was stood, holding Anders's guitar, strumming with his thumb on the strings. 'Search them,' Big D said, and Lance looked over the damp clothes spread out on the tarmac. He got down and began picking up clothing and tossing it over his shoulder. Anders was on his knees now, still watching. He saw Lance pass a towel to Big D. He saw Big D sniffing it.

'Jesus, Dee,' Lance said glancing up. 'Anyone would think you've never seen a towel.'

'Just get on with it, Lance, before it rains again,' Big D said.

'You gonna hold it like that all night?'

'Just get on with it.'

'I am. I am. What do you think this is?'

Big D unclipped a torch from his belt. He put light on something wrapped in Birthday paper. 'What is it?' he said, 'Why is it wrapped in Thomas the Tank Engine paper?' Lance shrugged. 'You think it's what we're here for?' Lance shrugged again. 'Just get on with it. Open it.' Lance ripped the paper. He passed the contents to Big D. 'This is creamed corn.' He showed the label to Lance.

'I know. I just opened it,' Lance said. 'That's why we're here.'

'It is? Is it?' Big D smelt the towel again and looked at the can.

'I got the statement from Mrs Hibbs.'

'Well read it then. I wanna make sure.'

Lance unfolded a piece of paper. He read out as follows. 'Spectacled chap walking round my shop without reason. He begins to touch everything. My boy approaches him and chap with specs panics. He runs off holding a can of creamy corn. He trips over and destroys my display of cat food. Then he escapes with my son giving chase.'

'Okay I've heard enough,' Big D said.

'Well I was finished anyway,'

'I got what I needed.'

'What's that?' Lance laughed, 'the towel?'

'That will do about the towel now.'

'Okay, whatever, are we taking him in?'

'Well we haven't been on a stakeout for nothing.'

'And it's definitely him, the worm boy?' Lance pointed at Anders and told him to stop watching.

'Well I watched the footage myself,' Big D said, 'It's clearly Anders. He runs straight into the cat food waving the can. Then he gets up with young boy Hibbs on his tail, just like the statement says.' Big D was now laughing, 'The cat food,' he said, 'he takes out the whole display. Boy Hibbs put it on this new thing called YouTube. The footage is on there. I recommend you watch it.'

'I don't surf the net,' Lance said taking the can from Big D.

Big D lowered his torch. The guitar strap and towel were on his shoulder. 'You should,' he said. 'There's different versions, edited ones, some speeded up, some with Benny Hill music playing.'

'Well I'm not much into that, though I would like to get back for the game.'

'Fair enough,' Big D said removing his Stetson, and with the same hand, he moved his wrist over his forehead. 'Fair enough, bag it, tag it, and let's go.'

Big D sat on the passenger's side with his foot on the dashboard, watching Anders in the middle mirror while Lance walked round the car. The back window was slightly open. Lance stopped there. He leaned in with his arms hanging over, dropped handcuffs through the gap and told Anders to wear them. 'Put them on, slugger,' Big D added.

'He'll put them on,' Lance said, 'he better put them on.' Then he went to the driver's side and got in.

'Is this necessary?' Anders asked holding his arm forward. But neither looked at him, they just told him to keep quiet and to wear them as instructed.

Lance then drank from a flask and finished half a sandwich. Tomatoes and onions fell from his mouth as he spoke to Big D. 'I can hear a mouse farting back there.'

Big D lowered his Aviators and watched Anders again in the mirror. 'Put them on, slugger,' he said. 'It's procedure.'

'But my arm, it's broken.'

'Put them on, put them on, put them on,' Lance said throwing bread crust in Anders's face. 'I'm counting to ten. If you get to ten you'll have another broken arm.'

Anders clicked into the cuffs, keeping one slightly loose so it wouldn't damage the cast. But Lance was watching, and when he was done, he asked Anders to hold both arms forward while he checked them, though he was only interested in one, and he fastened it until the plaster began to crack inward. Then he started the engine and came onto the road. Big D took his foot away from the dashboard. He was leaning forward now, laughing at Anders's belongings on the car park.

'What's so funny?' Lance asked holding the wheel.

'That,' Big D said, 'all that shit. Go back. Go back and pack it up.'

'Ah, Jesus Christ,' Lance said punching the wheel. 'This kids nothing but trouble.'

Chapter twenty-eight

Earthy smells drifted in through the windows, wet dirt, wet shrubbery, and as they approached the meat factory, there were hints of fresh cow dung too. These smells, and the smells inside the car, where it reeked of stagnant coffee, raw onion and tuna fish, and those smells, mixing with the dampness of clothes, Anders thought, was almost nauseating. Now moving under a jumble of tops, bottoms, socks and pants, he sat up, looking as though someone had poured a dirty laundry basket over him.

'Damn it, Lance,' Big D said, 'You could've repacked his stuff.'

'I wanna get back for the game. He's comfortable enough.'

Peeling a sock from his forehead, Anders stared out the window and watched the meat factory for the last time, those cattle wagons, those cows, those staring faces between wooden planks, ready for nightshift slaughter, those big white eyes, those snotty nostrils breathing steam into the night air. Captured, like him.

'It stinks,' Lance said. 'They shouldn't let 'em shit in the wagons.'

'What are you suggesting, Lance,' Big D said. 'They go before the journey?'

'I don't know,' Lance said. 'I'm not suggesting anything. That's not for me to figure out.'

He swung the car right. They drove down a narrow road with lots of bends and nothing but farm life on either side. There was a faint bleep inside Anders's pocket, then another, then a little vibration. Lance moved his tongue over his teeth. Big D stared in the mirror. 'You haven't patted him, have you?' He threw his arms up in the air. 'Have you and there's contraband back there.'

'Apologises, Dee, missed that one.'

'You better pull over.'

'Copy that, Dee.'

They stopped beside a barbed wire fence. Sheep were there on the pasture, staring, enjoying mouthfuls of lush, wet grass, baaing at the car lights and the ticking engine. Beyond them came a stone cottage, with smoke rising from its chimney, and its tiny windows were lit up, glowing orange in the darkness. Anders watched the smoke. Then he heard Big D's boots squelching in mud. He appeared on the roadside wiping his feet clean, dragging them on the gravel.

'I'm not happy with this, slugger,' he said opening Anders's door, showing him his soaked pants and muddy boots. He pinched the torch between his teeth, pushed the clothes aside and got in the back. Then he patted Anders's pockets, feeling inside them, taking things, holding each item up to the torch, arching his neck, dipping light on them.

'We got anything fruity back there?' Lance asked, speaking over the baaing sheep.

'I need more light,' Big D said, torch still between teeth, sounding gagged.

'Hold on I'll get mine.' Lance switched on his torch. He shined it in Anders's face.

'That's so unnecessary,' Anders said lifting his cuffed hands.

'I'll decide what's necessary,' Lance said. 'You got contraband. Now we investigate. Am I right, Dee?'

Big D didn't answer him. He arranged everything neatly on the back seat, phone, wallet, paracetamol, snus tin. Then he smoothed out the bus ticket over his thigh and examined it under the light.

'What we got, Dee?' Lance asked pushing off his seat, leaning forward, almost between them.

Big D showed Lance the ticket.

'So he was getting out, he's more slippery than a greased up body builder.'

'Yup,' Big D said bagging the items in clear plastic, bagging everything but the snus tin. 'Here,' he said, 'take these, we're all out at the station.'

266

Lance placed the tin on the dashboard. Big D didn't get out again. He stepped on Anders's stuff with his muddy boots and climbed through the middle to the front seat. 'We'll hold these for now,' he said waving the plastic bag.

Anders closed his eyes. He asked what he had done, why they had cuffed him, where they were going. But they said nothing and Lance kept the torch in Anders's face. He asked again, squinting as he spoke. 'What have I done?'

'Well,' Lance said finally dropping the torch, facing the open road. 'You're wearing clothes this time, so scratch indecent exposure off your list.'

The phone bleeped again. Big D opened the plastic bag and took it. 'Think your battery is running low, slugger. And look at that,' he said showing Lance, 'one new message.' Lance rubbed his hands together vigorously, telling Big D to read the message. Paper cups and sandwich wrappings rustled under his shoes as he moved his feet. Then he was beeping the car horn. The sheep scattered. He laughed. He kept beeping.

'Read it, Dee.' Beep! Beep! 'Read it loud. Read it clear.' Beep!

'It's from a chick named Lindsay,' Big D said pressing buttons with his thumb. 'You been rooting someone, hey, slugger?'

267

'She sounds hot,' Lance yelled. 'Read on. Read on my brother.'

Big D cleared his throat and began. "Broccoli is green. But cauliflowers are white. Watching you pick cabbage was pure delight."

Anders dropped his head forward. He swore quietly and blushed.

'Ugh,' Lance said, 'pass a bucket, I wanna throw up.'

'Does she like vegetables?' Big D asked, still facing the text. 'She waitin' for you in Cairns?'

'You do things with cabbage?' Lance chimed in. 'Eh, do you, you sick bastard?'

Anders sighed. He pulled himself up a little, glanced down at his cuffed hands, and regretting it instantly, explained that Lindsay was a man.

'Well shit,' Lance said beeping the car horn again, 'in that case you better pass me two buckets.' Beep! Beep! 'We got a woofter. We got a woofter.'

'Silence yourself, Lance,' Big D said. His face had gone rigid, he pushed Lance's hands away from the horn, again telling him to silence himself.

'Sorry,' Lance said. 'I forget sometimes.'

'Just don't say it again, okay, you copy that? Drive on now, we need to move.'

Chapter twenty-nine

They were on the road again. The clouds were low and the air was misty. Anders looked through his window at the sheep and the grass, the openness of the pasture and the mist between everything. He watched these things while they drove, and, after repeatedly asking what he had done wrong, Big D had suggested a game. A test, as he put it, to make an honest man of Anders, suggesting that he should tell them. He gave him three guesses, and, if he got them all wrong, (which he would, Lance said, because he was a lying little shit) he would have to wait until they reached the station, where Shiny would explain everything. Lance then argued that worm boy should only get two guesses, adding he'd already ruled out indecent exposure for him. Big D agreed that that was fair, and now, after wasting a guess on his clash with Steve, Anders sat carefully thinking, with one guess now remaining.

They swung right following another road, a wider one, completely empty, no cars, no buildings, no farm life, no people, just dark forest on both sides, and lines of streetlamps. Anders faced between the two front seats, watching the lit road, thinking about scenarios of weeks gone by. He decided not to mention the LSD. Silence on that subject had served him well so far, and he saw no reason to change tack now. Other images passed through his memory in random order, like a strange silent movie - Henry smoking weed, the dead cows on the conveyer belts, Marian's bloody cheek, being naked in the dirt and sand, the Blonde, Sammy and his fishy hands, the needle, the Possum on its perch, and Buttle's extraordinary white teeth, all came to him. And for a while, nothing seemed worth a guess. Then there was something else, a flashback to weeks earlier, when he was back in cell five, in that hot cell with Big D strutting round, was that it, he thought, was he caught standing naked, thrusting himself behind Big D, was there CCTV, had they found footage? Had they decided to make an example of him?

'I think I know,' he said, 'It looks worse on camera, I understand that.'

'Good,' Big D smiled, 'seems we're making progress.'

'I didn't want to do it though. I just thought you wanted me to.'

'What the heck, Dee,' Lance said arching his brow. 'You were there?'

Big D lowered his Aviators. He looked in the middle mirror giving Anders that wonky-eyed stare of his, eyes moving to places on his body, which places Anders was unsure, but they moved, he saw that.

'Of course he was there,' Anders spoke confidently. 'I couldn't get rid of him. He was strutting round like a randy peacock.'

'What's this all about, Dee?' Lance asked.

270

'It's just the kid,' Big D said putting his Aviators back on, 'he's a damn fool.'

'Admit it, Big Dee,' Anders said. 'You forced my hand, so I did it, so what. I stood there naked, thrusting it back and forth. I did it, so what.'

'You didn't mention this, Dee?' Lance said. 'Was you there? Is there footage of him naked, and you, and Benny Hill music playing?'

Anders noticed Big D leaning forward, reaching round his feet in the front. He came up with something and tossed it over his shoulder. The can of creamed corn landed on Anders's crotch. He winced for a moment, then opened his eyes and saw it there.

'You see it now, huh,' Big D said, smirking, locking his fingers together and resting them over his stomach. 'Look at his face, Lance, it's a picture.'

'That shut him up,' Lance said. 'I thought worm boy had you for a moment, only for a moment though.' He looked at Anders in the mirror. 'Check him out,' he said. 'Kid's shitting beans back there. Pop that mouth shut, worm boy, before you catch a fly.'

'Where's this from?' Anders asked.

'Oh he's good. Ain't he, Dee? Ain't he good?'

'He is. He's a slippery one.'

'He is slippery.'

271

Anders held the can in both hands. 'Something funny is going on, either I find out now or at the station,' he spoke as if they were the ones in trouble.

'You got some nerve talking that way, worm boy, some nerve. Anyone would think you're trying to agitate me.' Lance pushed his fringe to one side, and with the same hand, keeping the other on the wheel, he extended a finger and moved it inside his shirt pocket. 'Dee, I'm getting agitated.'

'Stay cool, Lance,' Big D said. 'Stay cool and watch the road, I'll handle him.'

The car began to pick up speed. Anders dropped the can and turned himself sideways, feeling through the clothes for his seatbelt. 'You planted it,' he said. 'You messed with my stuff. I watched you at The Old Crow, on the car park, messing with my stuff.'

Lance rubbed a finger over his gums, sucked it and then turned. 'He calling us corrupt now, Dee?' His finger made the journey again, shirt pocket, dip, up to gums, rub rub, back down, dip. 'I don't take that shit, Dee. You know I don't take it.'

'Don't play his games, Lance.' Big D touched his partner on the shoulder. 'He nearly got me just now, he's good, remember that.'

'I'm getting agitated, though.'

272

'Watch the road, Lance. It's a death trap, potholes everywhere.'

Big D yanked the steering wheel left. The car swerved. Anders reached for a seatbelt. 'Let me out,' he yelled. 'You've set me up. You're both corrupt.'

'One more word and we'll show you corrupt,' Lance was screaming suddenly, sweating and screaming and rubbing his gums. Big D looked at him. Anders looked at him. 'I'll pull in,' he said, 'I'll pull right in and let Big Dee drop his pants, and you and that pathetic A-hole of yours won't know what day or month or year it is. I ain't keen myself, but I don't mind watching. I've watched before.'

'Lance for Christ sake,' Big D said. 'Watch the road, the road, the road.' He reached over, brought the wheel left again. The car went over more potholes and they bounced on their seats, the tops of their bodies moving forward and back, rocking as though on a rollercoaster.

'I'm getting agitated,' Lance said with his finger in his shirt pocket, spilling white powder everywhere. He rubbed his gums, pressed his foot on gas, rubbed his gums again. Anders clicked into one of the seatbelts. Big D reached for his too, clicking in one handed whilst trying to take the wheel.

'Enough,' he said, watching the car swerve near the edge of the road, near a dip. 'We pass Hudson Hospital soon,' he said. 'They walk the

273

crazies here. They walk 'em every night.' He pulled the wheel. They came level with the road again. He slapped Lance's leg.

'I'm okay,' Lance said, 'just a little agitated.' But his eyes were squinting. He leaned forward with his face almost touching the windscreen, his breath marking the glass. 'Something is out there,' he said.

'They walk 'em,' Big D yelled. 'I told you. They walk 'em.'

'This one's alone.'

'Slow down!'

'Why's he alone?'

Through the mist came a gowned man. He ran towards the car gambolling about barefooted.

'I don't like this. Why's he alone?' Lance pressed the gas pedal.

'Don't be a fool,' Big D said reaching for the wheel, but the car ran another pothole, flinging him back over to his side.

The gowned man stopped suddenly. He held two red sticks with sparks coming from them. Big D seemed to notice and quickly, he began turning a handle, closing his window. Anders noticed too. He held his seatbelt tightly and pushed his feet into Lance's chair.

'Who's kicking me?'

'Put the brakes on.'

'Be quiet back there.'

'Easy, Lance, easy now.'

'I'm in control.'

'Stand down, Lance, that's an order.'

'Someone's kicking me back there.'

'Stand down I said.'

Lance ignored him and rubbed his gums with cocaine. He drew his eyes together. 'I remember him,' he said pointing at the gowned man, 'that's...' he paused, leaned on the wheel. 'That's Maniac.'

Big D swung with his fist. 'Enough on the gas I said.' He punched Lance on the throat. 'Stand down I said.' He swung both feet over Lance's legs, bringing everything he had down on the breaks. 'You bastard, Dee,' Lance choked on his words, 'You bastard.'

The car was slowing enough for Maniac to climb aboard the car bonnet. They hit more potholes. Big D fell back to his side and the car rolled on. Maniac's hands were now empty, Anders noticed, and the sparking sticks had been dropped through Lance's open window. Maniac steadied himself. He held the windscreen wipers and kept his body spread-eagled on the bonnet. He laughed at Lance through the window, watching him choke and stare wildly over the sparking sticks on his lap.

The car rocked over another pothole sending Big D's head into his window. His shoulders dropped suddenly and he arched forward, lifelessly, just hanging there in his seatbelt. Lance looked at him then reached down for the sticks. But it was too late. They exploded over his crotch and he jerked back grinding his teeth together, staring upward, eyes wide, red and wild, and veins pulsating on his forehead as though ready to burst. His screams and horrid smells filled the car, burnt flesh, burnt tyres, gunpowder, fish, onion, coffee. For a moment, Anders found the expression on Lance's face hilarious. Then he remembered the danger he was in. Nobody was at the wheel. Fear came over him and the journey became even rougher. They all rocked inside the car, and Lance, who was without seatbelt, took it badly. Anders watched him bounce forward and back, side-to-side, head bumping on the roof, up down, up down. 'My dick,' he screamed holding his bloody hands in the air, 'what if I lose my dick?'

Anders coughed. He felt the seatbelt cutting into his neck and stared forward through the clearing smoke. Another pothole was coming. He saw it was a big one. He pushed his feet into Lance's chair again and trying to forget about the pain in his broken arm, squeezed his seatbelt with both hands, holding it as tightly as possible, eyes now closed. Maniac slipped further down the bonnet, his eyes staring at Lance, eyes

276

influenced on a cocktail of medication and excitement, staring and laughing. Anders kept his eyes closed, but some things he could not escape, like the sound of Maniac's nails scratching the metal bonnet, or his palms squeaking as he slid, or his laughter, which seemed euphoric considering the circumstances.

He was slipping and disappearing beneath the car, first his legs, then his lower body. He was just head and shoulders now, and each time they ran a pothole, his face would hit the car. His nose was bloody and smeared across his face, yet he continued to laugh at Lance, showing broken teeth and blood on his gums.

Lance's hands were trembling as he managed to clip into his seatbelt. He had spit on his chin and sweat all over his face. He looked at Maniac and took the wheel again. He was back in control. He brought his foot down on the gas pedal, brought it down and kept it there. Anders tensed up feeling the car regain its speed. He listened to Lance screaming. 'Die, bastard, die.' Anders opened his eyes. He saw Maniac swinging left to right, hanging off the front of the car and laughing without a care in the world. He kept swinging that way, face bashing the bonnet now and then, and showing more blood on his teeth. Then he was gone. The wheels rocked over his body and Anders closed his eyes again, listening to the popping and snapping sounds. He listened with a pang of guilt, as though by being in the car, he'd played some part, as though his weight on the backseat had just helped crush a man to his death. But he didn't think about that for long. There wasn't much chance for reflection, not with the shattered glass spraying his face, not with the car flipping over the way it was.

Chapter thirty

Anders woke in the long, wet grass. It curled over his face and he lay there catching water droplets on his tongue. Somewhere he could still hear the car's engine ticking, and the sound of bullfrogs and crickets, and water passing over stones, maybe a nearby stream, he thought. And he lay there enjoying the sounds, imagining tiny fish of many colours swimming below the stream, going in and out of ancient pottery. He smiled. He tasted more droplets and watched many thick clouds passing slowly above him. The moment was a pleasant one, he thought, and he was enjoying himself.

When he woke a second time, Lance was speaking to him. 'Worm boy, where are you?' he said. 'The car is wrapped around a tree, there's smoke coming from somewhere. Where are you? I'm hurt badly. Anders, help me.'

'Be quiet,' Anders said. 'I'm listening to the fishes.'

'Help me, Anders, go for help.'

'I'm in the grass and watching the clouds. The water is good here.'

'But I'm bleeding badly.'

Anders tasted another raindrop. 'It's rather nice here.'

'Help me.'

'Try a raindrop, they're delicious.'

'Please don't leave me here.'

There was no answer after that, and Anders was busy now fixing his knee. He felt where the glass had stuck and tried with his fingers to pull on it. Then leaning over to his left, he took grass in his teeth and held it there. It was crisp, sweet, refreshing. It was long and thick. Never had he had so much grass in his mouth before, and finding it so ridiculous, he began to chuckle.

'Stop laughing, go for help.'

'I'm in the grass,' Anders mumbled.

'What was that?'

'The grass, I'm in it.'

He brought both hands over his knee, it was there, sharp against his fingertips, stuck deep, long and thin like a golf tee. He pinched it, pulled it, and dropped it. Blood began warming his leg and suddenly the grass tasted rancid. He thrashed side to side silently, spitting grass, hands clutching his knee. Then he crawled out of the grass and onto a large gravel patch, where he saw the car and Lance's face in the driver's window, looking white and sweaty. He pleaded for Anders to get help, but Anders sat on the gravel ignoring him, ducking out of his sling, undoing its knot with his teeth, then standing and tying the sling around his knee. The blood held. He looked at Lance and staggered towards the wreaked car.

'Are you getting help?' Lance said gasping between his words.

Again, he ignored him and began packing his stuff, bunching shirts together with his cuffed hands, stuffing them into his backpack and frowning at Big D's muddy boot prints. He found an old cap from when he worked the farm fields. He put it on then pushed the bag out of the car with his feet, and following tyre marks up a dirt slope towards the roadside, dragged it with him. Lance watched in his wing mirror, his wet fringe stuck flat to his forehead, his shirt soaked with sweat. 'Don't leave me here,' he said. 'Please don't leave me.'

At the top of the slope, for as far as Anders could see there was glass, bits of car, metal plates, black oil, skid marks, rubber tubes and bent pipes, and somewhere between all that, was a dead body. For a moment, he waited looking left to right for other cars, but as before, the road was empty. He sat down planning his next move. The engine continued to tick and the drip-drip of oil spilled over tree roots. He was about to leave, but he knew he would struggle with cuffed hands, and part of him wanted to check that Big D was okay. On his bottom, he slid back down the slope and got up looking filthy.

Big D hung forward in his seatbelt, as he was earlier, sleeping. His Stetson was by his feet. His forehead was bleeding and through a broken window, tree branches hung over his face, hiding him. 'He is fine,' Lance said. 'Stop looking at him and get help.' Anders listened to Big D. He was breathing, that was something, he thought. Then he turned to Lance and looked down at his trembling hands, covering a damp fleshy patch of tattered genitalia. 'Those firecrackers exploded on my dick and my balls,' he yelled. 'Please, please, get help.'

Anders raised his cuffs.

'What?'

'I want the keys.'

'No way, we're taking you in.'

'That's not happening now,' Anders said, smiling, liking the confidence in his voice. 'You want help and I want the keys. Now give them to me.'

Lance reached into his wet pocket, groaning with each movement, head back, teeth showing. He held a ring pinched between thumb and finger, two tiny keys swung on it. 'There,' he said. 'Now please, there's still time.'

'Be quiet,' Anders said, keys now in his teeth, ducking to each cuff. 'It's pathetic and you're pathetic. You're an arsehole too. Have I mentioned that before, no, well I'm mentioning it now, aren't I? You're an arsehole. I don't like you. Please understand this. I think you're a royal shit.'

He rubbed his wrist, moved his fingers and checked the cast, poking at the cracks and sunken parts around the bottom, crushed where the cuff had been. It was now redundant, a meaningless aid to his broken arm, nothing more than a wreaked shell, like the car. He slung the cuffs high over trees and watched them disappear into forest.

'Look at this,' he said poking the cast. 'Was it clever handcuffing a man with a broken arm, make you feel big?' He pulled more and more plaster. The cast became so soft, so broken, that the whole thing came away from his arm. 'Well did it?' he asked now waving it in Lance's face. Lance coughed. White powder puffs appeared around him, blanketing over his skin, adding to his paleness.

'It's procedure,' he said coughing. 'That's all,' cough-cough, 'we had to,' cough, 'I just follow procedure.'

Anders pointed at Lance's crotch. 'And how's that working for you?'

'Stop messing with me, go and get help.'

'I will,' Anders said climbing across the backseats into the front, 'I just need my stuff first.' He leaned over Big D's legs, opened the glove box. In searching for his stuff, he came across several pots of scented

Vaseline, some candles, a demonic mask, and a Coldplay album.

'They're not mine,' Lance said.

The plastic bag was there. He took some paracetamol and stuffed the rest of his things into his pocket. Then he began searching for his phone, keeping low on Big D's side, feeling round his feet, patting the floor. It was dark. He found Big D's torch and switched it on. He reached under more seats, felt down the sides, nothing, and returning to the back and shining the torch everywhere, nothing. Then he lay across the backseats, laughing. 'You look like a clown,' he said holding the torch in Lance's face. 'You're so white.'

'That's enough,' Lance spoke furiously. 'I've had enough.' He stared at his white face and purple lips in the mirror, much spit dribbled down his chin. 'Quit messing back there, my piece is hanging on by a thread.' His eyes followed Anders back out of the car, extending his neck out of his window, plaster all pasty and grey on his cheeks. 'By a thread,' he yelled, thrusting his forefingers over the burnt fleshy bits, pointing down. 'By a thread,' he repeated, 'a thread.'

'Yeah,' Anders said, 'you look awful, so white and sweaty. You need a doctor.'

'Yeah, no shit. What I been saying, you even listening to me?'

'This is what I'm saying. You need help. You got a phone?'

284

'Yeah, I got a phone.'

'Hand it over then.'

'Why?'

'So I can call for an ambulance. Hanging on by a thread, right?'

'This better work,' Lance said groaning again as his hands moved to places that he didn't want to touch. 'Here, make the call.'

Anders took the phone. He keyed in some numbers. 'Did you say by a thread?'

'Stop talking, just make the call.'

'Copy that, Lance, I got this.'

Anders's phone began to ring in the distance. Lance looked side to side extending his neck even further, nose pointed upwards as though someone was dangling a carrot in front of his face. 'What's that, what's the idea?' He watched Anders climbing the slope, pumps squelching, pants wet and torn. 'Come back,' he screamed, he stared, he spat, he sweated. 'Come back here!'

With Lance still screaming and glass crunching under his feet, Anders walked along the road passing carnage, a broken windscreen wiper, a scratched number plate, a can of creamed corn, which he kicked into a ditch, and further on, near his snapped guitar, he could see his phone, ringing, spinning, vibrating. He picked it up and kept moving, limping, passing more bits of wreckage. Lance's police badge was there. He opened it. It showed him in his younger days, he had more hair and looked very serious. Anders laughed at the photograph and pocketed it. Then he came to Maniac, all bent and curled and missing an arm, with eyes wide open and a rictus grin on his face. He knelt beside him and switched off Lance's phone, placing it in Maniac's curved hand, which was already stiff. 'Make contact with the Clown, old comrade,' he said, 'report we completed our mission.' Then he closed his mouth and eyelids for him. 'I better go,' he said standing up, and he dropped off the road again, hiding in the shelter of the forest, following the roadside as a point of reference, with Lance's voice haunting him in the background.

'Come back here, worm fuck. Come back here, I said. Are you coming? No? Well in that case I will kill you. I will kill you for this. I will find you first, that's job number one, and then of course, I kill you. That's how it will go. How does that sound, worm shit, worm fuck? I'll find you, and then I'll kill you. Come back. Come back here. Finding you is only the first part. Then I kill you. Come back here now,' and that's how Lance went on, and for almost an hour later Anders was sure he could still hear that screeching voice, so much so that he kept checking his shoulder, to be sure that Lance wasn't there. 'I find you to kill you,' he heard. 'I find you to kill you.'

After a good trek and keeping off the roads as much as possible, Anders appeared in the shadows of Rockhampton bus shelter, and felt his cap before entering. Instantly, a tramp in a straw hat sat greeting him, looking up from the floor, as though roosting in his soiled nest of newspapers, beer cans and used cigarettes. He took an empty soup cup and smiled with it in the air. 'Got something for me, fella?' he asked in a gruff but cheery tone. Anders smiled back at him. He liked his thick beard. He was a proper tramp and his beard was the colour of dirty snow.

'Here,' Anders said placing the ticket to Cairns in the tramp's yellowy fingers. 'Now where can I find toilets?' The tramp sniffed, cup in one hand, ticket in the other, staring between both, the way a child stares after finding a tangerine in their slipper at Christmas. He took off his straw hat now and sniffed again.

'Sell it,' Anders smiled, 'you got twenty minutes.'

The tramp stared with his drunken, muddy-eyes. He stared for a long time, as though hoping someone might pass and offer to sell the ticket for him. He began moving the empty cup through his beard, back and

287

forth, cup on nose, scratching, back of neck, more scratching. Then he pushed the ticket underneath a brown leather jacket, and, without getting up, pointed with his soup cup to a newspaper stand and information booth, and there, between them under a gloomy light, was a sign for public toilets. Anders thanked him. Then, oddly, as Anders was walking away, the tramp asked if for the price of fifty dollars, he would like to buy the ticket back from him.

Chapter thirty-one

The stench of urine was inescapable. He battled it one handed, pawing like a mad man swatting flies, nose scrunched up, thrusting with his good hand, one swipe, two swipe, repeat. Then stooping he made the O shape with his mouth, and blew air through it, hands on thighs, eyes watery and glazed, throat making retching sounds over brown puddles and paper towels dampening in them. There was ash over the sink, fag ends blocking the plughole, and old tissues stuck on the ceiling, where they'd been wetted and now dried. A cool breeze caught his neck and, looking up at the air vent, he heard rain coming again. He shivered. He held his arms. Then he emptied his pockets and undressed.

In just his underpants, cap, and scraggy sling that he'd tied around his knee, he stared at himself in the mirror, feeling his bruised ribs, body cold and shaky. He saw tiny cuts on his face, old and new, and blood seeping through the stitching on his shoulder. He took some dark glasses from his backpack and put them on. Then he bunched together paper towels and held them under the hot water tap, but the water ran cold. He brought them over his face, dabbed cuts, wiped blood, and read the swear words written in black marker on the walls, and the numbers for drug dealers, sex lines and hookers.

There was a bin under the sink and when he had finished, he gathered his dirty clothes and patted them to the bottom of it. Then using paper towels and toilet rolls, he repacked it nice and high and urinated over everything to make it heavy. Then, as he was stuffing his phone and wallet inside the front of his underpants, it suddenly sounded to him, as though a baby elephant was charging the door. His eyes drew quickly on the latch. He touched it confirming it was locked, but it seemed the elephant was going nowhere. It banged on the door. It spoke in a panic.

'Hey, buddy,' the elephant sounded American. 'You gonna be much longer, buddy?' He was American. 'I got me a baked Twinkie ready to drop. I can't hold out much longer. Believe me my bestest-buddy I've tried.'

Anders didn't say anything. He stepped into a pair of baggy pants.

Thud, thud, thud, there was more knocking. 'Anyone in there?' Thud, thud. 'Anyone at all?'

'Wait, please,' Anders said now stepping into flip-flops.

'Sorry to push you like this, buddy,' the American sounded sincere. 'Thing is, I had spicy dogs with macho relish for lunch, wife warned me not to overdo it, everything was fully loaded.'

There were fart noises other side of the door. 'Jesus,' Anders whispered, tugging a purple sweater over his head, checking the sleeve, making sure it was long and baggy enough to hide the bandages of his broken arm. Then more fart noises. *Jesus!*

'I don't like to push, but is it possible to get an estimated time?' the American asked. 'I wanna know what I'm dealing with here,' he said before farting again, 'dang sticky ribs!'

'I won't be long.' Anders looked in the mirror. 'I'm nearly done.' He removed his cap. He wet his hair under the water tap, combed it with his fingers, put the cap back on.

'The wife gives me hell when I eat sticky ribs. It's the hot sauce, I guess.'

'Yep,' Anders said.

'What you doing though?'

'I won't be long.'

Anders looked in the mirror again. He liked the cap and the dark glasses, felt as though he was in a movie, Harrison Ford in the fugitive.

'What you doing though?'

'Relax, I'm nearly done.'

'But what stage are you at?'

'Jesus. I'm just cleaning up, nearly there, buddy.'

'But I've not heard a flush yet.'

'I'll flush you in a minute.'

'What was that, buddy?'

'Nothing.' Anders pulled the chain.

'Thank the lord,' the American said.

Anders picked up his backpack and paused, noticing bloody paper towels around the sink. He gathered them, threw them into the toilet, and catching the American's interest, pulled the chain for the second time.

'Double flush, huh,' the American said. 'I might need me one of those.'

Anders opened the door, and there, with soft peachy cheeks, wearing the smile of a child, and jumping from left foot to right foot, was the American. His camera, which he had attached to his shoulders by leather straps, swung as he danced, as did his belly, which sagged over his front almost hiding his fanny-pack. He waved his puffy hands in the air joyfully, and passing by, stuffed something into Anders's hand, thanked him and locked the door.

Anders followed a path with queued buses on one side and shops on the other. Drivers called destinations, final warnings, name calls. 'Coolangatta. Last chance. Biggs and Marshall.' Two lads of a similar age to him ran past, arguing with each other, out of breath. Then he passed a bakery and a coffee shop, warming himself in the smells of cinnamon, stewed apples and cigar smoke. Different blends of coffee ran under his nose, he tasted them, enjoyed them. He saw through the barker's window, croissants, shortbreads and cakes, and staring at them, noticed the baker behind his selection of goodies, looking proud, stroking his floury hands over his floury apron.

He kept walking. Outside the coffee shop he saw an abandoned table, where half a bagel sat on a plate. He snatched it, crammed it into his mouth. The butter was rich and warming. He kept moving, hugging himself, almost trembling. Then he remembered what the American had given to him. It felt soft like a packet of slugs. He unfolded the plastic, *crocodile jerky,* and passed the hideous looking snack into a bin.

Rain poured in through a hole in the shelter and an old man with dowagers hump mopped it and positioned buckets. Anders walked round his patch. He pushed through a line of people boarding a bus and came out again on the same side. He saw the old man as an undercover police officer, maybe the finest, maybe a big player high up at special branch. He knew everything, the trip, the indecent exposure, the creamed corn incident. He knew all about Anders and his two accomplices – Maniac and the Clown. Again, Anders got the feeling he was in a movie.

When he arrived for his ticket, he saw a large, trout-faced woman with a perm that could rival an eighties footballer. She sat at her booth with a magazine over her countertop. Her eyes seemed glued to the pages and when Anders approached she neither looked nor spoke to him, she just kept reading, pausing only to reach for her biscuits. Being undercover, being on the run and all that, her ignorance suited Anders just fine. He took out his wallet, studied the timetable, and decided on a new destination.

Chapter thirty-two

The girl studied Anders in his purple sweater. He lay now across four seats, at the back of the bus, hugging a bottle of whisky. Only they were there, and he was sleeping. The other passengers sat near the front, and, somewhere in the middle, hunched over pieces of fried chicken, was a fat man with greasy whiskers.

'Finally we're off,' a voice said as the bus left the shelter.

Heavy rain drummed the rooftop and sprayed the windows. It moved faster now, and over enthusiastic passengers cheered as they joined the road and the traffic. Then the bus stopped suddenly, causing the passengers to hold onto their seats. They sat silently while the driver leaned from his window swearing at a pedestrian in front of his bus. Anders was swearing too, he had fallen from seat to carpet and opening his eyes, looked up at the girl with his cap askew.

'Are you okay down there?' She stayed on her knees looking over her seat, pulling a curl of hair with her fingers. When he sat down again he decided, seeing her snub nose with freckles, seeing her big green eyes and smiling face, that he was in love. 'You look familiar,' she said, offering him some gum.

'I get that always,' he said, and he took the gum and pocketed it.

'You're the one that got attacked, aren't you?'

He put on his dark glasses and felt the seats for his whisky. Then, moving his hand in circles, he cleared steam from his window and looked through it watching the bus make progress. 'What's your name?' he asked.

'Debra, but I hate that name, call me Debs.' She giggled into her hands. 'You're Anders, right, or is it Andros?'

'Andros,' he said rubbing the window. 'Call me Andros.'

She chewed her bubblegum and looked at him. 'You're famous in this town after that incident.'

He felt his cap and cleared away more steam. 'Where you heading?' he asked.

'Brisbane,' she said. 'And you, where you heading?'

'Gatton, an old friend owes me some money.' He burped quietly tasting whisky. Then using his sleeve, he cleared away the steam completely.

'Oh, I see,' she said.

'What about you?' he said. 'What you doing in Brisbane?'

'I'm doing a pantomime.' She watched his face on the window. 'Aladdin, you ever seen it?'

The bus turned onto a new road, one he knew well, one that he had limped along almost three hours ago. He felt his cap again and breathed heavily.

'Are you okay?' she said. 'I was saying about Aladdin.'

'Yeah sure,' he said keeping his face on the window, angling his body to see further down the road. But there was nothing, just rain, streetlights and dark forest. 'Robin Williams,' he said.

'No, silly,' Debs laughed. 'Not the cartoon, the panto.'

He wanted to say more but his mouth felt as dry as cotton. He wet it with some whisky. Then moved his stuff to the other side of the seats where an emergency exit was. Debs, now giddy telling about the pantomime, had barely noticed.

'We're doing the Princess Theatre,' she said, 'from December tenth to Christmas Eve.' She pulled her bubblegum, coiling it round her finger. 'It features some big names.' She giggled, she felt underneath her knees and lifted her panto script. 'You know, Jay-Dee being one of them.' She made circles with her finger to unwind the gum. 'Jason bloody Donovan, eh.'

Anders laughed and she watched him, waiting for him to speak.

'Jay-Dee,' he said not looking at her, because Jay-Dee was all he had heard.

'Yep,' Debs said lifting her script, smiling proudly. 'He's an Aussie legend.'

'Who's that?' Anders said.

'Donovan,' she said, 'what we're talking about.'

'Oh yeah,' he said lifting his cap, pressing his forehead on the glass. 'Good act, Hurdy Gurdy Man.'

Debra frowned on her script as though she'd missed something, whispering gurdy, gurdy, gurdy. 'Never heard that one, gurdy, thought I knew them all, gurdy, gurdy,' she repeated, stuffing the script inside her handbag.

'What are you saying?' Anders said.

'I was saying about Jason Donovan,' she said. 'You don't seem to be listening.'

'I am,' he said. 'I had a T-shirt with him on.' His eyes stayed on the road, there were skid marks and lights ahead, flashing blue and red colours.

'Oh classic,' Debs said bouncing on her knees. 'Was it classic Jay-Dee, eighties quiff an' all that?'

'Yeah, I think it was.'

Debs patted the top of her seat. 'Jealous,' she said smiling, 'you still got it?'

The bus was slowing, the lights getting closer.

'What did you say?'

'The T-shirt?'

'What? Sorry. I mean no.'

He saw more skid marks, broken glass, a sodden blanket over Maniac's body, his stiff feet poking out at one end. Then a truck with a long chain, dragging the wrecked car back up the sloped hill on its flattened tyres. Further on were two parked ambulances and a queue of police cars blocking the road ahead, their beacons spinning, flashing in the darkness, then paramedics in green uniforms, and police officers in Stetsons and waterproof ponchos.

'Bummer,' Debs said about the T-shirt.

'Yeah,' Anders whispered as the bus stopped. 'This is a bummer.'

Passengers began standing near the front, one by one, rubbing steam from their windows, ducking, looking at the lights, the officers, and Maniac's bare feet. 'This is unusual,' a bald man was saying, and he stood with his fingers hooked in his pockets. Then he went and stood behind the driver, watching everything through the bigger window. 'This is better,' he said leaning on the driver's chair, and more people followed him, all hanging round the driver.

'Keep to your seats,' the driver said.

'I'm not,' the bald man said, 'This is interesting.'

Debs had cleared her window and was watching too. All watched apart from the fat man with the greasy whiskers. He just stayed with his chicken, sucking his fingers, pinching more wings.

'What happened?' the driver asked opening the bus doors.

'Yeah,' the bald man said, 'we'd like to know.'

An officer stood on the ground, flashlight in hand and rain coming over his Stetson, rolling down his poncho. 'This road is closed,' he yelled in the rain. 'This whole area is a crime scene.'

Anders was listening. He moved to the emergency exit now, squeezing the door handle ready to go. Flashlights began shining in through the windows, officers walked up and down either side, scanning the bus, pointing their torches in from the outside. One officer paused watching a silhouette. He tapped his torch on the window ordering it to show its face. It did, its mousy hand made a circle on the glass and the officer pointed with his torch, staring as light glistened over the fat man's whiskers. He nodded. He moved on.

'Check that out, Andros,' Debs said without turning from her window. 'That guy must be dead.'

More passengers fell into the aisles, advancing towards the driver and the officer, lingering round their conversation. 'Make a line behind me,' the bald man said. 'Go on officer, when you're ready.'

'Some nut job escaped his unit,' the officer continued, 'sabotaged an arrest, a crazy guy named Maniac.' The officer looked at Maniac's feet. 'The name fits well,' he said. 'You wanna see what he did to our guy, damn near blew his donger off.'

'Someone's lost their donger,' the bald man yelled as more passengers came forward. Now they watched an ambulance, where paramedics stood round Lance, lay out on his stretcher taking gas and air. Thick padding covered his lap and tubes came out of him, leading to clear bags with liquid in them. The driver leaned forward on his wheel. He checked his watch.

'Trouble is,' the officer went on, 'he set free a friend of his, a fruitcake of equal measure who likes to show himself to people.'

The bald man swore loudly in the driver's ear. 'There's a fruitcake on the loose,' he then added.

Anders was finishing his whiskey. He had sweat on his lips. He rubbed them with his sleeve and even from the back seats, he could hear the officer telling the bald man that his updates weren't necessary. The whisky burned inside him. He watched the flashlights pass over his side then opened the exit and leaned forward, wetting his face in the rain. The rain was loud, but still he heard Big D talking nearby, addressing his officers.

'Put those pads and pencils away,' Big D said. 'And listen up.'

Anders felt good hearing his voice, was glad he wasn't dead, was glad to have whisky too. He finished the bottle and slung it into the forest. It made no sound. He then felt his heart thudding through his sweater, a good beat, he thought, good old whisky, he thought, putting his feet in the rain.

Big D arched forward with both hands over his knees. 'Put them away,' he said again, wearing a soaked bandage around his forehead, hair dripping over it. 'Listen up now.' Several officers surrounded him. They held dogs by their collar, and the dogs were going crazy in the rain, barking and jumping.

'Hey, Dee,' the officer by the bus door was calling him, hands cupped around his mouth, 'hey, Dee.'

Big D slapped his pants with both hands. Water splashed off them. 'What is it, Rookie?' he asked kicking a puddle. 'I'm addressing my troops,' he pointed, 'can't you see that?'

The Rookie took off his Stetson and looked at it. 'Sorry, Dee, but are we spot checking this one?'

'God damn these rookies,' Big D said while the officers nodded around him.

Then listening closely, the bald man punched the driver's chair and turned around. 'They're checking the bus,' he announced. 'They're checking the bus and that's just great.'

Anders had his backpack in one hand. He sat edge of the exit, legs in the rain, listening to Big D.

'Stop staring at me Rookie,' he heard Big D say. 'Is it going to Cairns or not?'

Anders was almost ready to jump, but he paused, and over the sounds of rain and barking dogs, he waited for the Rookie to answer. 'Nope. Not this one, Dee.'

'Then quit disturbing me,' Big D yelled and spat between his feet. 'Now listen in, boys,' he said. 'My partner and I are convinced he's heading to Cairns, he got himself a lover there named Lindsay.'

Anders closed the back exit. He moved across the seats again, silently on his bottom, back to his chair, back behind Debs.

'It's a bit crazy out there,' he said looking out of his window, seeing Big D divide his troops into two groups and send them into the forest.

'Yes, it's chaotic,' Debs said.

'What's going on at the front?'

'Nothing now, I think we're moving on.'

'Back to your seats,' the driver said waving his hands.

'You heard him,' the bald man added, 'back to your seats.'

'Just one more thing,' the Rookie said.

'Hang on,' the bald man said, 'there might be more,' and he stood in front of the driver asking the Rookie what it was.

'Don't tell anyone that this road is closed,' he said, but the driver had stepped on the gas, and the doors were closing in the Rookie's face.

'Did you hear that?' he shouted, running alongside the bus. But the driver just nodded and waved passively, eyes now scanning a map across his dashboard, planning a new route out of town.

'We need to check everything that's heading to Cairns,' the Rookie said staggering, slowing with his feet in the wet mud. 'Buses, trucks, cars, even cattle wagons.' The driver folded his map while the bald man watched him. Everyone else was now seated and the bus pulled away faster, leaving the Rookie behind in the mud.

'Well you don't see that every day,' Debs said coming onto her knees again, looking over at Anders. 'Are you okay?'

'I'm good,' Anders said dropping his wet cap. 'It was the body on the road, that's the only thing that got me, the body.'

'Yeah,' she said. 'That got me too. It's the second one I've seen in a week.'

'I had my whisky,' he said, 'made me feel better.'

'I could use a drop,' she said.

'Sorry,' he said, 'It's gone now.'

She smiled and watched him. 'How are you?' she said. 'You know, like after what happened.'

'I'm good,' he said. 'The headaches are easing, that was the worst bit.'

'Poor thing,' she said. 'I thought you were dead.'

'I felt dead,' he said. 'I mean, there was a point when I thought I was.'

'It was awful seeing your face.'

Anders looked up lifting his eyebrows. 'What do you mean by second one in a week?'

'What I keep trying to say,' she said. 'I was there, on the car park, I watched you get choked out.'

'Was you really?' he said pushing his flip-flops off with his toes.

Debs nodded. 'I played a footy match on the pitch next door,' she said. 'We often pop over to The Old Crow for post-match schooners.'

'I see,' Anders said reaching up on one knee, dragging his curtain to block car lights passing his window. Then for a pillow, he propped up his backpack and lay across the carpeted seats, hands clasped on chest, facing up to her like a child at bedtime. 'Does this team have a name?'

'We do unfortunately, Sisters of Australia FC,' she said looking over her fingernails. 'A rubbish name, yes?'

'Hmm, I quite like it,' Anders said.

She swiped her arm out playfully but he was too low, the tips of her fingers skimmed his shoulder. 'You're a crappy liar, Andros.'

'I've been told,' he said.

'I bet,' she laughed fluttering her eyelashes. He liked her that way. He hoped she'd keep doing it.

'How did the game go?'

'Oh, the game was terrible, we played the Redbacks, they're a tough bunch.'

'Your name is fine. Redbacks sound like sunburn victims.'

'Guess you're right,' she said, 'but they're a bloody good team though, dirty, but good. They were brutal that day, hammered us six – nothing.'

'Ouch.'

'Yes, ouch,' she said, 'was the poms fault, they fired abuse at our goalie all game, poor thing.'

The rain had calmed. It pitter-pattered now softly on the window. A few passengers stayed awake near the front end of the bus, lights on overhead, reading. The fat man slept, wheezing like an overfed bulldog. Grumbles over his sounds passed between seats, lights came on and off and heads popped up to look at him. There was no light at the back, and that's where they stayed, Anders looking up, Debs looking down.

'They were very obnoxious,' Debs went on, 'the poms.'

'Trust me,' Anders yawned, 'I know the type.'

'They sat in the stands,' she said. 'A skinny one and his large friend, both drinking wine from coffee mugs, wine from coffee mugs, yuck.'

Anders was laughing. He held his face.

'What, what you laughing at?' Debs began laughing too. 'What is it?'

'Nothing,' he said clasping his hands again. 'Go on, tell it.'

'They gave our goalie hell. She's a big girl you see, and each time she came out they began singing this awful song, "she's big, she's round, she bounces off the ground, she's Neville Southall, she's Neville Southall."

'I don't know that one,' Anders said.

'Me neither, but blimey, she had an awful game, they really killed her,' she said. 'The Redbacks went to town on us, one fired between her legs, one rolled under her boot, and one was a back pass from me, which she gave chase to, skidding, legs parted, following it into the net. It took five minutes to untangle her.'

'So it was bad.'

'Yep, very bad, we couldn't get to The Old Crow quick enough, and then we saw you.'

'What was I like?'

'You looked awful.'

'Show me,' Anders laughed, 'show me the face.'

'I can't, it's embarrassing.'

'Show me,' he said, 'you're an actress. I want to see you act.'

Debs blushed into her hands then came up clutching her neck, wobbling her head side to side and poking her tongue out over her lips. Anders laughed, one hand cupping his sore cheek, the other on his ribs.

'Was I that bad?'

'Worse,' Debs said looking behind to check no one had seen her, 'much, much worse.'

'I don't remember a thing,' he said.

'No, I bet you wouldn't,' she said. 'But I do, was one of the best things ever.'

Anders looked at her funny. 'Glad you enjoyed it so much.'

'Stop, Andros,' Debs said swiping her hands through the air. 'You know what I mean.'

'Do I?'

'It was the Possum,' she said, 'that was so great.'

He turned on his side, eyes gazing at her. 'Please keep talking,' he said.

'Well okay then.' She shuffled on her knees, her smile now gone. 'It was as though it was protecting you, a miracle almost. Some people have Angels on their shoulder, Andros, I believe that stuff.'

'Sure, me too,' he said, now sitting up and removing his glasses.

'I thought it was over when he dropped you, and he had to drop you because it was on him, all over him, nasty but beautiful.'

'It is beautiful, it's my friend,' he said.

'Some might've felt sorry for him, but not us, we saw what he did. We willed it to continue. It came again, everywhere, dodging and scratching, all utterly scary, all utterly exciting too.'

'And that's how he ended up...' Anders pressed a finger on his open palm.

'Yep, and we all ran with wood coming over us. We had to move fast, but our goalie was too slow and blood splattered her pants. Poor thing, she had an awful day.'

'That's great,' Anders said lying down again, rubbing his eyes, 'really great.'

'Not really,' she said, 'she had white pants on.'

'No, no, I mean the Possum, how it saved me,' he said. 'It's one of the best things I've ever heard.'

'Yes. You owe that Possum your life.'

'It saved me.' Tears appeared on his cheeks. 'It saved me.' He turned his back to her. He went silent.

Chapter thirty-three

The bus picked up speed now on the motorway, running smoothly on its pathway to Brisbane. The overhead lights were out, most curtains were drawn, and the passengers slumped horizontally in their seats. Those with partners leaned on each other, those alone leaned on their windows, some covered themselves with blankets, some used coats or big jumpers to keep warm. Heads rocked gently above the seats, and there was snoring.

Debs had sat down. She'd been studying her script and pausing now and then, peering at Anders between her seats. 'Andros,' she then whispered, 'are you sleeping?'

'No,' he said, 'are you?'

She giggled, 'shh, stop being silly.'

'I've got an appetite,' he said, 'but all I can smell is damp chicken and cardboard.'

Both giggled and shushed each other. Then she reached into her handbag, took a package and pushed it through the gap. 'Here, take this,' she said.

He opened the paper and took a sandwich. 'What is it?' he asked.

'Cheese and pickle, my mum made them for me. She worries when I don't eat.'

'That's nice,' he said, 'she sounds nice.'

'Eat the sandwich, Andros.'

'I am doing,' he laughed, and their giggles attracted grumbles from other passengers. Someone complained they'd not slept since Bowen. Another complained about the smell of chicken.

'This is yumbo,' Anders said, lay on his back eating.

'Say, Andros.'

'Yes?'

'Have you made plans over Christmas?'

'No, nothing,' he said biting soft bread.

'Well you can't do that.' She poured tea from a flask. 'It's Christmas.' Her hand went through the gap passing him a cup. Steam came from it, he held it over his sandwich and thanked her.

'What is it?' he asked.

'It's hot tea with sugar,' she said. 'You drink it.'

A double shush came from near the front. They watched each other through the gap, giggling with their hands over their lips. Tea spilt on Anders's sweater and he kept laughing.

'Visit me in Brisbane,' she whispered watching him eat. 'I'll get you a panto ticket.'

'Sure,' he said. 'Will you prepare more sandwiches?'

She laughed. 'Yes, I'll make sandwiches. Is the twentieth good?' she asked.

'Not the twentieth,' he said, 'I'll be in Gatton.' Anders drained the cup. The tea was hot and sweet. It felt warm and comfortable inside him. He closed his eyes and she turned away pinching her lip.

'Let's do Christmas Eve,' he said. 'That'll be nice.'

She leaned over her seat excitedly, her big green eyes glistening on him, her feet almost dancing. 'Oh no it won't.' She said using her best panto voice.

Then suddenly a man staggered into the aisle, he pointed to the back seats with his beer can and mumbled something, and in the darkness, accidently felt the bald man's head with his fingers. The bald man got up and went behind the driver. 'Can you believe that,' he said. 'I'll remember this journey for a long time.'

Other passengers woke to shush the drunken man. The driver ordered the bald man back to his seat and the fat man woke up, reaching for chicken. 'Billy bulldog is awake,' someone declared, and there were hoorays and waves of sarcastic clapping, and a man saying he hadn't slept since Bowen, not a wink.

Meanwhile Debs was over some paper scribbling a note for Anders. She added the address of the theatre and her contact number. She spoke excitedly, smiling over her moving pencil. 'The panto will be great,' she said. 'I know it will,' she giggled, 'and we can eat afterwards. There's this lovely place just round the corner.'

Anders said nothing. He was sleeping now, his sweater covered with tea and breadcrumbs, his half-eaten sandwich in one hand, and his chest moving up and down slowly, peacefully. 'Not sure I've mentioned this,' she said still writing, 'but Big D will be there too. He's a bit odd. But he's my uncle you see, and he always watches the show.'

The End

Printed in Great Britain
by Amazon

14148763R10181